MURDER VIRUS

SHAWN C. BAKER

To Kirsten. For everything, forever.

To Mom & Dad & Kim, for reading.

To John, Missi, Brown, & Keller. For support and inspiration.

To the corporate yahoos who destroyed a wonderful bookstore - look behind you.

We are not our memories.

If you seek to undo yourself, begin with what others have already forgotten.

Then, you can relearn your life as you see fit, and make of it what you will.

- **Uncredited man in bar fight, blood on his hands.**

PART I
ANGELA

CHAPTER 1

S tepping over the corpse of a college kid dressed in blue flannel and jeans, Detective Angela Miller entered the crime scene. The shooter's bullets had perforated the kid's clothing and the flesh beneath, leaving a veritable pool of blood.

"All that from one body?"

"Floor's canted," Jim Allen answered, pointing further into the building. Jim looked like the textbook definition of a cop - medium height, medium build, clean-shaven with a gym teacher's haircut and a single tattoo of a shark on his fore-arm. He exuded authority. The two had been partners for just over three years, not counting six months off in the middle while Miller was on leave. Angela followed Jim's line of sight to where five other bodies lay torn to shreds at the coffee bar. Miracle of miracles, the victims were all still on their stools, slumped face down on the counter, leaking viscera like five bottles of ketchup turned upside down. The blood had cooled, its color the grayish-brown that told the detectives they'd missed the party by just long enough for the trail to grow cold.

A tall officer named Sharp who had already introduced himself as one of the first-responders approached Angela with a smile. Angela knew what she looked like: a little rough-around-the-edges, manic, but her six-foot height and sleek build cemented her as something of an icon in the department. Most thought she looked more like an actress playing a cop than an actual cop. Anyone who underestimated her because of this, however, inevitably regretted it.

Angela could be quite mean.

"Coffee any good here?" Sharp asked, glib affectation in the face of horror.

"Any witnesses?" Angela asked, ignoring his tastelessness.

"None still livin'."

"Anyone get away?"

"Not sure."

"There a back door?" Jim asked, irritated. Angela sighed; Jim didn't like when other cops skipped over him to ask her questions, no matter how inane. Was it protective impulse or jealousy? Angela would have safely played her money on a combination of the two.

"In the kitchen, I'm assuming."

"Assuming? Gold star to the Millennial cop."

With an exaggerated flourish of disdain, Jim passed Sharp close enough that for a second, Angela thought he would clip the kid with his shoulder. His restraint maintained by a hair, Jim disappeared behind the counter and into the rear of the store.

"Back door," he shouted a moment later. Angela smiled apologetically at Sharp and followed her partner.

They found two more bodies in the back, one in the stock room, a twenty-something-year-old guy riddled with holes from automatic gunfire, the other a girl, maybe thirty. She lay half in, half out the back door, garbage strewed around her in a perimeter of chaos. Angela stepped over a banana peel and out the back door to where Jim stood by the dumpster.

"Looks like someone was taking the garbage out when the party started."

Emerging into the dingy concrete daylight, Angela stopped cold at Jim's discovery. A final body sat up against the dumpster, the top of its face torn to tissue paper, brains blasted across the dilapidated metal, an AR-15 still clutched in the man's hand. On the faded red brick wall beside the body, scrawled in what looked like neon paint:

KILL FOR THE SAKE OF KILLING

"Guess our guy only feels comfortable traveling in a group, eh?"

"That's disrespectful, Angela."

"Oh, fuck you, Jim."

"Whatever. Help me get this shit under control."

∽

Jim covered for her, and Angela cut out early. She hadn't slept in days, had reached a critical point with her insomnia. At 4:15 PM, she parked her car in the garage beneath her building. She didn't arm the alarm; it had been touchy of late, and the last thing she needed was complaints going to the super if it went off during the night. Angela was already on the outs with most of her neighbors.

By the time she stepped out of the elevator on the seventh floor, she'd already let her shoulder-length auburn hair down and swallowed a Vicodin. She passed a mirror in the hallway and saw bags under her eyes; the natural blue of her irises looked faded and vague, her cheekbones extra sharp. Angela hadn't been eating much, and her skin had a yellow tint to it.

"That's it," she said, telling herself she'd get some sleep even if she had to put herself into a coma to do so.

The door on the apartment kitty-corner from her's was ajar, and as she passed, Angela heard voices from inside. Hardly aware she was doing it, she stopped and peered through the opening. These neighbors were new, had only been in the building a few weeks, but since arriving, she'd already filed several complaints on them for noise and cigarette smoke. In the sliver of interior afforded to her by the open door, she saw a small man in an old suit. He smoked a cigarette, a magazine folded in his lap. Sensing her intrusion, the man's eyes rolled up and met hers.

"See anything you like?" he said and smiled.

"You know this is a no-smoking building, right?"

The man's smile flipped over, and he was on his feet and at the door a moment later. Watching him walk was like staring at an Armadillo flipped onto its back, tiny legs pumping.

"Fuck you, bitch."

"Yeah?" she said, but the door slammed tight in the jamb before Angela could deliver a retort.

She entered her apartment and kicked off her shoes. Another one of those days.

Around midnight Angela's cell woke her on the couch. Her head felt thick, mushy with wine and pills, but when she saw the text from Jim, Angela roused instantly.

Our shooter's a student at the Community College near the scene. Johnson Hughs. 25. Here's a link to his social media profiles.

Had Jim been working this late, or had he held the information until just before he turned in for the night, hoping she wouldn't see it until morning? Angela guessed option two; ever since she'd returned from leave, Jim had become notorious for plying her with help she didn't need.

"A good plan, Jimmy," she said to the darkened room, "but you forgot. I don't sleep."

Angela fired up her laptop and began to dig into Johnson Hughs.

CHAPTER 2

"Jesus, Angela, you look terrible. Did you sleep at all?"

"Don't you worry your pretty little head, Jimmy. I feel fine. What's more, I think I found something in Hughs's social media."

"This fucking planet. Jesus, psycho killers, and social media."

"Qu'est-ce que c'est."

"Fa fa fucking fa. What'dya got?"

"Well, facefuck is a wash. Looks like Johnson had joined so many other psychos and migrated exclusively to tweeting his bullshit at the world."

Captain Tavares barreled into the office, his ornery demeanor firmly intact.

"Miller, Allen. My office. Now."

"Hope whatever you have is enough to calm him down. Van Houten says Cap's in 'extra cunt mode' today."

"Everyone's in extra cunt mode around Van Houten. He's a cunt."

Angela took a quick detour to top off her coffee and then followed Jim into the Captain's office.

"Shut the door behind you."

"Captain, I think I found something on our shooter's social media profile."

"You what?"

Tavares drilled his eyes into Jim with enough force to suggest he might be trying to make him burst into flames.

"So she doesn't know. That means what, Jim? You did *not* relay my message to your partner yesterday because she wasn't really on the phone when I asked you where she was at Three O'Clock. Were you home, Miller? At the bar, perhaps?"

Angela threw Jim a look, but he remained focused on the boss.

"Look, she was tired. I thought she should go home, get some sleep. All we were doing at that point was waiting for an identity."

"And yet you sent her the social media info. This is bullshit. Your partner needs time off, she asks me. Don't cover for her again. Clear?"

"Look, Dave-"

"Don't Dave me, Jim. Do I detect something more than professional concern? Because I turned my back on that shit once before and look where it put her. That will not happen again, capiche?"

"Hello. In the fucking room."

"And thanks for showing up today, Miller. While you were at home yesterday catching up on your beauty sleep, District Attorney Valez visited to tell us the shooter just happens to be her stepson. She wants his profiles taken down before the press gets wind of their connection."

"Excuse me? Since when do we help politicians hide the skeletons in their closets?"

"NOT open for debate, Miller. Besides, by the time you

leave this office, Hughs's profiles will already be gone, so it's a moot point."

"And?"

"And what?"

"And what the hell do we tell the public?"

"Oh, come on. No one's gonna bat an eye at another shooting on a college campus. Happens all the damn time, these days."

"Jesus Christ, Dave, glad to know rubbing elbows with the District Attorney and her friends in city hall hasn't jaded you."

"Angela," Jim had a hand on her arm; she shook it off.

"No! fuck that. I have a lead."

"He's a lone gunman, Miller."

"Yeah? Well, I may have found information that contradicts that."

"Jim, will you take your partner here out for a long breakfast and teach her the ways of the force before I suspend her for insubordination?"

"C'mon, Angela."

"Dave-"

"Captain Tavares, Officer."

"Captain? This? This is fucking bullshit. I hope you're right, but just so you know, you're not."

"Today, Jim."

"Goddamnit, Angela. C'mon."

～

"So you must'a found something good to get that angry."

"I found *something*. Look."

Angela pulled her phone from her jacket pocket.

"His profiles are all down, remember?"

"Screenshots, rookie. Try it sometime."

"Ha!"

Angela passed Jim her phone.

"What am I looking at here?"

"Okay. So this post here? The one with the hashtag?"

It took a moment, then he saw it.

"#KFTSOK?"

"Our graffiti? Kill for the sake of killing. It's the name of a book by this guy here."

She took the phone back, juggled the windows to a live profile.

"Abramelin Harvest? Never heard of him."

"No reason you would have unless you're into his books."

"I read. Lots of Horror, too. Barker, King. You name it."

"I'm not talking about big box stuff. This guy publishes on Amazon, through a tiny company called Jonestown Books."

"Christ."

"Yeah. So flip back to the screenshot. See how our boy Hughs liked this post? Well, it's a link to an excerpt from Harvest's newest book. Guess what the title is."

"Hug time in Puppy Town?"

"Kill for the Sake of Killing."

Light bulb.

"So our boy Johnson gets mad at his DA step mommy and decides to emulate his favorite horror story."

"The subtitle of the book? 'An exploration of macro-cosmic surgical techniques to rid the world of the human disease.'"

"Jesus."

"Wept. I was smart enough to save that link. Here," leaning over her partner's shoulder, Angela opened the browser on her phone. Long lines of text appeared.

"How do these guys make any money if they give the thing away online?" Jim said, scrolling through seemingly endless pages of text, "Who the hell's gonna read this, anyway?"

"I did."

"Seriously?"

"Yeah. It's… truthfully it's fascinating."

"C'mon, Angela. The last thing I need is you finding religion on me."

"Not likely. See how three other people liked this same post?"

"Friends of yours?"

"Haha. Watch," Angela took the phone, flipped around the screen for a moment and handed it back to Jim, "That's one of the other users who liked it. Recognize that picture?"

"Should I?"

"Look closer. I'll wait."

Jim stared at the screen for a good thirty seconds before he got it.

"Shit! This is that shooter in Iowa last week."

"Bingo. Say hello to James Donald Rowland, number two of four people we know of Harvest's fanbase who've gone on a killing spree since this was posted."

"That strike you as ominous?"

"It doesn't you?"

"Maybe I should read this, show it to Tavares."

"I'll send you the link later. In the meantime, I found the address for Jonestown Books, thought we should take a ride."

"We stop for coffee first?"

"Sure. You're buying."

"What else is new?"

~

J onestown Books sat in a building on the outskirts of Downtown Los Angeles, in an old warehouse that had been converted into alternative workspaces. The kind of place where artists rented studios or bands practiced late into the night. Angela drove while Jim attempted to read the excerpt from Abramelin Harvest's book on her phone. After fifteen minutes motionless on the 110, he set the phone down and rubbed his temples.

"Trouble?"

"Never been able to read in the car. Gives me a headache."

Twenty minutes later they parked on 7th street and made their way to the building, which was in a small alley. The afternoon sun crested the tops of the buildings, empty condo units stacked across the horizon like dominoes, converted real estate that would probably end up section eight in five years, instead of fodder for the yuppie appetite the developers had hoped to exploit.

"Never ceases to amaze me. All the money in this city and it's still the filthiest downtown area in the entire fucking country."

"Yeah," Angela responded, watching a homeless man chase a rat the size of a small dog. The rodent led the man through a mountain of debris packed against the fence of a nearby parking lot; it looked like a wave of garbage had broke and rolled back, leaving piles of trash in its wake.

"Not a fan of DTLA. I've got a cousin that lived in one of these. Thought it was an investment in the city's future."

"How'd that work out for her?"

"She was attacked in an alley. Sold the place and moved to Kansas."

"Wow."

They walked to the door, a simple glass number with a

logo and the words *Jonestown Publications* stenciled at eye level. It was locked. There was no buzzer.

"Probably don't get many visitors," Jim said and rapped hard on the glass. They could hear the percussive sound echo out in a big, empty room.

"Think it's a front?"

"Who knows? I guess we're not going to find anything here."

Behind them, the homeless man had stopped paying attention to the rat, shifted his focus to the two detectives.

"I think we're creating a stir."

"It's your sense of fashion," Jim said. He shined his flashlight through the glass door.

"Hey, I think I see something in there."

"Really?" Angela asked, still watching behind them. Five homeless men - one of them over seven feet tall - had moved into a half-circle around them.

"What's that zombie show everyone loves? I saw an episode once, kinda looked like this."

"Angela, someone's in there. POLICE! Open the door."

Angela turned and strained her eyes to follow Jim's light past the glass. She saw someone move, but the room was dark.

"What are they doing in the dar-" Something lifted a strand of her hair, and she spun, caught the arm of the seven-foot homeless man in her left hand and drew her firearm with her right.

"Back the fuck up, dude!"

"If hairs be wires, black wires grow on her head. If snow be white[1]-"

Jim trained his piece on the advancing bums, his eyes wide with that, how-did-we-get-here look of surprise.

"You heard the lady. Back the fuck up."

The bum let Angela's hair fall and retreated a quick three steps, bowed at the waist while continuing his recitation.

"-why then her breasts are dun. Coral is far more red than her lips and..."

Behind them, a loud CLACK caused both detectives to spin. A short, black-haired woman of about forty stood holding the door open.

"Can I help you?"

"Detectives Miller and Allen. LAPD. We need to come in and ask you a few questions..."

"I'm just the cleaning woman. I don't work for-"

"Doesn't matter. Won't take long, 'kay?" Jim said and forced his way in. Angela followed, relieved to shut the door behind them.

CHAPTER 3

"That was fucked up."

"Right?" Jim said, holstering his weapon and fixing his stare on the cleaning woman. He seemed as jumpy as Angela after the encounter.

"All bums around here quote Shakespeare? Or just the giant ones?"

"Got me," the cleaning lady said, clearly unsettled by their intrusion, "I'm not supposed to let anyone else in here while I'm working. I could lose my job."

"Relax. Anyone asks, we'll speak to them," Angela said, showing the woman her badge.

"What's your name?"

"Carrie O'Sullivan."

"Okay, Carrie. Do you work for the building or an outside vendor?"

"Vendor. Spotless Vistas."

"Awkward name, no?"

"Their boat, I just row."

"How long you been cleaning this particular building?"

"I only do this office, probably last six months."

"Did somebody else do it before that?"

"I guess, but if they worked for us, I wouldn't know."

"You girls don't trade stories?"

"Never met anyone else on the staff. It's like Uber - there's an app, when you get hired you put it on your phone, the company uses it to assign you clients."

"Interesting."

"So, do you always do this particular office?"

"Like I said, for the last six months. I do this one, a couple homes in Baldwin Hills, and a diner in Inglewood."

"Wow. They keep you moving, huh?"

"I guess. It's LA, what do you expect?"

"Point. So, you ever meet anyone that works for Jonestown Books?"

"The owner. Nice lady. Guinevere Speck. Gave me a Christmas bonus."

Angela turned to look back out onto the street. Their friends had dispersed.

"Wow. That must'a come in handy, eh?"

Carrie made a point of dismissing Jim's comment with her eyes, fixed her attention on Angela.

"This going somewhere? I really need to finish and get on with it."

"Just a few more questions about Miss Speck. You read any of the stuff she publishes?"

"Nope. I'm studying to pass the Bar, don't have time for reading anything but law journals."

"Wow. No shit? A cleaning lady who wants to be a lawyer. Don't that just beat all?"

Angela elbowed her partner in the ribs and he lost his breath.

"Damn. *Cough*"

"I'm sorry, Carrie. My partner's not usually such a condescending asshole. Thank you for speaking to us."

"I'm sorry, okay?" Jim said, holding his chest.

Angela turned to lead them through the door.

"Hey, you guys talk to anyone else about Miss Speck yet?"

"No, why?"

"I was wondering if anyone mentioned when she's coming back."

Curiosity trumped Angela's embarrassment.

"How long since you saw her last?"

"A while. It's fine, I have a key, I was just wondering if I should start trying to pick up another gig. You know, if they're closing or something. I don't think anyone but me's been here in at least a month."

Jim met Angela's eyes. The shape of something terrible was forming around them, they just couldn't see it yet.

"You have a card, Carrie? In case we find anything out."

"Give ya my cell number."

"Perfect."

~

"So what do we have?"

They were stuck on the 110 again. The sun had vanished, and the temperature had dropped to a chilly fifty-seven.

"An author with a provocative book. Four people on social media who acknowledged liking it, two of whom became spree shooters. A potentially missing publisher."

"Don't forget the seven-foot-tall bum who quotes Shakespeare."

"Sounds like a lotta conjecture tying this together. We don't go somewhere with this soon, we'll be catching again."

"Might be a good thing. Look, I'm gonna drop you at your ride and head home. I haven't been sleeping."

"Angela-"

"You didn't let me finish, Jim. I haven't been sleeping *well*, okay?"

"Okay. Just remember, you promised you'd let me know if it started happening again."

"And I will. *If* it happens. Which it won't."

"The meds are working, then?"

"I guess. I don't want to kill myself anymore, if that's what you're asking."

"Good. Because I like you, Miller."

"Don't start."

Jim reached out and wrapped a lock of her hair around his index finger, adopted a terrible British accent, "Rapunzel Rapunzel, let down thine hair."

"That's not Shakespeare. Idiot."

They pulled into the station forty minutes later. Angela was home and in bed by nine.

∾

When she slept, Angela dreamed. Rough, deep dreams that would leave her exhausted and disturbed. In a few days, she would remember her bout of insomnia fondly.

In the dream, a faint siren pulsed through an empty night. It was cold, and Angela could see her breath. She was dressed in something tiny and sheer, and when she realized the siren was the doorbell, she moved to a large glass door and let Jim inside. He was dressed in a suit, but within moments they had each other's clothes off, were rubbing and sweating, cupping and licking one another in a rage of unchecked passion. This part of the dream was modeled after and extrapolated from the series of liaisons they'd shared two years before. This was just before Jim's divorce, before Angela was forced to take psychiatric leave following an IA investigation into the shooting of a high school principal.

Miller and Allen had been investigating word of a potential terror threat at a high school, and while working the case, they'd inadvertently discovered the school's principal had a thing for photographing his female students in their locker room. When they confronted him, the man actually pulled a handgun and shot Jim in the leg. Angela dropped him with one between the eyes, and all hell broke loose.

The dream-room morphed under the strain of their passion, and soon they were horizontal on the bed, Jim inside her, their movements pumping the breath from her lungs as he impaled her against the headboard. Dream Angela closed her eyes and held her breath, only to burst into orgasm a moment later. Jim went quickly after, and as he collapsed, exhausted, Angela laid the barrel of her revolver against his left temple and pulled the trigger. There was a burst of light, but no sound as blood erupted in a geyser from the split in Jim's forehead. Angela tossed the gun to the floor, crawled over Jim's dead body. She ran her fingers, palms, and forearms through the blood-soaked covers, picking up the color of her partner's expired life, drowning in a tidal wave of ecstasy, terror, and adrenaline. Angela saw that the room around them had filled with onlookers, and furious, she leaped from her throes on the bed to the floor, picked up the handgun and began to shoot them one at a time. But there were too many of them; her shots made no difference in the otherwise overcrowded room. She turned her head to the floor and began to scream...

~

Angela started awake, a sharp breath caught in her throat. It felt like she was choking on something. After a few moments of existential panic, she realized she wasn't.

Once she had herself under control again, Angela looked

at the clock and saw that she had only been out for four hours, give or take. Not what she had been hoping for, but she'd take it. From somewhere in the corridor outside, she could hear shouting and smell cigarette smoke.

She showered, made a pot of coffee and went back to reading Abramelin Harvest's book. The man was a compelling writer, no doubt about that. Harvest's words unfolded inside her head in a way that made complete sense.

After an hour she took a break, poured more coffee and checked the author's social media feed. It was generally a pretty active profile, but since landing on her radar, there'd been no new posts. Where was he? Where was Guinevere Speck? And most importantly, did either of them know Johnson Hughs or James Rowland? Answers seemed further away than they had when she'd laid down.

Angela went back to reading, but now there was a tickle in the back of her mind like she'd forgotten something. She lay her phone down and walked to the window; another day loomed before her, but it already felt sapped of strength, as though everything they would do today would ultimately be for naught. That was the way of the world these days, when an out-of-control population strangled everyone's lives, from hers to Jim's to the planet's; nothing worked because everything was broken. Everything was broken because none of it had been set up to accommodate a population that continued to grow unchecked, year after year. She thought of the bodies in the coffee shop, the fact that none of those college kids would live to reproduce - if they hadn't already - and she began to see the thing she had previously felt take shape around her. Harvest's book wasn't wrong; the only way to save the planet was to thin the population, and the only way to do that was to...

"Kill for the sake of killing. Jesus Angie, this is what no sleep does, remember?"

She poured the remainder of the coffee into a thermal mug and left her apartment. It was four-forty-seven AM; Jim wouldn't be at the office for a few hours at least, but maybe she could find something in the computers there to tie Hughs and Rowland together.

In the hall, she punched the elevator button and watched the arrow rise slowly from the ground level to the seventh, where it dinged softly and opened to reveal the new neighbor, leather jacket and cigarette hanging from his lip like he was James Dean. Next to him stood a tall blond girl who couldn't have been more than seventeen.

"Ah, the nosy neighbor. How are you, nosy neighbor? You going for a walk?"

"You deaf or just stupid?"

"What?"

"You heard me. I wake up smelling your filthy smoke, hearing your loser life. Keep it to yourself, dickhead. I'm a cop. I can fuck you up."

"Whoah. You got some mouth on you, girl. I like that in a woman; a filthy mouth."

They stepped from the elevator and Angela tried to make eye contact with the blonde, who she could now see had a doozy of a black eye. The girl kept her eyes pinned to the tan and green carpet that lined the corridor, refused to meet Angela's gaze.

"How'd she get the black eye?"

"She does MMA, but she's not so good. I've been trying to teach her a thing or two."

"I'll bet."

"Could teach you, too."

The elevator door began to close; Angela caught it with her right hand, stepped in and punched the button for the garage.

"Maybe some other time, huh?"

The door had almost closed when she caught it again, went through and in one perfect motion pulled her gun from its holster and brought the handle down hard on douche bag's nose. Blood burst from it like a water balloon with grape juice inside. Angela's neighbor howled in agony. The girl finally met her eyes as she dipped back into the elevator. As the doors closed, Angela smiled and said, "Don't be with him when I return."

When the elevator stopped at the garage a few moments later, she could hear Davey the Night Steward's radio before the door even opened. It sounded ominous, and she braced for the consequences of her actions.

"Detective Miller. S'pose they rousted you outta bed for this shit on Melrose, eh?"

"What shit on Melrose, Davey?" she asked, relieved.

"Didn't your people tell you? 'Nother shooting, this one big."

CHAPTER 4

"How long you been here?"

"You don't wanna know," Angela answered, lowering the phone. Jim caught sight of the page of text on the screen, regarded her with a funny look.

"You reading that book again?"

"Thought we should know as much about this guy Harvest as possible."

"You really got a thing for this, huh?"

"You think I'm wrong?"

"I don't know. Shit, people are extra crazy today, especially anyone that reads books on their damn phone."

"That a crack?" Angela smiled. Just like that, they were flirting. Her dream lingered for a moment, the feeling of his body in her hands, his blood on her face.

Jim smiled back, tossed his coat onto the driver's seat as he slipped from his ten-year-old Impala, just about the only thing he'd been allowed to keep in his divorce.

"You sleep?"

"Couple hours."

"That's something."

"I guess."

"So what do they know about this guy?"

"Nothing. Now ask me what *I* know."

Jim narrowed his eyes with suspicion.

"Okay, bite. What do *you* know?"

"The guy inside? The shooter? Her name's Abigail Kurtis. Thirty-four, married, no kids. Her social media handle is Killjoy 667."

"Really? Jesus, kinda skews the statistics, doesn't it?"

"I'll say. Thirty-plus married female? Definitely something we haven't seen before. Recognize the name?"

"Kurtis? Like, ah, Tony?"

"No dipshit, the social media name. She's one of the two remaining folks who liked that post by Harvest."

"Okay, then we can't ignore this anymore. Gotta find the fourth."

"Little busy at the moment."

"Hostages?"

"Not sure. There was some shouting inside after I arrived about an hour ago, but nothing since."

"Anyone try to talk to her?"

"So far? It's just me, and no."

"Well then, looks like I showed up just in time."

"Haha."

"What? You don't think I can pull this off?"

"Pull what off, Jim? We don't know anything about the situation. Wait 'til someone from the HRT shows up."

"Wait? C'mon. Don't be a pussy."

Jim walked toward the building, a small bookstore situated in the belly of a strip mall rounded out by a Dry Cleaners on one side and an empty storefront on the other.

"Do we know if there's a connecting passage between the shops? I mean, last time Hughs went straight out the back door with the garbage and the grunts missed it. I'd hate to think Ms. Kurtis slipped out a side door and I'm standing here talking to my-"

Jim's words were split by gunfire, a single shot followed by the sound of one of the windows in Angela's car exploding.

"Jesus! Jim, get down!"

Jim ducked behind another car that was parked in the lot, drew his weapon.

"Ms. Kurtis? This is Detective Jim Allen with the -"

Another shot, this one ricocheted off something metal nearby, ended up embedded in the concrete of the empty storefront. Jim looked to Angela, who'd also drawn her weapon. There was no movement from inside.

Not anxious to move back out into the open, they stayed in their spots for nearly ten minutes, waiting on the cavalry.

"Where the hell's back-up?"

"Got me," Angela said and pulled her phone from her back pocket. She didn't want to risk going for her radio, but she could call into the station, see what was keeping them.

Something on the screen caught her eye. It was a push notification from the social media app:

Fire-Johnny7, Drink_deathLord, Riteovpassag187 liked a post by Abramelin_Harvest.

"Jesus. No way…"

The idea crowded her brain so suddenly that she never doubted it, was rewarded by a sight that inspired the first thing in her life that felt like pure, unadulterated horror. When Angela opened the app with Harvest's post, she saw the likes on his excerpt had quadrupled, was, in fact, chiming over and over again as the number of Likes continued to climb before her eyes.

17 Likes.

22 Likes.

37 Likes.

46 Likes…

"Jim? We're in trouble, buddy."

"Yeah? You mean besides being pinned down by an active shooter?"

Another bullet served as their quarry's rejoinder. The rearview mirror on Jim's cover exploded in a mandala of glass and plastic.

In Angela's head, the same scenario played out all over the city. Shooter after shooter, all inspired by Harvest's doctrine. There was no back-up coming because everyone on the force was already in the same position. She had to tell Jim they were on their own, but she didn't exactly want to advertise the situation to their perp. Thinking fast, Angela stood and hoped the little bit of hostage training she'd had would keep her head from being blown off. Much to her surprise, Abigail Kurtis was already standing in the doorway to the store, gun lowered. She was coming out on her own accord.

"Abigail, this is Detective Angela Miller, LAPD. Toss the gun to the ground in front of you. I'll do the same thing if it will make you feel better."

They stood face to face, not more than three hundred feet between them. Eyes locked, the tension was thick enough to make Angela's palms sweat. In her back pocket, her phone continued to issue faint chimes every time Harvest's post received a new Like. It sounded like a Vegas jackpot.

"I'm not alone. You know that, don't you?" Abigail said.

"We know," Angela responded. Her left eye stayed trained on Abigail, her right stayed on Jim, who looked ready to pop up and empty his clip into the girl. Not wanting to make any sudden movements, she spoke plainly.

"Abigail, my partner Jim here has been shot before, so I need you to understand that he's a little edgy. I'm going to turn my head and talk to him for a second; do not shoot me, okay? I know you're not alone and I want to talk to you about it. About the ideas in Harvest's book."

"You've read it?"

"I have. But before we talk about that, let me talk to my partner, okay?"

"Okay."

Angela turned her head to Jim, still crouched behind the car.

"Jim, do us all a favor and set your gun down, okay?"

"You outta your fuckin' mind, Angie?"

Angie? He hadn't called her that since they'd slept together. That tawdry motel, the cigarette burns on the bedside table. She'd held him tight inside her that night, one hand clamped on his ass when he tried to pull out, thrilled by the perversity of it, the absolute abandon she'd surrendered to. Several weeks later, she'd taken a pregnancy test. Two days after that, she scheduled an abortion. It was the right thing to do; she'd never questioned that. Too many people already. So how was Harvest's philosophy any different? Sure, it was murder, but so was clogging the planet with more mouths to feed. More consumers to leave their carbon footprint. And if you listened to the billboards that sprang up in the poorer neighborhoods - because the Wealthy and the Just knew their target audience - heartbeat begins in only a matter of weeks, so no matter when you decided, it was already a crime.

"Not out of my mind at all, Jim. I just want to make sure Abigail and I can have a real conversation."

"A real conversation? Jesus."

"Jim."

"No, Angela."

"Abigail, it's alright. Jim won't-"

Angela heard the door behind her open a split second before she could process the sound for what it was. She watched Abigail's line of sight swoosh left. Riding on instinct, Angela raised her .45 and squeezed off one shot, hit Abigail in the side of the face, sent her cartwheeling to the pavement. Jim stood to her right, his gun still trained where seconds ago Abigail had stood.

"Nice shooting, Angie-"

Angela turned and put two in Jim's chest. His body bounced once against the car before coming to rest on the curb, his firearm hanging limply in a puddle of garbage that had collected atop a drainage grating.

Behind her, two twenty-something-year-old guys had come out of what might have been an apartment building. She saw the look of terror strike them right before she spent the remainder of her clip on them. All discernible life in the area quieted, Angela exhaled. Her posture settled, and she lowered her weapon. Faintly, in the distance, she could hear gunfire and sirens. At that moment, they sounded like heaven to her weary ears.

PART II
GERALD

CHAPTER 5

For just a moment, I listen to the sound of the glass as it breaks against the wall. My eyes glow red with the tears I've rubbed from them these last few days. In the distance, days ago, miles away, hours from now, there is a perfect form of grief that defines itself clearly and with precise borders for those it touches. That is not me. My pain is an ocean, above which the constellations of madness and grief that encompass my life have inspired in me the need to hurt somebody.

My name is Gerald Henry but my friends call me Hank. Only problem is, as of last night, all my friends are dead. Roy was the last of them.

When the call came in, it felt like I was reliving the past. Sixteen years ago, another friend died because of me, because of my business, and I've never been able to stomach that one either. Now Roy.

Fuck. Let's check the scoreboard then, shall we?

Danny: dead.

Roy: dead.

Candy: currently painting pictures of dandelions in an asylum.

It was Roy's boyfriend Marej who called. He didn't say, "Hello Gerald, how are you?". He didn't make small talk. We've had our differences, Marej and I, but we both loved Roy.

After I hung up the phone, I stood and stared out the window for a long time. I remember feeling a ball of stress form in my stomach, followed by the dull, throbbing sensation in my head that had begun accompanying life's little tragedies. When you hear about a psychic, you figure if they're legit, they've got their shit together. You know, that they know how to use what they have.

Not necessarily true.

I left the office in a daze and walked around the corner to Shag's, the neighborhood tavern I'd taken to frequenting. It's a rough joint, and I wouldn't have it any other way. The air in Shag's is full of smoke, perfume, and hormones; it feels thick and sweet in the back of my throat.

After thirteen bottles of bad domestic beer, I get my wish in the form of three stooges who accost me as I pass the pool table for putting something other than 80s hard rock on the jukebox.

"What is this shit? Hey, you listening to me?" The voice asks in such a way that I intuit it is repeating itself at this point. I don't care. I'm barely paying attention.

"Ellington. Duke Ellington. If you'd stayed in school past the first grade, you might have learned something," I say to my new friend. All three of them are big, muscle-bound biker types with tats and halitosis. The one speaking is the Alpha, and I'm making him my project.

"Fuck off," I add, the match on the gas.

He scowls at my response, snaps his pool cue in half, and brandishes the jagged result like a weapon. I get a flash of a tattoo that reads DIO on his knuckles and laugh.

"I'm gonna fuck you up," he says.

This is supposed to scare me. It does not.

Behind him, on the television that plays soundlessly over the bar, there's one of the recently inescapable Public Service Announcements about MV-20. A highly contagious, fast-acting virus, the Los Angeles County Health Officer stands beside the Mayor, raising the stakes on an already spiraling situation poised to completely remap modern life. Shelter-in-Place orders are inevitable, they say. This virus is spreading quickly through major population areas. I'm about to ask the bartender to turn up the volume when ol' Ronnie James lunges at me, frantic to save face before his cronies.

He's letting his emotions get the better of him. No focus. I'm no Ralph Macchio, but I know a thing or two. Ronnie winds up with his two front teeth sticking out of the table's green felt. Meanwhile, Daryl and Daryl beat a hasty retreat, muttering vague suggestions about my mother.

I watch them go, dust my hands off, and return to my seat at the bar just as the tears return full force. My chipper, adrenaline-inspired facade recedes into the bottom of a glass of beer. I finish what's there and order another. Still, I know no amount of drinking or fighting will change the fact that my friend is dead.

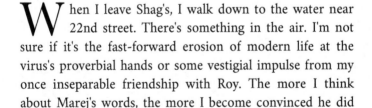

When I leave Shag's, I walk down to the water near 22nd street. There's something in the air. I'm not sure if it's the fast-forward erosion of modern life at the virus's proverbial hands or some vestigial impulse from my once inseparable friendship with Roy. The more I think about Marej's words, the more I become convinced he did not tell me everything. If Roy is dead, I have to know why.

What's more, I need to know who, and then I need to punish that person the same way I did the fucker who killed

Danny: unmarked grave in the middle of nowhere. Dig a hole, disappear a person. I don't like it, but that doesn't change the fact that it's what has to happen.

Standing on the edge of the pier, I close my eyes and try to address what I've come to think of as the 'aether.'

A stupid name, admittedly, but you gotta call it something; aether always seemed as good a name as any.

On that strangely cold night, surrounded by the city of Los Angeles on all sides except the one that surrenders to the ocean, I scan the horizon, trying to see my way across the twelve-thousand miles that divides me from Roy's adopted home in Seattle. I get nothing, which means I'm going to have to go there. It seems risky, with everything going on at the moment, but what can I do? I have to follow my gut.

This is just before the killings began.

CHAPTER 6

I knew all along that once Roy's death dragged me into this, I'd eventually become a target. Occult knowledge, *hidden* knowledge is like that. You strike a match in the darkness, you can see better, but you also give away your position. I'm the type that, well, let's just say I get involved. I returned to my meager apartment just off Gaffey and booked a flight. Six hours later, I hired a car from SEATAC, landed in Pioneer Square, and began to nose around.

Violence moved through the city like a plague. Small fires and broken glass decorated the formerly peaceful streets of what Roy used to jokingly refer to as "Amazon Town." Fights lay revealed around every other corner, literal orgies of malevolence spilling from restaurants and storefronts into the street. I caught visions of blood everywhere I went, as well as a recurring hallucination that changed people in my peripheral to monsters: boney, spikey things. I tried to pin this down, but direct attention shifted them back to their standard demeanor. I thought of Adriane Lyne's film *Jacob's Ladder* and immediately regretted doing so.

I interviewed anyone I could strike up a conversation with, mostly elders and college kids. Some told me stories about neighbors, friends, family members who had recently gone off the deep end and attacked people. The newspapers were soaked with seemingly random acts of violence and staggering promises of Martial Law. Page four related the tale of a pallbearer who beat a grieving man to death; page two, a Police Captain who massacred every cop under his precinct's roof and then stalked out into the street to pick off fifty-seven people before turning the gun on himself.

This might sound like chaos or mass hysteria, but it's not. I've caught glimpses of something very precise at work here. I can almost see its face, and it has something to do with Roy's death.

It's been several years since I last visited Roy. On that trip, he introduced me to his dealer and guru, one Marej Careb. Marej eventually became Roy's boyfriend. Domesticity loomed, larger than life. I remember being surprised. Roy had always been wild. Had his hedonistic nature finally got the better of him?

I didn't think so.

One thing I knew about my friend, he would never let a contact like Marej go, regardless of how the romance turned out. Fast-forward to the present. I'd arranged to meet Marej at his earliest convenience, location his choice. I'd expected one of the city's higher-end coffee shops or some swank lounge near his place. Evening came and I'd not heard back, so I had time to kill. I walked around until I found a place that had Roy's fingerprints all over it, metaphysically speaking.

The Diamond Access Bowling Alley was not the kind of place I would have expected Roy to frequent.

One round at the bar and wouldn't you know it, Mack, the owner, told me he knew Roy.

"Had to throw him out last week. Was in pretty bad shape, even for him."

I left a message on Marej's phone and proceeded to spend the rest of the night there, waiting. No call, no show. In lieu of my intended quarry, I drank like a fish and talked to anyone I could. Not about Roy, but about the city. Something was off, something more than what was happening outside. When I tried, it was almost as if I could sense a guiding hand amidst the chaos caused by MV-20.

On the television behind the bar, the same PSA I'd seen the night before in LA played every fifteen minutes or so. The statistics had worsened by a considerable amount.

At two A.M., I made my way back to the King's Inn. The walk back was tense. Police were everywhere, violence still erupting on every block. Also, I couldn't shake the feeling I was being tailed. Whenever I tried to sneak a peak, I came up empty, but you always trust your gut. I made it to my room, downed a handful of Ibuprofen and hit the sheets. When I woke up again, I realized I had slept clean through to the next evening. In my absence, the world had changed.

CHAPTER 7

Shelter-in-Place order, effective at midnight. Not a moment too soon. The streets are occupied exclusively by roving packs of violent marauders and trigger-happy police. National Guard coming soon. I barely make it a block before the feeling of being watched returns. I begin composing a strategy to draw my tail out, but find myself in the midst of what looks like a scene from *The Warriors*. A crowd of middle-aged men charge one another, baseball bats and chains, glass bottles, and at least one gunshot. Blood and teeth fall like rain, and I barely make it out before shooting one of them in self-defense. I kick another in the nuts and disappear down a tiny alley. When I stop to catch my breath, I call Marej and finally get through. He gives me his address. It's not far, a swanky condo in the most expensive district.

When I arrive, I'm surprised to see a large group of people there with him. Dance music is loud, lights are low. It looks like a club. An Asian kid who can't be a day over eighteen lets me in, takes me to where Marej reclines on a white, Italian leather sofa. He's a mess.

"I'm still in mourning," he says and apologizes for last

night. "I've been on a bit of a bender since... well, you know." He apologizes again and offers me cocaine to make amends.

Just like I remember him.

I find out this was Marej and Roy's place; they'd bought it late last year, just weeks after Marej had his head caved in by gay-bashers. There's a fireplace to the sofa's left, on its mantle a framed print of Roy and me Senior year in high school. Memories flood my head, and for a moment, I'm transported backward in time.

"Gay-bashers? Jesus Christ, what fucking year are we in?" I say over the music, which has now doubled in tempo and volume.

"You'd be surprised."

"I guess so, but it's not like we're in Okla-fucking-homa."

"Ignorance, it seems, remains its own reward for some."

As Marej speaks, I see the scars etched permanently into the bridge of his nose. It makes me hate the world even more than I already do, which is saying something. Humanity lost its 'get out of jail free card' with me a long time ago. Extinction feels both right and inevitable.

On cue, the TV on the far wall soundlessly runs the MV-20 PSA. I want to ask Marej what he knows about it, but I can't get a word in edge-wise. It's all I can do to follow the conversation over the sensory overload of the room.

"Roy was the best type of man. He spent the last several weeks reconnecting with University friends who did charitable work. He was excited about working with a company that handled donations to local impoverished school districts."

"What kind of donations?" I shout, surrendering to temptation and throwing back a fluffy white line from the obsidian table before us. No sooner than it's gone, Marej has one of his entourage cut me another. I hesitate but ultimately follow through. If booze helps my abilities, blow turns them up to eleven; I remain confident I will need all the help I can get. Or that's just an excuse.

"Books mostly. Some other outfit handled the food and clothing. Not sure why they never pooled their resources, though it may have something to do with Murph's ties to the publishing industry. Still, isn't that just like Roy? Always trying to save the planet."

"Who's Murph?"

"A friend."

Marej does a line himself and then paws wantonly at a young kid, African American, with a bald head and a ton of metal shit in his face.

"I miss him terribly. He truly did make me complete," Marej is fucked up and reminiscent, and I take this as my cue to exit. On the landing outside his door, I write the name Murph in my little black book.

~

Outside, I veer toward the seafront. There's no hired cars and no cabs. I catch sight of a tank in the distance, and I'm suddenly regretting being here. Then, I catch wind of something that feels familiar. Not Roy, but something related to him. It's hard to say how my 'gift' works, and even harder to know exactly when it's going to work and what it will tell me. In this case, I still have Marej's vibe in my head. I think I'm probably projecting it because the feeling that Roy is walking next to me becomes paramount.

The cocaine has my head buzzing like mad, moving my feet without my conscious mind having any say. I turn a corner and find myself replaying scenarios that feel like the antenna in my head has plucked them directly from Roy's memory:

The long walk from the Diamond Access to the condo.

Words, an endless expanse of words jumbled and falling, slamming into and out of my mind, controlling me with their delicate suggestions.

The song 'Rise' by Doves.

Maybe the world isn't meant to go on. Maybe we're not meant to suffer these tragedies.

Lying. Cheating. Everything... so black and horrendous.

The idea that life is scarier than death because at least with death, you know where you stand.

Sniper.

I'm trying to shake these thoughts off, but I can't, and I stumble. My eyes focus backward on the past. I see Roy talking to his mother about the Algonquin blood in their family. Folklore. We both have Native blood; it's what brought us together as friends in the first place, dark skins in an otherwise spotless white community. Day in question, I'm smoking a cigarette, and Roy says something about being a messenger. Something about his father, who he never knew. We're eighteen, and I'm staring at him. Then, suddenly, I've time-lapsed back to this moment. Where am I? There's a fire; I'm staring at the flames. There's a flash, and someone across the street sees me fall and runs over to steady me, but it's no use. I collapse into strong arms.

And that's when I see them again, only clearer, monsters with mangled, elongated flesh, every one of them. They only look like humans. Inside, they are killers.

CHAPTER 8

S taggering through the streets, I see soldiers and hear gunfire. For a moment, I think I get hit; I'm not, but I get swept up in a group of people. Engulfed in their mass, I'm taken to what I think at first is a church. Candlelight, low, drone-like singing. Glass breaks, and a bearded man addresses the crowd. It's some kind of secret meeting, or... I don't know. 'Meeting' is the wrong word, but gathering, yeah, that works.

At some point, I realize we're not in a church at all. We're outside, standing in the shell of a skyscraper in the early stages of construction. People in hoods warm their hands over garbage cans with small fires burning inside. The scene looks like it's from the end of the world. I keep hearing that fucking refrain from the Doves song, and I have an image in my head of something dreadful. It's not my imagination, more like what I would describe as some low-fi psychic broadcast. The images are disturbing—a man strapped to a table with a large beaker of thick, black liquid to his left. The opaque solution travels through an IV into his arm. He starts to scream, then his eyes turn backward, revealing a second set of pupils beneath. There's an explosion, followed by a rain of... garbage? Nearby, someone is laughing.

The images disappear as suddenly as they came on; I look up, and the person laughing is standing in front of me. I know them...

Time skips. It keeps doing that. It's like I blink and suddenly I'm sitting in the dimly lit bar at the Diamond Access Bowling Alley. There's a bottle of cheap beer in my hand, and a woman sits across from me who I recognize instantly. The pure cosmic serendipity of my life flexes, making me feel both insanely powerful and as insignificant as a bug.

"Detective Angela Miller. Holy cow. Everyone's looking for you."

Just before the call about Roy, the big news in LA was how Detective Angela Miller gunned down five people in the street, only to disappear from a locked cell a day later. Public outcry ensued, the families of Miller's victims taking to social media to raise a citywide series of protests at the spree-shooting cop's ability to fly the coup and leave a city in mourning. In the case of Jennifer Flores, sister of Luis Flores, one of the victims, she hired me to track down Detective Miller. I tried to make Ms. Flores understand that the police are a brotherhood. They protect their own. She didn't care; she wanted justice.

The thing that surprised me about Angela's case was that one of the people she murdered was her partner. My research shows Detective Jim Allen was a well-liked and highly decorated officer. Hard to believe other cops would help his murderer escape, but who knows? The thing about organizations like the police is everyone has an agenda, from the beat cops to the Commissioner, and they're often at odds with one another.

I hadn't made any progress when Marej's call came in. I

hadn't thought about Detective Miller or Jennifer Flores since, and now here I am, sitting across from my quarry.

Detective Miller bores daggers into my forehead with her eyes. I try to keep up a dialogue just to lighten the mood of the room.

"You're never going to believe this, but you just helped me solve a case and make five thousand dollars," I say with a smile that quickly inverts when something cold and metallic digs into my back.

"It's not my imagination; there's a gun at my back."

"Gerald Henry, Private Investigator. Meet Special Agent Joseph Killacky and his gun. What's your gun's name again, Joseph?"

"Woo."

"As in John Woo, the director?"

"Yeah. I like shoot 'em ups. Get it?"

I turn my head slightly to get a look at this Joseph guy. Fit, mid-thirties, maybe. His unnaturally thick eyelashes trigger a memory of seeing him shoot someone in the face back on the street. A couple of someones, followed by the sound of our shoes echoing on the rain-slicked pavement as we ran out from beneath the skyscraper's skeleton. I remember passing through an alley, then he led me back here to the Bowling Alley.

"Loud and clear."

"Okay, so let's cut the shit. That okay with you, Mr. Henry?"

"Call me Hank."

"Mr. Henry, we don't have time to get to know one another. There's a rampaging murder virus turning the population into kill-happy drones and we're here to stop it. When Joseph pulled you out of the building we raided, you said something about knowing how this all started. We need that information from you now, or Joseph will shoot you in the head and we will move on."

"The two of you raided that place?"

"There were more of us. An entire task force, to be accurate."

"Murderheads are up a few points, eh?"

I hear Joseph's chair slide on the tile a second before he cold cocks me in the side of the head with the gun. I fall to the floor, reality crackles for a minute. When I regain my composure, I decide to play along, at least until I can kill one of them.

"What we have to offer you, that's as good as it's going to get, Mr. Henry. And it won't ever get that good again. Capiche?"

"Yeah. Sure," I say, rubbing my head. I make a mental note to punch Joseph in the mouth first chance I get.

"You said something about monsters when we were running outta that shit hole," Joseph says from behind me.

"Look, I don't know what the hell that was. I have these episodes sometimes…"

"Ah, yes. That's right. You're not just a PI, you're psychic, too. How's that working out for you?"

"Apparently not as satisfying as being on the LAPD."

"You're trying my patience."

"You should hear me play piano."

"What do you know about Abramelin Harvest and his murder virus?"

Even though I don't remember ever hearing that name before, something comes back to me from my fugue. At that meeting, a homeless man with an enormous beard and dirt-smudged face whispered in my ear:

"They figured out a way to make murder a virus. There's no use; we're all going to catch it. You're friend knows. It's why he sent for you."

Roy? Was he talking about Roy? I decide to play along for a while.

"The virus is… I think it started here, in the city. A month ago, maybe?"

"If that's true, that puts it before Iowa," Joseph says.

"Fits with Rowland's trip to Bothell," Angela responds, jotting something down in a small, brown moleskin.

"If you know all this, why are you asking me?"

"We ask the questions, Mr. Henry."

"Fine. At least tell me what you know, so we're all on the same page."

"Alright. An indie-published manuscript by a right-wing fascist named Abramelin Harvest has gone viral, literally. The virus started infecting only those who read the book; however, something changed in the past seventy-two hours. The virus now appears to be as infectious as the flu or the common cold. Of course, the media had to have a nickname, so colloquially, the virus has become known as MV-20."

"Sounds like Science Fiction."

"Haven't you noticed? We're living in a world that looks an awful lot like Science Fiction. Deal with it, Mr. Henry."

The jukebox kicks on. Wouldn't you know it? *Rise* again. I get the feeling the Universe is trying to tell me something. I close my eyes, the little engine in my head goes 'Click.' I feel the psychic residue from a wave of dead people push up against my brain, knocking on my door, trying to get in. Little pigs, little pigs…

"Okay. Here's how this goes. I'm psychic."

"We've covered this."

"Shuddup, will ya? Now, when I close my eyes, I'm going to allow someone else to come inside me."

"Hot," Joseph says, and I push up off the chair and spin. Catching him unaware, I snatch Joey's piece with ease, eject the clip, and fire the chambered round into the jukebox. It sputters and dies. Bye-bye Doves.

I sit down again, straighten my collar, and smile. Joseph clocks me one but it doesn't hurt. He's shaken at my speed. I allow him to take his gun back. He doesn't scare me.

"So like I was fucking saying. During the possession, this body in front of you will not be me. Gerald Henry, PI, License Number 19771 will be a television tuned to static. White noise. You can imagine how vulnerable this makes me."

"Now we're getting somewhere. I need you to contact James Rowland. He-"

"That's not how this works, okay?"

"So then tell us, please, how this works."

"I can channel whoever's near us at the moment, metaphysically speaking. It will be your job to protect me during that time. Got it?"

"What if the person you channel attacks us?"

"Subdue. Do not mortally or critically wound. Do I have your word?"

"Yes, Mr. Henry, you have my word."

"Alrighty then," I say as I lean back in my chair and become someone else.

CHAPTER 9

EXCERPT FROM KILL FOR THE SAKE OF KILLING: AN EXPLORATION OF MACROCOSMIC SURGICAL TECHNIQUES TO RID THE WORLD OF THE HUMAN DISEASE, BY ABRAMELIN HARVEST:

*E*very human being on Earth has thought about killing another person. It does not matter who you are or what you believe. Beliefs do not hold together as a cohesive preventative operating system. Why? Because every human being has a multitude of different "people" inside them, and not all of them are nice. The "I" program installed and continuously updated from birth is a convenient device to weather the chaotic currents of existence; however, that device is not real. There are too many disparate entities inside each of us, all vying for control.

I call this the ego-scaffold, and it is what makes each person on the planet unique. It is also how we deal with those often contradictory thoughts, personalities, desires, etcetera. This infrastructure is the scaffolding we build around the swirling masses of chaos inside our heads, the suit of armor we show to the rest of the world. These suits may change slightly, depending on the situation, but in effect, in form and function, they are consistent. However, these suits are fictions and never precisely who we are because there is always a chance that a new situation, a new idea, or desire can be introduced and change our course completely.

Some ideas are self-propagating. Before the internet co-opted *the word meme, it was a scientific term. Coined by the scientist Richard Dawkins, a meme is an idea that is as alive as we are. Like us, memes harbor an impulse for procreation. How does an idea reproduce? By manipulating people to espouse it, they spread it to others in their words, writing, expressions, analog, or digital. Subsequently, I hypothesize when considered in this manner, it becomes clear there has never been as strong an idea in all human history as murder.*

In a world that otherwise holds us helpless, we obsess over the ability to inflict ourselves on our environment in any way possible. To affect those defiant forces of nature that can crush us like flies, that can remove everything we are, everything we have ever accomplished. Murder occurs every day. It blasts its way across the world in gunshots, stabbings, explosions, endless avenues to accomplish its goal. Murder can also occur in massive, Earth-shattering proportions, like when the United States dropped the atomic bomb on two cities in Japan.

Murder is in our plays, our movies, our books, our art. It is in our religions, and our bedtime stories, our pastimes, and our love lives. Moreover, in a staggering evolutionary leap, murder has emerged from the digital age's chrysalis in a newly perfected form. You will find that the truth of this text is that the planet needs murder to reassert itself and stop the infection choking it to death. The infection is us, and murder is the cure."

PART III
OTHER VOICES

CHAPTER 10

BILLY WICKERMAN

"State your full name for the record."

"William Howard Wickerman. Seriously though, I hate being called William. Billy. Please."

"Next, can you confirm that your name is not now, nor has it ever been Gerald Henry?"

"Who?"

"Good enough. All right, Billy. Tell me about the first time you saw the book *Kill for the Sake of Killing*."

"You a cop?"

"I'm not going to arrest you if that's what you're worried about. However, if you don't tell me what I want to know, I'm going to have the man standing behind you do something excruciating. Understand?"

"Since you put it that way, sure."

"Good. Start at the bookstore. Charters."

"Okay, well, the night I found the book, our GM Tony was there. So was our District Manager Lola; pretty sure they're fucking. Anyway, it was slow, and Tony told me to clean out the lost and found. That's where I found the book."

"You took it home?"

"First, we all went out for drinks. Tony's kinda an old Goth dude gone corporate, same with Lola. On nights we'd go out after work, we usually went to this Goth/Fetish club called KNOCK KNOCK. Pretty cool. I was sitting at the bar by myself, and I started to leaf through the book. Before I realized how much time had passed, the lights came on and security started herding us toward the door."

"That's when you went home?"

"Yeah."

"What did you do then?"

"I laid down but found it impossible to sleep. I tossed and turned for a bit, but there were these... I don't know. Things, pictures in my head. Eventually, I got up, opened a beer, and went back to the book."

"How did reading the book make you feel?"

"Better, I guess. It feels like... like the book gets *inside* you. It blots out everything you think of as 'you.' It's not *just* words. They're like these fucked up, crazy images, too. That's what I saw in my head when I wasn't reading it. Nothing I recognized, but these images, they were made of, like, syntax. Syntax, and punctuation and verbiage; things you associate with language, but not specifically language. Shit, I don't even know if that makes sense. But the things I'd see, they floated there, in this new place, this room inside my head. And the pictures, they kept changing. Shifting, like a lava lamp or Rorschach cards: houses, cars, highways... a dark black ocean and a raft made of bone."

"A black ocean and a raft made of bone? Oddly specific."

"I guess. All I wanted to do was sleep, but the book, it wouldn't let me. I read all night. At some point, I heard my roommate Brodie wake up for work. He walked back and forth in the hallway outside our bedrooms for about five minutes, making a shit ton of noise. Brodie was my best friend, but he was also an inconsiderate asshole. I got angry, you know, blamed him for not being able to sleep. I started imagining killing him. Only, it was so real, those thoughts. I saw myself attacking him with my bare hands, ripping his head off his shoulders, splitting his ribcage open. Very vivid, right down to how his flesh would feel beneath my fingers as I tore him apart. I could even hear the blood as it poured out of Brodie's body and splashed in a soft, satisfying pool around my feet.

"This image, it made me sick, but it also made me feel powerful. Like nothing I'd ever experienced before. Here was this root-black thing inside me, running an instant replay in my head over and over again. It was all I could do to sit perfectly still. I had to keep telling myself that something was wrong with me, that this wasn't normal. Because after reading that fucking book, it kinda felt normal, you know?"

"Did you kill Brodie?"

"At some point, I reached my limit. I stood up and went out after him, but he was already gone."

"What happened next?"

"I don't exactly know. One minute, I was in our crib, fighting the urge to kill something or someone. The next? That's when I understood."

"Understood what, Billy?"

"There's a fine line in everybody, one between the crazy thoughts that run through your head and the ones that balance you out. But the way things are now, in this society, all that really does is make a thin little shell of sense and routine. That's it. That's what we call sanity, just a little bubble where we think we've found a safe place to reside.

"For me, that line had disappeared. Erased overnight as I lay thinking of that black sea, Harvest's words cycling through my head dozens of times from start to finish. By morning it only took me twenty-seven seconds to mentally run over the entire book. How is that possible? And the clarity of playback, word for word, was nothing short of extraordinary.

"It was because of this newfound clarity that I finally understood what the images had been trying to tell me. They were a map, an arrow pointing in one direction. I couldn't point to that direction; it wasn't like up or down, left or right. But I knew how to get there."

"How?"

"On a raft of bone and an ocean of death.

"Amped, I stumbled from the house out into the street, my senses blazing like I'd just taken the strongest hit of acid *ever*. That's when I saw the two joggers on the other side of the road.

"My vision went red, and I crossed the street and headed straight toward them.

"My approach must have set off an alarm because I saw them exchange an anxious glance. The joggers picked up their pace. I picked up my pace, too.

"It began to rain.

"I laughed. I knew they could hear me, and I knew they were scared. The woman kept throwing anxious looks at the man until their pace turned into an all-out run. About a quarter of a mile ahead, a grocery store came into view.

"It was like I could taste their fear. I made my intentions more and more obvious because, as sick as it sounds, I was totally enjoying myself.

"About one hundred paces from the store, the rain became a torrential downpour. My joggers slowed, no doubt exhausted from fighting a losing battle against both the rain and what must by now be overwhelming concern about the maniac chasing them. It was only early afternoon, but the clouds made it look like midnight. I suddenly understood the brightly lit place in front of us was the only comfort these poor fucks could hope for.

"My daydream from earlier came back to me. The one about killing Brodie, the blood, and how it made me feel to have it cover me, head to toe.

"I started chanting:

"Blood.

"Blood.

"Blood.

"I don't know if they could hear me over the rain, but my prey slowed as they closed in on the store. Exhausted, their shoulders slumped, and they started to stumble.

"Within about fifteen feet of the entrance, I finally overtook them. I made one final push, launched myself through the air, and landed smack on top of the woman, using my momentum to drive her face into the concrete.

"It was fucking awesome, ya know?

"I could still feel the book running through my head. It was, like, an endless, twenty-seven-second loop. I rammed the woman's face into the street, chunks of her flesh and hair catching on the blacktop. On the second impact, a tooth dislodged and stuck in a groove. On the fifth, her right eye popped and left a streak of slime on the road beneath us.

"It was only a matter of seconds before the man tried to intervene. Was she his wife? Girlfriend? Mistress, sister, cousin, lawyer? It didn't matter, because my bloodlust was all there was at that point. It took me about five seconds to kill him. He tried to meet my attack head-on, but I caught his first punch mid-swing and used his momentum to catapult him forward and into a parking block, where the front of his face broke off like the ash on a cigarette.

"I could hear his neck snap as he landed, but I couldn't be bothered. I was too busy continuing to drive the woman's pulverized face into the curb. I started to sing *Mary Had a Little Lamb*.

"When I finally finished with the joggers, I stood up and

brushed the brain matter and pulverized bone from my shorts and found myself staring at the holy grail. These were the places of the living and, thus, where I would find my targets.

"I moved toward the grocery store."

CHAPTER 11

EXCERPT FROM KILL FOR THE SAKE OF KILLING: AN EXPLORATION OF MACROCOSMIC SURGICAL TECHNIQUES TO RID THE WORLD OF THE HUMAN DISEASE, BY ABRAMELIN HARVEST:

*I*n *the mid-2000s, there was a rash of animal attacks on populated human areas. While it is true some incidents involved mountain lions, bears, and, in one isolated case, a cougar, all entering major US cities and killing people before being captured or killed, the phenomenon occurred primarily in populated areas where nature still had something of a foothold in the environment.*

In Africa, elephants stormed into villages in packs, killing people at random. Unprovoked, these magnificent creatures would destroy residents, their homes, and their crops. Several smaller villages in India were likewise devastated beyond repair.

Around the same time, England saw a significant spike in attacks by several species of giant owls. The birds of prey began to swoop down in broad daylight and grab children and smaller adults, carrying them off and, in some cases, killing them. There were several reports of owls attempting to pluck full-grown men and women.

In beachfront areas, squid would perform suicide missions into shallow water, attempting to drown as many human beings as they could before they died.

Why?

There are too many humans. Humans are destroying the world, and in an effort to thin our numbers, the Planet has built-in defense mechanisms it can trigger to counteract a population that has become out of control.

Here then, is another of those triggers. This manuscript was dictated to me by the Planet, with instructions to pass it on. Following the ethos and systems laid down in this text will lead to an understanding that we must all take up this fight. Those violent urges that litter the background of our daily lives must now be acted upon, not dismissed.

Think of the Planet.

CHAPTER 12

When I open my eyes again, I can tell whoever just came through me must have given my host useful information. Angela sits scrawling notes in her moleskin, nodding her head as if in time with some inaudible rhythm.

"Right, right, that was the massacre at the supermarket where you killed... how many people?"

"Sorry to interrupt, but Billy's gone. Good old Gerald is back. "

Angela's eyes pin to me like lasers; I can feel the heat.

"Well, that sucks," she says.

"Yeah, well, it's not like you have anyone else who can do it any better."

She flips through her notes for a few moments.

"Okay, this makes sense, after all. There were reports that the police aced Billy during the massacre at the supermarket. Is that how this works? We reach the end of whoever's in your head's life, and then, what? Once they're dead, they're out of your jurisdiction? That doesn't make any sense. I mean, they have to be dead to channel them in the first place, isn't that how this works?"

"It's the Death Event. The trauma of dying severs the link. That's not always the case, but usually. Once, I followed some guy straight off a cliff into the afterlife."

"Oh, come on."

"Seriously."

"What'd you see?"

"You'll have to wait until I retire and write my book."

I smile, and she throws her glass at my head. I just barely dodge it in time. It hits Joseph. Good. Fuck him.

"No, seriously. That's where it ends with Billy Wickerman. Interestingly enough, however, it feels like I've got someone else on deck."

"Really?"

"Billy would appear to be the first link in some kind of chain, and the next person in line is already knocking on my head, eager to talk to you. Word spreads fast in the afterlife."

"Who is it?"

I close my eyes and instantly feel the aetheric Rolodex flipping by in front of me. The air I'm breathing gets thicker, then starts to thin back out. I see images of people's faces flit by until my internal search engine stops on someone: a tall, middle-America looking guy, black, no older than twenty-five.

"Tod? Tony Tod? Really?"

"What?"

"Not a horror movie fan, I take it, Angela?"

"What we have outside is enough for me, thank you very much. Now stop wasting my time, Mr. Henry."

"Right. Fuck me," I say before welcoming in our next guest speaker.

CHAPTER 13

ANTHONY TOD

The woman in front of me is gorgeous. She says she's a cop, but the sour puss on the goon reloading his handgun behind me suggest they may actually be something more dangerous than police.

"Mr. Tod, are you the General Manager of Charters Books in downtown Seattle?"

"I am. Good store. Come in, you'll see. We've got a better selection than any store in the Pacific Northwest. Especially for Horror and Sci-Fi. All the good stuff."

"Drop the sales pitch. Are you familiar with the book *Kill for the Sake of Killing*?

"That's what this is about?"

She nods, and I detect a dangerous fatalism in her expression. Unless I do something quick, I'm dead.

"Okay, well, ah…"

I jump up unexpectedly, thinking I'll catch her by surprise, run for the door. No dice. The goon smacks me upside the back of the head, and I fall face-first to the floor.

"I guess I'm fucked, huh?"

"You're not in trouble, per se Mr. Tod. But I need information from you about that book. I need to know how you first came across it. What it did to you. What you think about it. If you answer my questions, you'll be free to go. If you continue to give me trouble, Joseph will begin breaking things on you. Are we clear?"

"Crystal," I say, settling back into the cheap, single-mold plastic chair. I recognize this chair because I know this place pretty well.

"What's so funny, Mr. Tod?"

"I took bowling as an electorate in college. Yes, I'm aware how much money I wasted doing that, but truth is, I developed something of a taste for it. Ever since, every Wednesday night, I play league here. You can even see my jersey from our winning tournament on the wall in the other room."

"You must be very proud. I, however, do not care about bowling. I only care about-"

"The book. Right. Sorry."

Something catches my eye: my reflection. Like every bar in every bowling alley I've ever been in, the walls in this place are mirrors from the middle border up. My host moves her head to the side, and I see myself. Only it's not me. I open my mouth, he opens his mouth. I raise my hand, he raises his hand. I can't help think my mother would turn over in her grave because her handsome, black son is now stark raving caucasian.

"What the hell happened to me?"

"In a nutshell? You're dead, Mr. Tod. You're dead, and I'm using a psychic to channel you. Got it?"

I stare at this chick in awe. What she's saying is insane. Then again, my entire life has been crazy of late. So maybe...

"Joseph, do something terrible, would you please?"

"Wait!" I say, "Just give me a... just give me a minute, okay?"

"Mark," she says and rests her eyes on her phone, clocking the time.

I think back to the last thing I remember before waking up here, and unfortunately, what she says makes sense. That I'm dead, I mean. I remember the ghostly figure laughing at me from the shadows, the tunnel, the sniper above the elevator. From there, it's like a thick, dark blanket of stars swallowed me whole.

"Let me get this straight, just for the record. I'm dead, and you're having someone channel me?"

She nods, and I can tell by the uptick in the corners of her mouth that she's impressed I came around so fast.

"My grandma used to tell me her mother could do shit like this, back in the old days."

"Again, don't care."

"Fair enough. But here's a question for you: if this isn't my body, why would I care if you torture it?"

"Good question. Maybe you won't, but I'm betting you will. Shall we try? Joseph?"

The goon is on me so quickly I barely have a chance to acquiesce.

"Fine! My bad, just call off your dog." Luckily, I have an ace.

"Sit, Joseph."

"Fuck you, Miller. You keep that shit up, I'm leaving you in the ladies room with two holes in your head."

Awkward! The tension between these two is thick, so I sit quietly and wait to see what happens. Eventually, hostilities cede, and we pick up where we left off. Time for the ace.

"The book, Mr. Tod."

"What would you say if I told you that book is responsible for the wave of violence that currently holds the city in its thrall?"

"I know that to be a fact, Mr. Tod."

Shit. That was my ace.

"How bad is it?"

"Joseph?"

Behind me, Joseph stands and turns on the television mounted to the wall.

"... Where the lower floor of the Chihuly Exhibit was found literally piled seven feet high in some places with corpses... *Channel Change*... killed thirteen people inside the store, then opened fire on a bus full of children parked outside... *Channel Change*... at which point Warden Mansfield killed every prisoner housed under his supervision, firing on them through the bars of their cells, reducing them to little more than trapped animals left to his -" CLICK.

"I see."

"You don't. You really don't. This thing is pandemic proportion now, and I have reason to believe the outbreak may have started at your store."

"Outbreak? What is this? Violence, murder, they're not contagious."

Gunfire sounds from just outside.

"You sure about that, Mr. Tod?"

"I... I guess I thought all this would just, you know, blow over. I mean, it's not like we're talking about a best seller here."

More gunfire; she doesn't even need to say anything.

"Charters started in the Midwest, but really came to power here in Seattle. Did you know that? When I was in college, there were still quite a few stores. But, last couple years, well, you know. The internet."

She's making the hurry-up gesture. I realize my nerves are moving my mouth; I'm having trouble thinking beyond the idea of violence as an epidemic.

"Can I start at the beginning? Just to, you know, get the

ball rolling? I'm having trouble right now. I think this guy I'm in might not be as smart as me or something."

"Mr. Tod..."

"My store? It's one of only a handful left. I'd been there for a few years as a bookseller, one of those poor schlubs who have to look up the new Oprah book for middle-aged women or self-help shit for wannabe start-up yuppies. I worked hard, paid my dues, and got the Manager gig about a year ago."

"I don't care about your fucking career path. The Book. That's all I want to hear about."

"Alright, but-"

"Joseph. If the word book doesn't come from Mr. Tod's mouth in the next thirty seconds, please shoot him."

"Love to."

"Book! See? Getting there, I swear. One of our constant chores is to recover the items people pluck off shelves and abandon all over the store. Creative hiding places, too. Sometimes I find stuff wedged into small spaces, bent and twisted beyond the salvageable limit. Sometimes they are simply, masterfully destroyed. And sometimes, well, sometimes you find things that don't belong in the store in the first place. Sometimes, those things are books."

"Finally," she exhales like she was about to explode.

"The title sounded like one of those cookie-cutter Thrillers guys like Patterson and his contemporaries churn out, like, a dozen times a year. Boring. Anyway, my nighttime cashier Billy-"

"Billy Wickerman?"

"You know Billy?"

"We've met. Continue."

"Well, Billy brought it to me one night. No SKU, no ISBN, or UPC. Tattered and chewed, the book looked homemade.

The front cover was devoid of anything other than the title, so I flipped it open and tried to find identifying marks.

"This is first-generation then," she says over my head to the goon.

"Sounds pre-first generation. Like someone printed the ebook at home and made a physical copy."

My host nods for me to continue.

"So yeah, homemade isn't a stretch. Inside, from what I glanced at that first night, the text looked thick and unremarkable.

"What'd you do with it?"

"Told Billy it wasn't ours, he should throw it in the lost and found. Fast forward a couple days, here's Billy with the same book. It's a slow night, and he'd been cleaning out the lost and found, saw that no one ever claimed it and asked if he could have it. I told him yeah.

"We left early that night but didn't go home. Billy had become a friend, and our DM was visiting, so we all went out for a drink."

"What's the DM's name?"

"Lola. She'd come from my store, actually. In fact, we kinda had a thing. Well, we started fucking. After that, she used my affections for her tireless vagina to weasel a recommendation out of me, knowing full well I would not pay attention to what I was recommending her for. Two weeks later, she was the new District Manager and, subsequently, my boss."

"Smart girl."

"Yeah. Girl power, right? Well, I was pissed at first, but whatever. Eventually, I realized that with her new position and a little guilt, I could get her to slather me with biased and undeserved favoritism. Plus, we kept fucking."

"Anyway, so that night, we went to KNOCK KNOCK, a sort of Goth/industrial place nearby. From the moment we arrived, Billy could not keep his nose out of that book, which seemed weird, but I was distracted. First order of business was to score some blow from the bartender. Fast forward near the end of the night, Billy's still sitting at the mostly empty bar reading, Lola and I try to fuck in the john, only I'm so high I can't get it up, and the lights come on."

"Where does Billy go afterward?"

"Home, I guess. Only the next day? He doesn't come in for his mid-shift. Which is weird, 'cuz this kid's reliable. I get a little worried. I kept seeing his face buried in that book. There was something in his eyes. I don't know how to explain it. He looked... possessed."

"Two hours after we open the store, I see it on the news in the break room. An as-yet unidentified attacker killed thirteen people at a grocery store down the street from Billy's house. Not sure why, but something clicked. The cops hadn't ID'd their killer yet, but there was no doubt in my mind. The killer was Billy.

"The rest of that day felt like a hallucination. I kept thinking about how I'd just seen Billy. What had happened between the time I left the bar the night before and this... massacre? What the hell was going on in this kid's mind?

All I could think of was that stupid book.

It sounded crazy at the time, but the idea that I had caused this nightmare simply by letting him take that book home became inescapable. I tried to put it out of my head, but more and more, the idea possessed me. Finally, I set out to make sure I could find the damn thing before anyone else did.

When I arrived at Billy's apartment, I knocked, but no

one answered. I knew Billy's roommate Brodie; he'd worked at the store for a few months last year until we found him Sweet-hearting Manga to teenage girls. The kid was a nob, but right now, I hoped to find him home.

When Brodie finally opened the door, he looked like absolute shit. Bags under his eyes, long hair scraggly and unwashed, dressed head-to-toe in black. He looked like he was either high out of his mind or had been crying.

Turned out it was actually a little bit of both...

As soon as he saw me, Brodie's eyes went wide with terror. He slammed the door so hard I thought the thing would break off at the hinges and topple back on top of him. Alarmed, I tried to reassure him through the door.

"Brodie. You know me. We've met. I'm Billy's boss."

There was a pause, and then the door opened again. The kid looked even more disturbed now: frantic and agitated.

"You gave it to him."

"What?"

"The book, man! Where did you get it?"

"You mean the book he brought home?"

"You know the book I mean, man! Where'd you get it? Tell me or... or I'll go to the police."

The traces of white powder that clung to the flesh at the base of the kid's nostrils suggested this was a bluff.

"Look, can I come in?"

I have serious drug radar, and right now, that shit was howling like the sirens in Dresden, 1945.

"Where did it come from?"

My back buzzed like a swarm of insects. I could feel the hunger in my blood.

"I'm not going to talk about the book or any other fucking thing standing out here where the whole complex can hear us."

Brodie stood fast for another moment, then his shoulders slumped and I knew I had him. He turned around and walked back into the apartment. Anticipation mounting, I followed.

I counted the steps it took to cross the living room and enter the small corridor that terminated in two bedrooms. Twenty-two. The door on the right was open. Inside I could see a computer, a still image of pornography on the screen. Below that, a bed and a glass table with long, thin lines of white powder cut out on it and a large bag of the same stuff at the far end. Brodie either didn't care that his vice had been left out for my scrutiny or was so high he didn't realize it. The door to the other bedroom was closed.

"In here," he said, indicating the closed room, which I assumed was Billy's. Business first, I told myself, giving the drug a wink and a kiss. I'll be back for you later, beautiful.

The kid opened the door to the other room. As we entered, I passed him and, in doing so, caught a particularly vapid scent from his full head of unwashed hair. I recoiled from the odor. The little shitbag seemed blissfully unaware of his stink.

"There it is, man."

The room was small, most of its space taken up by a shabby king mattress and an elaborate computer desk. It was the kind of thing that belonged to the previous decade when computers and media took up considerably more space. The book lay open on the desk, the walls around it covered in words. Words scrawled in neat, enormous sentences, as though the room itself consisted of four giant pages. I feel it's important to note that withough having actually read the book yet, I inherently understood the words on Billy's walls had been copied from it.

I felt like Wendy Torrance or Alice tumbling down the rabbit hole. Seeing this tangible evidence of my employee's madness, I had the distinct premonition that my life would never be the same again.

CHAPTER 14

I could feel the book's power from across the room. It had a presence, a kind of malevolent inertia that devoured your attention. I hadn't noticed this that first night Billy found it, but now it was undeniable.

I mean, I actually forgot about the drugs. For a moment.

I watched Brodie; for all his fear of this sinister volume, he was drawn to it. Rubbing his nose, his eyes glossed over once they settled on it. He drifted over to the open pages, and I saw he had no more motor control than a somnambulist. When he began to flip through the pages, he did so as though he were in a trance. It was at this point I noticed the ink stains on his fingers. It became clear that if Billy had started the macro-transcription onto the apartment's walls, Brodie now continued it.

I decided to test the waters. I walked over to the desk and picked up the book.

"Hey," he yelled, snapping out of his trance.

"What?"

"Don't touch that!" he said. I didn't relent, and he snatched the book from my hands.

"I thought you were afraid of it," I chided, trying to down-play my immediate reverence for the book. The fucking thing pulsed at me like it *needed* me.

"I... I don't know. I don't understand what's happening to me."

Tears of madness and confusion stained his cheeks. I tried to look understanding, but really the only thing I could think about was beating this snot-nosed Millennial to death with my bare hands.

This seemed as good a time as any to broach the subject of the drugs.

"I think it might help both of us to talk about what happened to Billy," I said, stepping back out of the room. "C'mon. Tell me what happened."

Brodie led us back to the living room where I plopped onto the jaundice-yellow couch and heard the wooden support beams snap beneath my modest frame.

Definitely hand-me-down furniture.

Everything in the place reeked of thrift stores or dead aunts. The kind of stained, sagging furniture that bachelors in their early twenties live with until a girl takes an earnest interest in straightening them out. Brodie disappeared into the other room, brought out the bag of white powder, started cutting it up on the glass-topped coffee table that separated us.

"Hey, ah, I didn't have time for an Americano before I came over, so..."

Brodie rubbed his nose like a magic lamp and stared at the drugs. Had he only just realized the compromising position he'd created for himself?

"There's a coupla' cans of Red Bull around here some-where," he said half-heartedly. He already knew where this was going.

"How about a little..." I raised my finger to my nose to finish my thought, and he hung his head, defeated.

Game set and match, bitch!

"So, I take it you've read the thing?" I said, hoarking back an Ozzy-sized line.

Ninety seconds later, we were taking turns with the straw; of course, the blow greased the wheels. Now I couldn't shut the little fucker up.

"I tried to ignore it, but... man, sounds crazy... it's like the thing talks to me."

"Did you read it?"

"Yeah. A couple of times. I just... I wanted to understand why Billy did it. I mean, it's Billy, ya know? He never hurt, like, anybody."

I could hear Brodie's voice as the confessional continued, but I could no longer see him. Instead, the image of the words scrawled on the walls in the next room danced behind my eyes. I've never had a very crisp memory, but suddenly, it felt photographic. My brain remembered every word. It panned back over them all now, deliberate, like I was reading the actual book. The experience was alien, almost like the words were going over me, not the other way around. Like *they* wanted *me* to think about them, wanted me to *remember* them.

"... and then I dreamed about the thing. It was like, Hi-Def, ya know?"

My host prattled on, an AM radio in between stations. In my mind, a scenario played out as if in real-time. Brodie lowered his face for another line and I drove my fist down on the back of his head. The straw went straight into his brain, and his face slammed through the glass. Impaled by shards, his eyes turned the consistency of cottage cheese. I gathered a mess of his hair and used it for leverage, hammering him against the table's wreckage repeatedly. When I finally pulled him up to get a look at his new mug, I saw a large shard sticking out from the bridge of his nose, right between those delicate, chewy organs of sight.

"Hey, man, fa-fuck off!" the vision ended. I became lucid to find Junior brandishing a kitchen knife at me. In my audacity, I'd apparently forsaken the economy-sized lines he'd been cutting out for me, going instead to snorting directly from his bag.

I reacted violently, to say the least. With the words from the wall still echoing through me, I watched as if from outside myself as I nabbed the little bastard by the back of his nappy ass head. In one swift movement, I brought his face down to meet my right knee.

BAM! He actually flew backward and away from me. Blood arced across the room, splattered on the wall while his head collided with the deep red mahogany armrest of that hand-me-down sofa. The sound his skull made when it broke open was like the sound of an eggshell when you crack it against the edge of a stainless steel sink.

I grabbed the book, the coke, and a juice box from the fridge and was on my way."

CHAPTER 15

That night, I barely slept. It wasn't the drugs. I mean, they didn't help, but what was really driving me was the book. That's the wrong word, though, isn't it? I mean, a book is something you read, something you take into yourself. This? This takes *you* in. I came to see it as a manifesto, written by someone who understood all the things about the world that I did not. Someone who saw humanity and its creations - the Internet, the News, Consumerism, Capitalism, Socialism, etcetera - for the diseases they are. Abramelin Harvest had communed with the Earth, and the Earth had told him its one and only wish.

End Humanity.

By morning, I felt wrought with epiphany, I ducked out to the corner liquor store. That's where I had a premonition. I was waiting in line when a PSA for the MV-20 virus came on the tv behind the counter. This is before these became so ubiquitous. I mean, now there are billboards, a celebrity PSA, Emergency Broadcasts. It's been the number one trending topic on Twitter for days. Everyone knows what it is and how rapidly it's spreading. Shit, even the fucking President finally acknowledged it. Things were getting scary, violence in the streets, and supplies running low. That's when it hit me: the virus had started with the book.

I needed to start stockpiling if I was going to make it through what I suspected was coming. I bought a couple bags of essentials, but when the cashier refused to sell me liquor because it was still too early in the morning, I lost my temper and killed him. It wasn't until I'd used the customer bathroom to wash the blood off my hands that it occurred to me I'd compromised myself. Murder, once something so frightening and alien, now seemed so calm and rational.

It seemed so *right*.

I locked the front door and left through the back. It was only ten blocks to my store. I walked the entire way so as not to arouse suspicion. In case the Police had already been called. It was early enough that we hadn't opened yet, so I disarmed the alarm and went to my office. After taking stock of my supplies, I fired off a quick text to Lola. I was pretty sure she was still in town and would roll through around 10:00 AM. My plan hinged on her presence, but I wanted to have everything ready, just in case I couldn't convince her to play along.

No one but Lola and I knew this, but in the room that housed the store's server, behind the computers, there's a door that leads to a seldom-used basement. This would be my new home for the foreseeable future.

If you've ever done the Seattle Underground Tour, you know there are tunnels beneath the streets of the entire city. The Seattle we know today is built on top of an older one. A failed metropolis that poor civic planning installed atop a tideland that eventually flooded. The fact that our store - located in a historic building at the Eastern end of Pioneer Square - had a basement wasn't weird, but we hadn't known abou it until a drainage problem forced me to hire a plumber a few months back. Said plumber also unearthed a secondary access hatch connected to the tunnels that crisscrossed below the rest of the city.

Perfect for my purposes.

I needed a place to hole up and see if I could come at this book thing in a way that might help me get a leg up on it. I could feel changes taking place inside me, like two totally different minds. One was familiar and had been with me my whole life. The other thought murder was an acceptable response to, well, everything. I was, I believed, infected with MV-20, the result of my exposure to what Billy had transcribed on the walls of his apartment. If this was the case, if a few glances were all it took to enter my system, then the city - maybe even the world - was fucked.

I needed to know what we were dealing with if I had any hope of surviving it. I wouldn't be able to do that if I succumbed to the increasingly persistent urge to kill everyone I encountered. Thus, isolation.

When I finally got situated, I called Lola's cell. She was five minutes away. When she arrived, I was still above-ground, waiting for her, but in bad shape. That sound Brodie's skull made when I broke it open? It'd become a melody. An ear-worm that ran through my head non-stop. This created what I can only describe as intermittent fugue states. Reality slipped beneath hallucinatory reveries of murder. Elaborate, blood-spattered fantasies I could feel pushing me toward something horrible. I kept seeing myself killing people. Beating the shit out of them with an encyclopedia, or, better still, with the revised, hardcover edition of *Infinite Jest* I kept behind glass in my office. One customer, a regular who always - and I do mean always - made it a point to get in my face about something, received my favorite imaginary death. In the vision, I watched myself stalk alongside him in the Fiction section while he browsed, waiting for the right moment to pounce. At the precise moment he picked up the copy of Salman Rushdie's *Shalimar the Clown* - the one he put on hold every other day but never bought - I sprung. Grabbing the braids in his hair, I twisted them around his throat like rope and used them to strangle the fucking life out of him.

When Lola arrived, I could tell that she knew something was wrong. I decided to play the sympathy card.

"Gads, you look like shit, Tony. What's going on?"

"IBilly killed like a dozen people in a grocery store."

"Our Billy?"

"Yeah."

"Excuse me, do you work here?"

This was no vision; the store was open, and Lola and I were standing on the sales floor. Before us, the first customer of the day.

"Yes, ma'am," Lola answered when she saw I had no intention of acknowledging the woman.

"I said, do you work here?" the woman demanded.

"And she said yes, we do. Time to clean out those ears, eh Grandma? I think I have a steak knife in my desk, be right back," I turned to go, and Lola caught me by the shoulder. The look of horror on her face was priceless. The look on the old woman's was even better.

"How can we help you?" Lola offered, trying to assuage the woman's outrage.

"What?"

"YES! Yes, she said YES, we fucking work here!"

Lola stared at me aghast, possibly recognizing by my enraged breathing and hunched posture that I was two seconds from tearing this bitch's throat out.

"I... I..."

"I'm sorry, ma'am, Mr. Tod just, ah, well, someone we know just died."

Lola with the save.

"I... I..."

Lola turned quick and whistled for Andy, another employee nearby.

"Andy, help this lovely woman find whatever she's looking for. It's on us," Lola said these last three words looking me dead in the eyes so I would understand what she was really saying was, "We need to talk."

CHAPTER 16

Lola took the seat behind my desk and began to interrogate me.

"Are you fucking high, Tony?"

"No. Well, yeah, but that's not the problem."

"Oh, it's not?"

Lola put her hands together in a contemplative steeple and tried to look stern. All in all, a weak attempt at putting me in my place. Her posturing made me mad; I imagined fucking her to death, then quickly shook the image out of my head. This was Lola, one of the few people I counted as essential to my life. Also, if I wanted my plan to work, I needed her.

"What about Billy? What the fuck is going on?"

"Look! I need time to figure things out; that's what I was trying to tell you on the phone," by the look on Lola's face, she wasn't buying any of this. I'd have to amp it up a bit.

"I think... I think I might have stumbled onto the reason."

"The reason what?"

I remember thinking it was a good thing this one could

fuck, or she'd be hemorrhaging blood from all orifices right about now.

"The reason Billy killed all those fucking people! Try and keep up, will ya?"

"Sorry, sorry. It's just..."

"Forget it. Just help me out, okay?"

"Fine, Tony. What do you need?"

To pull off what I had planned, I knew I would need someone to help me. I also knew the only person in a position to do so was Lola. As a locally-based District Manager, she could cover for me with Corporate *and* physically run my store. It would also put her in a position to bring me supplies or deliver messages on my behalf. I'd decided I wouldn't be leaving my little hidey-hole anytime soon, lest I end up like Billy, so I asked her to lock me in.

This, of course, took some explaining.

I didn't go into detail. I didn't want to try and explain what I could feel happening to me. Besides, judging by the way she began to physically distance herself, I'm pretty sure Lola suspected I might have contracted MV-20. The PSAs had switched to "Social Distancing" instructions. These now played ad nauseam, the newest version containing several big name Hollywood stars pleading with the population to "help fight this monster." Judging by what few updates I received from Lola, things had gone from bad to worse.

The world outside had begun to show escalating signs of contagion. This crazy fucking virus was making people murder one another en mass, working its way through the population, turning everyone from adolescents to senior citizens into mindless killers. No one else had worked out the connection between Harvest's book and the disease yet. How could they have?

Regardless of whatever Lola thought about me, she agreed to help with a series of increasingly strange requests. I'm guessing this was due to an alchemical combination of fear and attraction. She was afraid of me, but we fit together so damn good she couldn't live without me.

Boy, did I miss the mark on that one. But we're all narcissists at heart, here in the twenty-first century.

That night, locked beneath my store, I used a portable LCD lamp to claim a small circle of the damp, cold concrete as my own. I began to read the book properly, page by page. As I poured over the words, something strange happened.

At first, it felt like I'd fallen asleep but stayed lucid. Like my consciousness had shifted into a kind of dream world. I was no longer in the basement but adrift on a dark ocean, a raft of bones the only thing keeping me afloat.

"Hold up a second," my friend across the table interrupts me, "A dark ocean and a raft made of bones?"

"That's right. Mean something to you?"

She jots notes in an old, brown moleskin and then motions for me to continue. I guess we're not sharing information here.

"The bones that made up the raft, they'd been fused together. As I sailed away toward an unsure horizon, I realized something about the scene looked familiar. It was the future-primitive plane of a world without humanity. A map I'd found in the back of the book outlined all this in crude, almost childish scrawlings. In my head, I followed this path, destination designed by a hunch, and soon found myself at the heart of the problem."

"Which was?"

"Time. If humanity was scheduled to end, I was running out of time."

CHAPTER 17

After a few days, I knew my original, non-murder persona was hanging on by a thread. The deck was stacked too high against it. I hadn't slept. I was beside myself most of the time. My old self looked in as though from outside, forced to watch the crazed automaton that had replaced him ranting and raving about, well, killing everyone and everything.

I was obsessed with extrapolating current events. News agencies continued to beat the armageddon drum, using terminology like "a virtual army of unidentified assassins" and "the contagion of mass murder." CNN tracked the body count like sports stats, and Homeland Security released graphs and charts that illustrated "The Evolution of the Homicide Virus." MV-20 for short.

Here's some food for thought. According to the U.S. Census Bureau's website, the world's population was closing in on 8 billion people when this outbreak began. Keep in mind the Census folks have a website that updates almost every second with population tracking data. That's how fast humans multiply—every second.

That's pretty scary, right? Herein, we find what I believe to be the real genesis of the outbreak. Harvest's book is merely a result of a much more deeply rooted cause.

It's a well-known fact that nature has a way of balancing its scales. Throughout human history, we've observed and recorded population adjustment periods in other species, so why would we think ourselves immune from the same effect? It makes me angry to think how arrogant we are, how sure of ourselves as the dominant form of life on this planet. Recognizing this as a misconception was key to Harvest's text. Humanity's population was out of control, and we'd ceased being the dominant form of life on the planet in 1881, the year the Supreme Court of the United States granted Corporations Peoplehood.

From Harvest's text:

The ruling modified the fourteenth amendment, which passed in 1868, after the Civil war, to protect recently freed slaves from discrimination. In 1881, as a ploy to avoid what they deemed 'unfair taxation,' the Southern Pacific Railroad argued that Corporations were people, too, and thus, should have the same rights. When the Court ruled in favor of this argument, human beings ceased to be the dominant form of life on planet Earth. We became nothing more than the cells within a more complex organism, The Corporation.

Harvest's book argues that when a person contracts Cancer - which is essentially a harmful overpopulation of white blood cells - treatment entails using radiation to lessen the amount of those cells. Harvest, a self-described Planetarian, introduced his viral text as an analog to radiation treatment, literally killing off the overabundance of cells. In this case, the cells are us.

You can't even imagine what it was like for me to come into these epiphanies. I spent days pacing around that dank room, laughing and crying, sometimes in the same breath.

There we were, on the cusp of this massive Event - possibly an Extinction Event, no less - and no one else had any idea of the magnitude of this thing. Not even the infected, running around out there, doing Harvest's bidding.

Humanity's refusal to acknowledge scientific fact, coupled with our inability to treat other species as anything but inferior, ultimately proves we deserve this. The Root Cause Analysis for all the problems in the world? Too many people, end of story. From pollution to government ineffectualness, immigration to disease, it's all because there are too fucking many of us. I mean, you want things to work, and no one wants to see a couple of million people die, but to quote the B-Boys, something's gotta give.

I, for one, could not wait to do my part.

CHAPTER 18

I t was about this time that I noticed the hole for the sump pump, my bathroom for all practical purposes, was beginning to back up.

Shit. Literally.

A welcome distraction from the manuscript, even if an unwelcome problem, it was the smell that first alerted me to the situation. I tried to ignore it, but then strange gurgling noises began issuing from the hole. I wondered if it was affecting the store upstairs.

By the middle of what we'll call the fourth day, I could no longer sit on the hole to take a shit, as the back-up had crested the threshold. After the first time I attempted to find a way to stand or lean over it, well, let's just go the easy route and say I gave up.

Time began to malfunction. I found myself suspended in a thick, viscous syrup. Hours, minutes, seconds, all increments of the clock swirled and swam around me. The straight-ahead, tick-tock version of time that we're trained with from birth lost all meaning. I experienced what I came to think of as a total freefall chronology. The only incremental passage to judge it by was the duration of a song I could hear through the ceiling. 'Rise' by Doves on an endless loop that winnowed away my sanity with its haunting melody. I wondered who Lola had given control of the store stereo to. Or if the digital vendor Charter's used for in-house music had succumbed to the rising tide of violence, leaving their playlist stuck on a single track. This would have been cause for alarm in the world I'd known less than two weeks before. Several days into forced isolation? Not so much.

I re-dedicated myself to the task at hand with a new curriculum: I stayed high, willed myself to eat as little as possible, and waited for Lola to open that fucking door. Fear or no fear, she *had* to come back at some point. My attempt to outlast or undermine my infection had managed only to prime my bloodlust.

I used the rapidly dwindling mountain of blow to stave off hunger, as I was increasingly afraid of the confrontation with my sump-pump a bowel movement would demand. Likewise, I began to freely piss in the far corner of the room. I found several old buckets of paint that, once pried open, I poured over the urine to kill the smell. Unfortunately, with next to no ventilation, the fumes lingered. They were rough and probably toxic, but they beat the soggy smell of days-old urine. This, too, added to the ongoing altered state I'd created for myself.

How many days until I realized Lola had not returned? There was no way she could have forgotten me, so I figured she'd either abandoned me or been murdered in the chaos.

Soon after, I decided I had no choice. I had to clear the sump pump.

I removed my shirt and lay on my belly in front of the pump's hole. A thick crust of shit and piss covered what had once been an opening with about a three-foot radius. There was no pretty way to do this, so I closed my eyes and thrust my hand directly into the scabrous matter. It felt like I'd pierced the outer skein of a wound. My breath caught in my throat as the puncture unleashed a noxious bouquet of horror, unlike anything I'd ever experienced. Tears streaked from my eyes, but I plunged my arm in further, all the way up to the elbow, searching for the blockage that would release this blackest of nightmares. Soon I was in up to my shoulder and still, nothing. I fought to keep my chin from touching, but eventually I slipped, and my face landed gently in the tepid mess. I could taste the salty sweat of the thick black sludge on my lower lip, its cold, oily kiss on my cheek.

~

My stomach churns at the memory, so I stop to take a drink. That's when I notice the look on my host's face. Far from the sickened reaction I had anticipated, she is all smiles.

"You okay hearing this?" I ask, trying to be considerate.

"You weave a most harrowing narrative, Mr. Tod," she says and reaches for a glass of auburn liquid that sits on two ice cubes in a tumbler before her. As she does, I realize something.

"Humor me for a moment?"

My host's left eyebrow arches, indicating curiosity.

"Raise both hands above your head."

Now the other eyebrow turns down, as do the corners of her wonderfully red lips. Lips that inspire in me a mournful memory of Lola.

"Fuck you."

"I thoughts so," I say and turn to Joseph.

"So you're not her stoolie; you're her jailor."

"You heard the lady, Mr. Tod. Keep talking before you unearth a pile of maggots."

"I eat maggots for breakfast. Remember? I'm dead."

The room devolves into a stalemate that, of course, my inquisitors win. I just can't keep from talking about myself.

"So, what happened next?" my host asks, reasserting control.

"I vomited. Repeatedly."

"After that."

"After that was right about the time I found the tunnel."

My hand brushed against something. No, not against something. Against *nothing*. With my arm in this hole all the way to my face, I suddenly felt an open pocket of air. I had to ask myself: what's below the lowest level of a city with an underground tunnel system?

Answer: Folklore. Something forgotten, whispered about, a fantasy that went down much further than recorded history would like us to believe. We're talking below sea level here. Deeper, unexplored catacombs that lay forgotten by time. Thrilled by my find, I decided then and there; it was time for me to make my escape.

As soon as I could dig out enough of the sludge to shimmy through the opening, that is.

I redoubled my efforts, and just moments before I had a workable entrance, I heard the latch on the door behind me and turned just as Lola and Tim, the Regional VP, entered the room.

Oh, what I'd give to know what went through Tim's mind that first moment he laid eyes on me.

"See, I told you he was down here," Lola said, accusingly.

"And I am sorry I didn't believe you, Lola. I mean, well, just what the hell have you been up to, mister?"

I'd met Tim a few times. He was the kind of guy people

put a picture of in the center of their dartboard. The way he spoke reminded me of that religious neighbor on *The Simpsons*, and at the moment, I could think of nothing that would make me feel better than ending his life.

"Anthony, Lola tells me you haven't been on the job in two weeks. She said you've been, ah, living here in our basement?"

Our. That was the kicker. Not that being shoulder deep in excrement, strung out on drugs, and infected by a rampaging murder virus wasn't enough. But that stupid corporate idea of 'our.' Our store, our product, our time, it pushed the nuke button on my hate. Violence welled up inside me, and I snapped.

"Well, mister? What do you have to say for your-"

Before Tim could finish, my arm came out of the viscous vacuum with a thick SLURCH, and I was on top of him like a demon guerilla at a zoo in hell. Weaponless, I drove my fingers - almost a week's worth of fingernail growth leading the way - deep into his throat. I used the jagged edges to pry his flesh open like a stubborn cupboard. Tim's skin broke, his veins popped, and when I found that most exciting of arteries, the holy carotid, I yanked it clean out of him like an errant thread from a thrift store sweater.

What resulted was a fountain of blood—a cliched way to describe it, but accurate all the same. Had I a penny, I would have tossed one at the rapidly growing pool that surrounded his freshly minted corpse.

The rage subsided just in time for me to hear Lola's heels on the unfinished concrete floor. She rounded the corner from my sight, and before I could even attempt to follow, I heard the door slam and lock. From the other side, I could hear her crying and screaming into her cell phone.

"He's crazy! He just killed our Regional Vice President, and now he's after me! Help! Help!"

Maybe it was my frayed state of mind, but at that moment, life felt an awful lot like a video game. A video game I had every intention of winning by wracking up the biggest fucking body count I could.

The police were no doubt already on the way.

I retreated to the hole, diving onto my stomach and sliding across the slop as if it were a child's Slip-and-Slide. Word by word, line by line, page by page, Harvest's text ran ceaselessly through my head. I could hear the Doves song again; only this time, there was a strange, high-pitched cyclical sound accompanying it.

'Remix?' My mind paused its frenzy to question.

As I reached back into the tunnel, my arm quickly returned to the open pocket of air below me. I tried to survey the space to determine if I would fit - no sense in getting stuck. I had just begun to crawl into the hole when I heard the police charge through the door.

'Here goes,' I said, excited and terrified. I took a massive breath, closed my eyes, and slipped into the sludge head first.

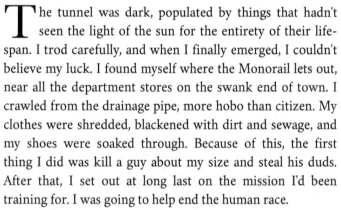

The tunnel was dark, populated by things that hadn't seen the light of the sun for the entirety of their life-span. I trod carefully, and when I finally emerged, I couldn't believe my luck. I found myself where the Monorail lets out, near all the department stores on the swank end of town. I crawled from the drainage pipe, more hobo than citizen. My clothes were shredded, blackened with dirt and sewage, and my shoes were soaked through. Because of this, the first thing I did was kill a guy about my size and steal his duds. After that, I set out at long last on the mission I'd been training for. I was going to help end the human race.

With the virus driving the meat suit, there's an ecstatic

elation that comes secondhand, a sort of pleasure reward for signing up. I remember it started as an icy feeling in my face, a lot like anger, only cut with an almost adolescent ache. Imagine Jason's mask coming off only to reveal Charlie from that Wallflower book beneath.

This delicious teenage feeling welled up inside me, like the rising tides of an acid frenzy, or the moment that precedes your much anticipated first kiss. That's what I felt every time I would attack someone, bludgeon them, batter them, stab, slash, rend. It hurt but felt good at the same time. Everything around me looked white - heavenly - and I couldn't stop smiling. It was all just too damn much.

Looking back on it now, I believe Abramelin Harvest's greatest feat was summoning an extra-worldly entity and disseminating it into the population as a linguistic virus. The infection is actually a conveyance method for possession by an extremely hateful entity - a demon I would say if not for the religious connotation - that wanted nothing less than the total abolishment of the human species.

Not a murder virus, but a murder monster. Living in us all. Ridiculous? Maybe, but mama raised a Catholic at heart, so I have that fear of the Devil and his demons deep-seated inside me.

The epiphany was almost too much to take. If I was right and there was some kind of monster at large, turning us into its murder drones, what did that say for everything we thought we understood about the world?

Unfortunately, my excitement made me sloppy. I charged into the elevator at the bottom of the nearest home goods store but failed to notice the police had set sharpshooters on the top level of the promenade. When the elevator door opened on the second floor, I caught a bullet between my eyes and poof! Here I am.

~

The room is quiet. I look at the clock on the wall behind the bar, remembering again that it didn't work.

"How long was I... out?"

"Henry?"

My vision disappears in a flash of white light, and for an instant, I see something, a bit of what my previous occupant said to Angela. There's a dark body of water and... whatever else disappears as I sense the next person in the chain that started with Billy Wickerman and has continued along a route of his acquaintances.

"No time. Incoming."

"What?"

Angela's question resounds as I slip through a hole in my mind and allow Lola Gibbets into my head.

CHAPTER 19

Excerpt from Kill for the Sake of Killing: An Exploration of Macrocosmic Surgical Techniques to Rid the World of the Human Disease, by Abramelin Harvest:

Killing one human being will not do ANYTHING. Killing two is better. However, working on an exponential algorithm, a person can unlock a tidal wave of extinction energy that, much like the wave a skilled surfer rides, continues long after the passenger has crested and fallen. There is Extinction Energy all around us, prepared by the Earth. One need but find the proper patterns to release it.

Take the trappings of the modern world. Cars? Buildings? Suburban communities and travel routes are designed in grand undulating schemes, patterns of delicate balance and proportion that lend themselves to killing human beings. The layout of the modern subdivision is not an accident. Nature is influencing us: our patterns and creations. It is contriving our eventual outcome, helping us to make it impossible not to kill ourselves.

Many modern buildings have been constructed with the Extinc-

tion Event in mind. Added floors, made to be forgotten, hidden behind and beneath the functional areas of the buildings can be found, if one has the right compass, the right ideas to point to them.

If you put your ear to the foundation of society, no matter the epoch, you can hear the rushing waters of Extinction beneath you: the invisible energies prevailing beyond the inertia of death. Energy cannot be destroyed. Humanity, however, can be.

CHAPTER 20

LOLA GIBBETS

"L ook, I'm not an idiot, okay? At least, that's one thing I can pride myself on. Not too much else I have going for me at the moment, but at least I'm not stupid.

When I started the job as a cashier at Charters, I knew right away there was room for advancement. I mean, they made Tony General Manager in, like, a week or something, and I had my shit *waaay* more together than he did. That said, I didn't want to risk showing him up, so I needed a plan.

Let's get this straight right off the bat. As a woman, I have never been opposed to what my mother used to call strategic fucking. It's fun, and it has served me well in the past. So when I saw the chance to get Tony in my corner, I took it.

Only things didn't work out the way I planned.

If I'd known what was going to follow when Tony asked me to lock him in the basement of the store, I would have done so and immediately went to the cops. That's not how things worked out, though. I guess part of that's because, against all odds, I'd developed feelings for him. Which ulti- mately prevented me from seeing things clearly. Still, how could I have known he was infected? As it was, I figured all this MV-20 shit was just a liberal hoax, designed to push the current guy in office right out on his ass come November.

Little did I know we weren't going to make it to November.

I remember driving to the market where Billy had gone nuts, just to see if it was true. I couldn't wrap my head around the little D&D geek I knew from the store being a mass murderer. Then I saw the absolute horror. I mean, even with all the fire trucks and Police Tape and emergency personal standing around, I could see that the sidewalk was washed in gore. We're talking GORE. It looked like a bomb had gone off, and I guess in a way, one had. The bomb's name was Billy Wickerman.

It was shortly after Tony went crazy that I began to suspect he was right about everything. Because, here's the thing, Tony didn't lose it until he went to Billy's apartment and ended up killing his roommate Brodie. Even then, I didn't think it was that big a deal. I mean, have you met Brodie? I want to kill him every time I'm around him.

But then the violence in the world around me began to escalate, and I realized some kind of conspiracy was at work.

"Hey, wait a minute…"

~

"**W**here the hell are my tits?" I ask, terrified.

"Thank you for joining us, Lola. Please, don't be alarmed."

Across the table from me is a woman that looks remarkably like me. Her complexion is perfect, like mine. Her nose sharp but attractive when juxtaposed with the long, thin lips that describe her mouth. And her hair - long, brown hair with a slight wave that I *know* she hates as much as I hate the one in mine. The fact that I have to spend thirty-odd minutes straightening it every morning is the one thing I hate about myself. This, however, no longer appears to be an issue.

"Who are you, and where the hell is my body?" I ask, immediately pondering that I've actually had occasion to ask such a thing. First the murder virus, then Billy and Tony, now this?

"What the hell happened to reality?" I say out loud.

"*That* old gray mare? Ain't what she used to be, I'm afraid. My name is Detective Angela Miller, and you, Lola Gibbets, are dead. You were most likely killed by one Anthony Tod. Now, with the bases covered, I need to ask you a few questions."

"Bases covered? How about, if I'm dead, how the hell am I talking to you?"

"You are currently inhabiting the body of one Gerald Henry, a - ahem - psychic detective. As you began to understand shortly before your death, there is indeed a contagion of murder running rampant through the population. Mr. Henry may have ties to its origins. Also, Mr. Henry happens to have the ability to channel the recently deceased. Any more questions?"

The incredulity of every word that has just come out of this woman's mouth cannot compete with what I know to be a fact. I realize the wall behind her is mostly made of mirrors, so I stand up and stare into the eyes of the man I wear like a suit.

He's dark-skinned, maybe part Native American? My own rounded, supple chin is gone, replaced by a square shape covered in five-o-clock shadow. The nose is flatter and wider, and the eyes are just the slightest bit too close together. The beautiful tits I paid several thousand dollars for when I turned thirty are gone, replaced by flat, dull pectoral muscles that are hardly defined. Couple this with a bit of a paunch, and I can't help but feel disappointed.

Dude could do a push-up or two once in a while. Just saying.

"Okay, so you got questions? Ask."

"I need you to tell me everything you know about the book *Kill For the Sake of Killing.*"

CHAPTER 21

Miller says the name of the book, and suddenly everything starts to make sense. Simultaneously, I become aware of an uncomfortable feeling in my pants.

"Oh."

"Something I need to know?"

"I think Mr. Henry has a thing for you."

"What?"

"Let's just say I might be new to this, but I wouldn't be in a hurry to stand up right now."

"I see."

"Yeah. So, ah, I guess I was going to tell you about the book."

"Please."

"What I never bothered to tell anyone else is, that copy ended up in Tony's store because of me. I mean, the time-line's a bit hazy on my end because I like to drink, but yeah, it came from me."

"And where did you get it?"

"Let's just say from a friend."

"What's this friend's name?"

"I don't remember."

"You don't remember your friend's name?"

"Look, I'm talking about a one-night friend, if you know what I mean. It's like this. I have a high-stress job, and to unwind, I like to go out, have a few cocktails, then get laid. I should probably be a bit more discerning about who I sleep with, but then again, look how things turned out, right? So… a few days or maybe weeks before that night at Knock Knock, I met a guy, went back to his place, and he's the one who gave me the book."

"Was this in Seattle?"

"Bothell."

"Bothell, Washington? By the college?"

"As DM, I travel between the different branches at least three days a week. Since the Amazonian War on Brick-n-Mortar stores eventually forced the company to downsize, I have Seattle, Portland, and Spokane. In recent months, totally against my recommendations, the company opened a small kiosk-type store on the U of W campus in Bothell. I was there, making sure it was up to snuff, and afterward, I hit the bars."

"You were exposed to the book before the others?"

"Yeah. We go back to this guy's place, do what we went there to do, and then, while we're lying around after, we start talking. Real philosophical shit. I was impressed, 'cuz this guy seemed like a fucking frat boy at first. Then, he starts in with all this deep shit, about saving the planet, humans are bad, yada yada yada. I agree with a lot of what he says, so he hands me this book. I forget about it at first, then, a few nights later, I come across it in my overnight bag. I started reading it and couldn't stop. I read the entire thing that night. Several times.

"I'd planned a napsturbation weekend; two days alone, reading and drinking wine, my new Bad Dragon vibrator my only companion. Only, once I opened that book, everything else faded into the background. I found it impossible to put down.

"So you had it with you when you went to Tony's store?"

"Yeah. But I'm pretty sure I didn't leave it there. I was auditing the store for Loss Prevention, left my bag unattended in Tony's office for about half an hour or so. My theory is Billy jacked it."

"Okay, that fits with what we already know."

"Which is?"

"I'll ask the questions. Suffice it to say we're trying to determine how many copies are out there. It began as a download, then was picked up by a small publisher called Jonestown Books."

"So, you've been on to this for a while."

"Almost since the beginning. Here's what I need clarification on, though. You said you had already read the book well in advance of it showing up at Tony's store. How were you not affected?"

"Yeah, well. Here's the thing. I could tell what the book was trying to do to me. It integrated with me in this way... I don't know that I can explain it. Leave it at, Harvest's words simply bolstered what was already inside me."

"Come again?"

"No harm in coming clean about it all now, is there? See, I kinda had a pre-existing relationship with murder before that fucking book ever came into the picture."

∽

"Look, that stupid book didn't make me kill anybody. I'd already taken murder as a hobby long before I ever laid eyes on the works of Abramelin Harvest. See, the reason Charters had to replace both their Seattle store's GM and that region's DM is because I killed the people who held those positions before Tony and me.

"Oh, I know Tony likes to make it sound as though he worked there for years, cutting his teeth as a bookseller and cashier. Nope. They promoted his ass like the week after he started because they *had to*, thanks to me.

"First, the previous GM, Kinkaid, was a tool. A Sales Manager position opened, and I figured I could get a tried-and-true Frat boy like Kinkaid to promote me if his cock kept ending up in my mouth. Trouble was, he had no intention of honoring his end of the bargain and promoted Tony instead. This pissed me right the fuck off, so one night, instead of fucking Kinkaid's brains out, I split his head open with a hammer and scooped them out with a ladle. This was a crime of passion, but it changed me. The release killing that piece of garbage provided me felt like a twenty-megaton orgasm. From that moment on, I knew murder was something I needed to explore, even if only to help me relax. That's always been an issue with me. High strung as a motherfucker.

"After Kinkaid, I employed a two-prong attack. First, I seduced Betty, the then-District Manager, to lull her into a sense of familiarity with me. Betty was a fifty-something man-eater; she'd had numerous abusive boyfriends and a history of drug problems, so I figured, fuck it, easy target. By the time I killed Betty, Tony had already been promoted to replace my first victim. It didn't take much to get him under my thumb, and he backed my play for DM without even realizing it. This created a little bit of a stink between us. Still, I actually liked Tony. I helped him overcome his issues by continuing to fuck him and do what I could behind the scenes to ensure his store remained number one in the company.

"But I digress.

"So I'd already developed a taste for murder when I read Harvest's book. If anything, its message just made me feel better about the things I had grown to like so much. Because the book tells it the way it is. We all know there are too many people in the world. We all know people are the root cause of every goddamn problem on the planet. But how many of us have the balls to do anything about it? No pun intended, because, you know. I have balls now. Weird.

"There are an awful lot of human beings walking the Earth today who don't deserve to live. Shit, just turn on TMZ or CNN. You'll see half of 'em right there. But seriously, you must see it. Everyone does; it's just a matter of being brave enough to acknowledge the fact that some people should die. It's not a matter of opinion that the planet Earth would be a better place without us. It's a scientifically proven fact."

"Had you killed others? Or just the two from Charters?"

"At that point? Just those two."

"But, you'd read the book?"

"Maybe she was immune because she'd already committed murder."

The voice is the first time I realize someone is sitting behind me. I turn and see a good-looking guy who's not even facing us. Instead, he's nursing a pint of beer and eating peanuts.

"Could it be so simple?" More to herself than her friend, Angela asks, "What happened to you after Tony broke out?"

"Nothing. I mean, I nearly shit my pants when he killed Tim right in front of me, not because I liked Tim or anything, but because I thought I was next. When Tony disappeared through that hole in the floor instead, I talked to the cops that showed up and then got out of there as fast as I could. I needed to grab supplies, then get out of the city as fast as possible. The only thing, well, I'm not really sure what happened after that."

"What about that first night at the club, after you left?"

I'm about to answer when I hear the chair behind me screech across the tiles. It's a loud, violent sound, and I flinch, turning in time to see dude quaff the last third of his beer, then hurl the glass at the bottles behind the bar. A bunch of shit shatters, and angry guy draws his gun.

"Shit," I saw under my breath and immediately intuit the faux pas in saying this out loud.

CHAPTER 22

"I should put a fucking bullet in his head right now, Angela. Then one in yours."

"What then? Walk out into the street and hail a cab to SEATAC? Because I don't think you really want to do that right now, Joseph."

"This is bullshit! How is any of this helping us?" Angry-guy's pissed, disproportionately so, and I wonder how long they've been sitting in his dank bowling alley bar, listening to the Psychic channel dead folks.

"I don't understand your question, Joseph."

I can hear Angela's attempt at re-establishing the control she maintains over this tool even with one hand shackled to the table. But dickhead is angry, and it might not be so easy.

"Oh, I think you understand the question just fine. I think you want answers for why *your* infection is the way it is. None of these people Henry's channeling are doing us any good when it comes to the bigger problem. Total waste of fucking time!"

This is news. My interrogator is infected? I watch her intently; she's quiet for a few moments. I want to ask how she got infected, how they happen to be in the thick of this. Are they actively trying to combat what's happening, or is this just a fact-finding mission?

"Okay. What would you suggest?"

"No idea, although the first thing we should do is put a slug in his forehead and get the fuck out of this bowling alley. We should be actively tracking down someone who is *currently* infected and, you know, alive."

"I understand what you're saying, Joseph, but how is it more productive to put ourselves at risk trying to subdue a live, infected person when we have someone in our custody who can channel them?"

"None of Henry's 'ghosts' sound like what we've experienced on the streets. This one, shit, she's so rational there's no way she has the same thing the others have. Just like you."

"You're right," she finally says, "None of the people Henry has channeled for us exhibit the 'Rage' symptoms that we've seen in the rest of the population. Same as me."

"That's what I just said."

"Don't you get it? Why? Why is it, with a cross-section sample of, what? Four people now, none of them are uncontrollably hostile?"

"Again, waste of time, Angela."

"No, jack ass. What's the common denominator?"

"I don't know. Charters?"

"Yeah. Or Henry himself."

"What about you? Kinda queers your theory, doesn't it?"

"I don't know. We're both from Los Angeles. Maybe there's a common person between us?"

"And her?"

"Well, unless Lola here knows Roy or Marej, we're out of options."

"Roy?"

Both my hosts look surprised.

"You know Roy?"

Don't you hate when you accidentally volunteer information that leads you to tell a story that paints you in a less-than-attractive light?

"We're waiting."

"Roy was the name of the frat boy in Bothell. The one I got the book from."

∾

"**H**ow many people has this psychic guy channeled for you?"

"Not enough. Now come on, is there anything else you can tell me that might be helpful?"

I pause, sensing a naughty little spark in the back of my mind.

"I want a drink."

"I want some answers."

"And I've given you some. Besides, I think a little Vodka might even me out, smooth out my nerves."

"Jesus Christ. Joseph?"

"I look like a fucking bartender to you?"

"Well, unless you want to undo my cuffs…"

Joseph grumbles but complies.

"Ketel and tonic, no lime."

"Popov it is."

"No tip for you," I say and shoot Angela a conspiratorial "Just us gals" smile. She doesn't go for it, but that doesn't matter. She's chained, and Joe is distracted, so now's my chance.

I'm up in a flash, heading toward the brightly lit corridor at the end of the room.

I emerge into the bowling alley proper. To my immediate left is one of those stupid games where you put a quarter in and try to pick up a stuffed animal from inside a plastic box. Only this one is out of order, and there's a small toolbox sitting on the floor next to it. Guess what's lying out in the open?

I stop to gank the hammer, but as I do, here's Mr. Angry, right on cue. He tackles me. When I open my eyes, I see I wasted my chance: the front entrance is directly in front of me.

So close.

The collision is all momentum so that we sail out the first glass door and into the small atrium with rubber floor mats that say 'Diamond Access Bowl' as if it's the greatest thing in the world, but just before I come through the second set of glass doors Joey brings his first straight down on my face and-

CHAPTER 23

EXCERPT FROM KILL FOR THE SAKE OF KILLING: AN EXPLORATION OF MACROCOSMIC SURGICAL TECHNIQUES TO RID THE WORLD OF THE HUMAN DISEASE, BY ABRAMELIN HARVEST:

K*illing people is not as easy as one might think. I'm not talking about the resolution it takes to smash hard-wired moral or socio-philosophical barriers, either. I'm talking about the actual act of taking another person's life. People, by evolutionary nature, are not that easy to kill. Sure, some of them are; the frailer, meeker, mentally, or physically disadvantaged. Even then, you'd be surprised.*

Stop and think about the sheer force of will it takes to live day after day, year after year. When you're younger, sure, it's easier because, although you don't have the momentum living builds as you age, you're fresh. Regardless of your age, it's not easy. And when you're older? Age hardens a body. It makes survival the point of the razor, so to speak. Only it's not just the point; it's the entire curve of the blade. People are hard to kill because the world, in its infinite wisdom, has been trying to kill them since conception. As a result, if someone has made it into or beyond their teens, they're by nature an adapting, surviving machine.

This survival gene is what makes people hard to kill. Especially with your bare hands. And yet, it also makes the actual act of killing a person that much more fun."

CHAPTER 24

A terrible sound brings me out of my current fugue. It only gets worse when I realize the sound is me screaming.

I open my eyes, and there's blood in them. It doesn't take long to realize it's dripping from my forehead. I'd been knocked unconscious.

Instead of Angela, it's Joseph that sits in front of me. He smokes a cigarette - one of those slim ladies' brands - and eyes me like a tiger stalking a piece of meat.

"Where's Angela?" I ask.

"Ladies' room."

I realize this is the moment to play the ace in my sleeve.

"You think she's gonna come back? I mean, you have her handcuffed for a reason, right?"

"You're a pretty clever guy. Good job, Skippy."

"Don't call me Skippy."

"Sorry, Skip."

"Bastard. Look, what the hell is going on? Why did you spring her?"

"Just following orders."

"Is she infected?"

"Oh hell yeah. I'd say ask her partner, but he's dead. You already know that, though, don'tcha Mr. Psychic Detective?"

"You're a real patronizing fuck, you know that, Joseph?"

"S'what they tell me. Hey, everyone has a specialty."

"When did she catch it?"

"Ya ask me, it was while working that first shooting in L.A."

"And how'd you end up with her?"

"Well, you know, ol' Ang is what they call a "consummate professional." Really just one hell of a detective. She connected their shooter in L.A. to one in Iowa and subsequently to the book. No one believed her until after her own arrest. Interstate homicide means the Bureau comes in, next thing you know, I'm called up out of my nice, quiet desk job in Hoover's basement, told to escort a "consultant" to Seattle."

"Consultant?"

"Yeah," Angela says from behind me. There's another suit with her now, one I didn't see before. He has her in cuffs and leg irons.

"Ah, Mrs. Lecter. I was getting worried."

"Detective Miller is the first person to be infected and live this long. Also, she appears to have some natural ability to block the effects of the virus."

"So why am I answering her questions instead of yours'?"

"Her questions are our questions. You think I'd have any idea where to start with this shit? Up until I pulled you out of that fucking Hobo murder church, I assumed all this was a liberal hoax."

The new suit passes Angela to Joseph. He rubs his cigarette out on the tabletop while Angela looks on in disgust.

"Filthy fucking habit," she says.

"So says those who quit and wish they still smoked."

Joseph surrenders the seat to her, removes the leg irons but closes one of her cuffs around the metal post that holds the table up. It's bolted to the floor with what looks in the dim light like four-inch Lag Bolts. Angela ain't going nowhere. With her free hand, she flicks the cigarette butt at him.

"Who's your new friend?" I ask.

"That's Doug. We have an understanding."

"Joey and Dee Dee, huh? Are Tommy and Johnny outside?"

There's a sound I can't place, and then I feel Doug's hand upside the back of my head. Not a Ramones fan, I guess.

"Gerald, what would you say if I told you that I had information about what happened to Roy?"

"You read something on the stall in the ladies' room?"

"For a good time, call Gerald Henry, Psychic P.I."

"Fuck off. Tell me."

"First, I'd like you to explain something to me."

"That is?"

"How is it you're able to channel these people, but you can't remember anything they have to say?"

"He's stuck," Doug says, still hanging close behind me, presumably waiting for the chance to strike me again.

"Stuck?" I say, turning to see if he's pulling my chain.

"That's what my grandfather called it. He had the same thing. That's how I knew you weren't full of shit."

"Oh, really?"

"Yeah. You got a birthmark on the back of your head that looks like Texas?"

I'm floored.

"Gramps used to channel his four dead wives regularly. According to him, everyone who has the gift has the same birthmark in the same place."

"Four dead wives?"

"Yeah. I always felt bad for him. All those ghosts did was wake us kids up in the middle of the night to tell us how small Gramps' dick was."

I laugh, unsure if this is a routine or not. No one else joins me, so I decide to rope things back around to the only topic that interests me.

"Back to Roy."

"You said Roy was gay."

"I never said that. Roy *preferred* guys, but in school he was what we called a raging, pansexual whore."

"So he fucked women, too?"

"Do you need a diagram? I mean, I don't know if I'd go as far as to say *women*. A woman wouldn't be interested in a guy like Roy. Girls, Roy was into girls and boys."

"He was a pederast?" Doug asks, shocked.

"No, but the word woman implies, I don't know, someone who's grown up and wouldn't have time for the kind of shit Roy was into. Trust fund baby; spent all his time partying."

"So, if I were to say he might have hooked up with the chick you just channeled, that might sound plausible?"

"Yeah, that sounds exactly like Roy."

"Then, there is a pretty good chance that your friend Roy was more involved in this than we previously thought."

At this point, I feel a precipice spread out before me. This thing is bigger than I thought. Add the background on Angela's police investigation with the addition of a second Fed, and I'm not entirely convinced of my safety inside or out. One thing is clear: my hosts know a lot more about what's going on than they're telling me.

"I'd be a lot more help if you looped me in."

"What do you want to know?"

"What happened to you?"

Angela hesitates for a moment, then her posture changes, and I swear I see something physically leave her.

"My partner and I ran down some leads after Hughs's coffeeshop massacre. Through our investigation, we traced the earliest incident related to Harvest's book to-."

"I already told you all this shit," Joseph sneers.

"Yeah, but I don't believe *you*."

Pain shoots through my scalp as Doug pulls my head back with a wad of my hair.

"Who the fuck do you think you are?"

"Look! If you know so goddamn much, what is it you're doing here?"

"What *they're* doing here is very different from what I'm doing here," Doug says. This guy makes Joseph look like Mr. Considerate.

"Because if Angela is infected? She's not behaving like it. That's what I want to understand. Angela, you're calm. Rational, not running around, foaming at the mouth, killing everything you can get your hands on. You're different."

"What can I say? Private school really does make a difference."

More machine gun fire from outside, followed by a burst of high-pitched screaming. None of my friends seem to care.

"Hey, yo! You Feds maybe wanna do something about that?"

"Fed?" Doug looks at me sideways, like I just called him a cunt, "You got the wrong guy."

"Wait a minute..."

"I'm the fed," Joey says.

"Then who the fuck are you?"

"Douglas?" a new voice says from the door to the kitchen. I turn and see a woman there. She's five-two, maybe a hundred and fifty pounds, "Douglas works for the people who wrote the book."

CHAPTER 25

At first, the woman who emerges from the shadows that grip the bar's kitchen enclave strikes me as familiar. Short, frizzy hair and a No-Bullshit demeanor, she reminds me of Roy's mother. With the recognition comes more memories to assault my frontal lobe, and I begin to experience an unpleasant disorientation. Past and present weave together, strands of confused tissue that sap me of my ability to accurately judge how the situation has changed.

Good thing Angela's never at a loss for words.

"Who the fuck are you?"

"My name is Guinevere Speck. I own the publishing house that released the first edition of Mr. Harvest's work."

Angela hisses, stands up too quickly, and the handcuff jerks her back down onto her ass.

"Careful," Guinevere Speck says, unable to hide a smile.

"I was at your office in downtown LA."

"Were you now? I haven't been back to LA for months. Not since first meeting Harvest's people.

"Why are you here now?"

"I'm here because your presence is requested in Paradise."

While this Speck woman talks, it becomes more difficult for me to focus on her words. Something is radiating off her that's throwing my abilities into absolute turmoil, and it only takes me a second to realize Roy's essence is all over this woman. It's literally radiating from her. Is this Roy's Mom?

"No, Mr. Henry, I am not Roy's mother."

Speck says this and my blood turns cold.

"How?"

"Please. Did you think you were the only person on Earth with psychic abilities?"

"Check her head," Joseph says, and I actually spit with laughter.

"No need. I do, indeed, have the birthmark in question."

"Why are you here?" Angela asks, "What is it, Psychics eat free, this weekend only?"

"This city is the epicenter of the last great event in human history. As civlization's lights go out, this city will serve as a beacon in the new night. Us psychics? We're drawn to it, like moths."

"What event?"

"My dear Detective Miller, isn't it obvious? I mean, you of all should understand. You've read the book. It's the Apocalypse, finally here."

"She's lying," Angela says, but no one believes her. It's too easy to think that what this Speck woman says is true. On some level, everyone in the world must know humanity has this coming.

"It's the Apocalypse, and you're here to invite us to Heaven?"

"Not Heaven, Mr. Henry. Paradise. I have something to show you. Something that will, in fact, explain the scope you've been grasping for in the dark, Detective Miller."

"A present? You shouldn't have."

"Not you," she turns to me, "He'll only talk through you."

"Who?"

"Take my hand and see."

Guinevere Speck begins to cross the room toward me, and I see Joseph's left hand slip casually toward the gun in his waistband. Speck stops mid-room and fixes Joseph with a look that inspires his hands to land empty, back on the table. She smiles, then pulls up a chair next to me and extends her hand.

"Take it. He'll only speak to you."

As soon as I take the proffered hand, I jump. A cold, severed appendage falls onto the table between us. It looks as though it once belonged to an older man. That is until someone cut it off him just above the wrist.

Speck smiles.

"What the fuck is that?" I ask, my voice cracking with disgust.

"Trust me."

I feel like if there's a book out there titled Who Not to Trust, "People who offer you severed hands" would be listed on page one. That said, there's something about this woman. Her continued Roy-ness makes it so I can't help but fall in line. With no small degree of hesitation, I hold my breath and retrieve the hand from the table.

When I do, the hand shifts in my grip until our palms touch. I choke back a wave of nausea as a trill of electricity passes between us. I watch in horror as the fingers intertwine with my own. I hear a voice in my head, and my dick stands straight up. The nails are jagged and dirty; one of them pierces my palm's tender flesh. The taste of iron floods my mouth as an infinite cloud of darkness descends over my soul.

CHAPTER 26

HARRY WEISBERG

Previously, it occurred to me that, with the kind of clout I have in Los Angeles, I could most likely get away with murder. Yes, this is an egomaniacal sentiment. However, that doesn't make it less true.

Remember that.

Everyone has thought about killing someone else. Murder is in the body's DNA; it's the mind that has learned to disapprove. Society has indoctrinated us with a Hoover Damn-sized blockade that says murder is an atrocity or, at the very least, has terrible consequences. These perceived mores usually come from how we were raised. With some, they go back to the bible. Once you have money, though, and the power that accompanies it, all of that breaks down on the subatomic level. You change. You become something more than your peers.

Thus, if you're smart, you can do as you please.

One afternoon a few weeks ago, my brother and I sat in on a pitch meeting. Only the guy who showed up wasn't' the person scheduled. At first, we assumed a mix-up had occurred. It's rare these days for either of us to actually sit in on these kinds of meetings, so I got pretty pissed.

The guy remained calm. He didn't say a word, just stared at us with this knowing look. Larry starts screaming at the secretary, and this guy doesn't budge. Security showed up, escorted him out, no problem. When he's gone, I see he's left something behind. A small cache of paper stapled together. The top sheet reads KFTSOK.

I'm still not entirely sure why I didn't just toss the thing in the garbage. I mean, I don't read scripts by nobodies, especially ones who break into our office. But something made me turn that first page and...

The opening was prose accompanied by pictures - *demonstrative illustrations* - all outlining the most efficient ways to murder large numbers of people at once.

At first, I couldn't understand what I was looking at, like a fog rolled over my brain or something. I remember there was this buzz in the air. It made me feel weird. I walked out into the hall and could tell right away no one else could hear it. Then a voice, more *inside* than *outside*, said, "This is the way forward, Harry."

Chills gripped me, and I barely made it to the restroom in time to puke. I couldn't stop the images from those pages running through my head. Ways to maximize stabbing patterns, how to choose victims. Sick shit. When I stopped spilling my two-hundred-dollar lunch into the toilet, I went back to the meeting room. Everyone was gone. Confused, I took one last look at the packet, then tossed the fucking thing in the trash. I couldn't get my breath, and my adrenaline was pounding in my ears, so I decided to go out and grab a beer and a bite to eat.

I feel the hand twist in my palm, and the fugue state changes. Now, everything is real time, as if I've traveled backward in time to relive some poignant moment in Harry's final days:

~

I walk up Sunset to my favorite diner, *Ginger's*. Along the way, I buy a *Variety*, a *Time*, and a *Newsweek*. Distraction is what I'm after, although I suspect nothing in any of these publications will be arresting enough to take my mind off the horrors contained inside that packet of papers. I cannot keep those images from perpetually running through my mind, like the tray on a typewriter, from one side to the other.

I enter the diner and take my usual spot at the counter. I wait until I catch the waitress's eye, order a beer, and head to the men's room to discharge the remainder of the day's caffeine. The sun is leaking through the horizon, time to switch from stimulants to depressants.

When I return, someone is sitting in my seat, reading my Newsweek.

"Excuse me," I say, more alarmed than angry. This person in my seat, I can't tell if they're a man or a woman. About five-foot-ten, skinny, with long, straight hair. They don't respond at first.

"Ex*cuse* me," I say again. They turn around this time, and I realize it's that hot new actor, whatshisname, from that terrible Reese Witherspoon movie we did last year.

"Oh, I'm sorry, were you sitting here?" He smiles and stands up, begins to move past me with my magazine.

"Hey, that's *my* Newsweek."

"Oh, right. Sorry," he hands it back to me and then leaves the diner. I watch him walk through the parking lot and disappear past the cars. No corresponding headlights exit the parking lot.

Shrugging it off, I sit down and go for my beer. I lift the frosted green bottle to my lips, then start when I feel someone at my back, followed by a voice in my ear.

"There's a great article on page one-eleven," I'm so startled I almost jump out of my seat. It's him, walking by me again, this time towards the men's room.

The waitress comes over to take my order. Sharon, the one I usually come to see, is off today. Sharon's substitute Chara is hot but lacks the enduring quality of corruptible innocence that makes Sharon my must-have. Sharon's absence on a day she usually works irritates me, but that's good. The irritation softens how unnerved I am by the encounter with whatshisname.

I order my usual: burger, medium-rare, the works. Another beer, too. I kill the rest of the first one in two gulps and hand the empty bottle back to Chara. Our eyes meet for an instant; I find myself wondering what the largest object is that this one has had inserted into her ass. This normally titillating question doesn't do half of what it does for me with Sharon.

Feeling slightly better, I relax a bit and open the Newsweek. I flip through articles that do not interest me for about ten minutes before my food arrives. I set the magazine down and begin to eat.

Halfway through the burger (which is perfect, regardless that it's not Sharon who serves it to me), I remember the actor's voice in my ear:

"There's *a great article on page one-eleven.*"

With the hand not currently holding the burger to my

lips, I reach over and flip the magazine back open. I skim back and forth for a while, then realize I've been pranked.

There is no page one-eleven.

I shrug, perplexed as to whether I'm on some kind of hidden camera show. I look around, but everything seems to be in order. Then I realize I haven't seen what'shisnuts return from the restroom yet.

It must still be the effect of that manuscript because something has me spooked. I don't even finish my burger; I drop a fifty on the counter and stand to leave. As I do, the magazine falls to the floor. From where I stand, I can see it has fallen open to, you guessed it, page one-eleven.

I snatch the periodical and make for the door. Once outside, I light a cigarette and exhale into the balmy Los Angeles evening. Feeling a little better, I open to the page and begin to read. As I do, my spine grows cold with a mixture of fear and disbelief. The article on page one-eleven is a reproduction of the manuscript left in my office earlier that day.

CHAPTER 27

I drive my Maserati along Sunset at dusk. The night has not yet pushed the sun from the sky; a thin, pink crack stretches across the horizon for as far as the eye can see. Gazing at this heavenly swathe of color is like looking at a cotton candy thunderstorm rolling in. When it finally starts to rain - it's been six months since the last drop - I don't engage the ragtop. Instead, I tip my head back and open my mouth, half expecting the sweet taste of the Midwestern summers of my youth.

Returning to the diner, I park around the corner from the entrance. I put the top up, then saunter over to the front door where I pop a squat on the sky-blue antique bench just outside. I light a cigarette, taking my time and enjoying the tobacco. I recite snippets from the manuscript to myself with each inhale, staring through the window at Sharon, my obsession, back on the job. I watch her deftly hustle the dregs of the dinner crowd and ask myself, is she the one?

A couple with one of those stupid little purse dogs walks past me. The man stops to extinguish his own cigarette in the small, faded blue beach pail filled with sand so ancient it's black. The word 'BUTTS' is stenciled across the bucket. For some reason, when I notice this, it amuses me enough to laugh out loud.

"Can I help you?"

I turn, amazed.

"What?"

"Something funny?"

"Nothing you would understand. Not yet, at least."

"Oh yeah?" he stands up straight, casts his shoulders back and takes a step closer to me, so the remaining sunlight becomes strained through his shadow over me.

"Why's that?"

Behind him, the woman with the dog reappears at the door. The dog lets out a tiny YAP.

"Alex, I got us a table."

"Just a sec, babe."

Anybody who uses 'babe' is automatically an asshole in my book. Not that I needed more convincing by this point.

I open my mouth to speak, but everything slips into slow motion. That pink light flashes so that everything looks like some kind of weird negative image. I no longer see my new buddy Alex as the comprehensive entity that he is, that all of us are, but rather as a collection of unimportant scenarios. A compilation of ideas, some realized, some not. Thoughts, feelings, urges, and pleasantries, that's what little boys are made of. The vision goes a level deeper, and Alex's skin disappears. Beneath it, I can see millions of tiny particles swirling in chaotic patterns. Personal inertia is all that keeps this 'man' together and presenting itself to the world, an expendable, five-dollar facade over a wasteland's threshold.

Seeing this, I realize I have only to say the proper thing to send one essential cell, one tiny piece of the whole spiraling into disintegrative chaos. The rest will follow.

"You know what I find most amusing about people, Alex?"

He looks at me with disdain, unable to move as words flow through me.

"The fact that everyone wants the same basic rights, even though so many of us aspire to transcend those rights. This quest for individuality is a ruse, a falsehood. People believe that their unique traits will inherently elevate them in the eyes of their peers. Acceptance and disgust. Herein lies the ultimate conundrum, the overall reason humanity's hidden motive is always, at its heart, self-destruction."

My new friend Alex seems struck at first, probably not expecting such a complicated answer. He waivers then tries to take another step toward me but cannot. A faraway look comes over him, and tiny beads of sweat form on his forehead and chin.

"Alex, honey?" the woman calls through the door again.

Without another word, Alex enters the restaurant. I watch him for a few moments, confident that I have introduced a mental itch he will not be able to scratch. I also somehow inherently understand that in two nights, he will murder his finance, kill and eat her dog, and then throw himself off an overpass into traffic.

Nice, huh?

Satisfied, I put my cigarette out in the pail and walk through the door, taking my customary seat at the counter for the second time that night. Behind me, I hear a voice I recognize.

"Well, hello there."

It's Sharon, offering me coffee. I turn my cup over in the saucer, and she leans in across me to fill it from behind. The tables are full, and she's busy. As she crosses over me, I smell honeysuckle, lavender, and something else. Something... familiar.

I can barely contain myself.

"Get ya a menu in a minute, hon. Riding out the last of the rush."

"No worries, I'm just having coffee."

"Sure thing."

"Missed you earlier."

"Car trouble. Chara covered for me. She treat you okay?"

"Oh, yeah."

"Good."

Ten minutes later, Sharon agrees to accompany me for cocktails after her shift.

I finish my coffee, leave and drive around the city for a while. I stop at a bar called Powerhouse and have a few cocktails before returning to meet Sharon at eight-thirty. Fifteen minutes later, she exits the building and seems surprised to see me.

"I didn't really think you'd be back."

"Be a man of your word, son. That's what my grandfather told me almost every day of my life until he died."

She smiles at this. I walk around to the passenger side of the car and open the door for her. This blows her mind.

"Such a gentleman for a Hollywood big shot. I didn't think there were guys like you left in this town."

"That's a pretty jaded view. What happened to make such a pretty girl so cynical?"

Sharon falls quiet, and I can tell I've hit a nerve. Something did happen, something bad. That's the smell: honeysuckle, lavender, and trauma.

We drive to my favorite little restaurant in Malibu, order two Martinis, and sit in the dark near the ocean.

"So, what's it like working in the movies?"

"Boring."

"Come on."

Her words slur, and I can tell the booze is going straight to her head.

"No, really. I wake up every day around one o'clock in the afternoon and drive to our office. My brother usually strolls in an hour or two later, hungover. We spend a few hours going over expense reports, maybe pop into the script room to see if anything worthwhile has surfaced. Afternoon hits, there's always a lunch meeting or two with agents, lawyers, sycophants, Brad Pitt, Jennifer Lawrence. After that, we usually head down to the studio to screen dailies from whatever is currently filming. You know the rest. That's when I come to you for dinner."

Sharon looks at me with something that can only be described as unbelieving awe. She's about to speak but stops and instead does the most adorable thing: she puts her head in her hands and bats her eyelashes at me. What decade is this chick from? My god.

We finish our drinks and leave. I drive us a little further down Highway One and park where we can walk down to the beach. Shoes in our hands, our feet sink into the cool, pleasurable sand.

"So Harry, how come you never asked me out before? You always flirt with me."

"No, you always flirt with *me*. I merely flirt back. Retaliation."

"Oh pah-lease. I'm not the flirting type."

I chuckle and stop for a moment, facing her. Nervous at my sudden scrutinizing attention, Sharon begins to talk again and ruins everything.

"You probably flirt with all the girls."

"Don't say that."

She stops abruptly, suddenly very worried she has said or done something wrong.

"I don't mean to sound angry, but when you say something so trite, you sound childish. I wouldn't be here if I did this to all the girls."

"I'm so stupid. You probably think I'm trying to sound like your wife or girlfriend or something."

I don't acknowledge this, but start walking again. I'm losing my cool, still preoccupied with those pictures from earlier, and my growing need to spill some blood.

"You say you're not the type, but you, m' lady, are a charmer. You need to see the potential that I see."

"Yeah, I bet I know all about the potential you see in me."

Gripping the knife in my pocket, I can hardly control myself long enough to say, ever so softly:

"You have no idea the plans I have for you."

Uneasy again, she smiles. I return the gesture and put my arm around her to bolster her self-esteem.

Wait for it. Wait for it.

Somewhere in the distance, I can see a bonfire on the beach. Faintly, I hear the strains of a song we used in a movie last year. I think the band's name is Dove. The chorus has haunted me since the first time I heard it. The stars look small and recessed as I lean in to tenderly touch the back of Sharon's head. Why can't every date be as sweet as this?

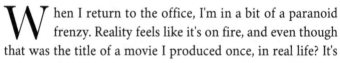

When I return to the office, I'm in a bit of a paranoid frenzy. Reality feels like it's on fire, and even though that was the title of a movie I produced once, in real life? It's not a good feeling.

High voltage doses of fear trigger a kind of atavistic response in me. My shrink says this goes back to a particularly nasty experience I had in the 60s. My brother and I were up in Redwood National Forest, taking hallucinogens with our buddy Abe. Somehow, I got separated from the others and ended up spending the night alone in the forest. During that time, I hallucinated that another version of Abe found me. This doppelgänger kept just out of my sight, taunting me from the darkness that swallows those woods. All night long, Evil Abe sang me songs that made me think I was going to be responsible for the end of the world.

It was awful.

Still no word from Larry. I go back upstairs to check the garbage in the meeting room for the manuscript, but it's gone. Then I hear the vacuum.

We contract out to a company called Spotless Vistas for cleaning. I tend to work later than everyone else, so I have a rapport with most of the regular girls they send us. As luck would have it, I recognize the one running the vacuum. Carrie O' something or other, real pretty Irish girl, mid-thirties. Going to school to be a lawyer, no less. I flag her down and am relieved to hear she just emptied the garbage moments ago. She pulls the manuscript from a bag marked SHRED. I'm so happy; I slip Carrie a fifty as a thank you.

"Must be some script."

"Carrie, honey. You don't know the half of it. This right here? This is going to change the world."

CHAPTER 28

"**M**ust be some script," I say as I emerge from this latest channeling session. This is the most vivid, lucid experience I've had in my life, and I've been doing this for closer to twenty years than I'd like to admit.

"Script?" Angela asks, alarmed. The mood in the room has shifted. Something happened while I was out.

"Was that really Harry Weisberg, the big-time Hollywood producer?"

Guinevere Speck nods.

I look at the hand on the table, and the pieces fall together.

"The MV-20 PSA I keep seeing, the one every station is playing non-stop."

Speck smiles as she tells us, "Harvest's book was only going to reach so many people. A broadcast PSA with Hollywood star power? Limitless."

"Jesus H. Christ..."

"Why would anyone do that?" Joseph asks.

"Harry and his brother have history with Mr. Harvest. Plus, they're jackals. The Council targeted them early on."

"Council?"

"All good things. Now, you're all going to have to psyche yourselves up to move. We don't have a lot of time, and we're expected."

"Expected?" Angela snarls. Her face tells me if she could, she would walk over and batter Guinevere's face in with her bare hands. "We're not going anywhere with you."

"Go look out the window."

"She can't," Joseph says and stands. He pitches the cigarette he's smoking so that it lands at Speck's feet, then walks directly up in her face and grinds it out with the tip of his shoe. It's the kind of dramatic, macho bullshit you always get from hostile authority figures in helpless situations. There's a brief face-to-face before Joseph walks over to the window. He lifts the metal shutter just enough to peer outside, then carefully guides it back to rest against the window frame. When he returns to us, he passes Speck with a wide berth, sits down, and lights another cigarette.

"We're fucked," he says. Is that a note of terror in Joseph's voice? I believe it is.

"What? What did you see?"

"He saw that the streets are mobbed with a surging mass of violence," Guinevere says, "He saw hundreds, soon to be thousands of people compelled by the MV-20 infection to vacate the safety of their homes and attack one another in the streets. Blood for breakfast, blood for lunch."

Then, another voice from the hallway outside the bar:

"He saw the beginning of the end of humanity."

My nervous system recognizes him before my brain does, and by the time I turn around, my arms have already come up for an embrace.

"Roy!"

We hug. It's good to see him, but my relief is cut with something unexpected: suspicion.

"Marej told me you were dead."

"I can assure you reports of my demise have been greatly exaggerated. Looks like I showed up just in time."

"What'd ya mean?"

"Gerald Henry, Psychic Detective ready to give up? C'mon, use that... what did you call it? Ether? Use that Ether and tell me what's what."

I'm blank until I'm not. It's obvious, especially after Speck and Douglas move into place at his side.

"You're with them?"

"Yes sir. Now so are you."

CHAPTER 29

"You're working with these people?"

Roy and I sit in a booth at the back of the Bowling Alley's bar. Across from me, my long-time friend looks different. Older, sure. He's also skinnier. No, wait. That's not quite right. Roy appears less... corporeal in some way I can't explain. He's drinking a beer, an import, but that's not Roy's style. Roy hates beer; always said it bloated him. Sure, in High School, you drink what you can get your hands on, but after we turned twenty-one, I don't think I ever saw Roy even look at a beer again.

Somewhere behind us, I can hear Angela and Guinevere Speck arguing. Through the frosted pane of glass to my left, Joseph paces back and forth in the lobby. Not sure what's up with him and this Doug character, but it's nothing good. Might be an angle to exploit to turn them against one another. If I don't, there's no doubt they'll kill me when my usefulness wears off.

Back to Roy.

"So you're telling me you've been to this... this Paradise place Guinevere wants to bring us to?"

"Oh man, Hank. It's awesome. Seriously. It's like I'm tapped into the most important event in human history. It clears everything else out, all the old cobwebs. All the poisons installed and incubated by society."

"Okay, you sound like someone who's had too much of the Kool-aid."

"You say that now, but wait until you're there."

"But where is there?"

"It's a direction you can't point. That's the only way to explain it. Below, but also Outside."

"Sounds like you're talking about some kind of Temporary Autonomous Zone."

"Yeah, except we don't call it that. Had to distance ourselves from the terminology used by anarchist pedophiles."

"Wise move. Now, cut the shit, Roy. You're all talking about this place, but no one's saying why we're going there."

Roy smiles but doesn't answer. In the ensuing silence that my question triggers, I hear faint strains of music. Where the hell is *that* coming from? The jukebox in the other room's screen is dead. I made sure of that. I chalk the sounds up to the slow unraveling of reality that began the second I stepped off the fucking plane almost twenty-four hours ago.

This drift, however, is what does it. This moment-to-moment ebb of anything substantially recognizable - not my friend, not the world, not the laws of fucking nature - it turns what should be a joyous reunion sour.

I look at Roy's smile, and all I see is an opportunistic jackal. I knew he had gotten into some weird shit, but this person sitting across from me is *not* my friend.

Will I have to kill him, too?

Roy is looking at me like he can read my mind and, shit, maybe he can. Who fucking knows anymore?

"You met with Marej?"

"I did. He didn't take your passing all that well."

"So sweet. Don't worry, Marej and I have since been reunited. We'll see him before too long."

"Really? He going to Paradise, too? Cuz, Roy, I gotta level with you. I'm not convinced, man."

"What would you do instead? You've seen what waits outside this building. The virus has spread, Hank. It's everywhere."

The word 'everywhere' comes out like Roy's speaking in the midst of an orgasm. I ask myself again, where's my friend? How did this happen?"

"I don't know. Find a car, drive north."

"North, south, east, west. MV-20 is everywhere now, Hank. Get it?"

"Well, maybe I should just blow my fucking brains out then, eh?"

"Bullshit. I see the way you're watching that fed. You forget, bro. I *know* you. You're assessing, waiting for an opportunity to do to him what you did to-"

"Careful about bringing up ancient history, especially when you fucking well promised me we'd never mention that again."

"Fine. My point is, they're watching you too, bro. How much longer until they decide to lighten their load? A psychic PI only sounds about as useful as you can throw him in a city where ninety-nine percent of the population has been turned to mindless murder drones."

"And you've shown up just in the nick of time to spirit me away to safety at the end of the world? To Paradise, no less."

"Yeah, man. Now you got it! I'm like, what's his name? Finn. Yeah, swooping in like Erin Finn to save the day."

"You mean Errol Flynn?"

"Whatever. Who cares? That's the old world, brother. Ain't gonna be nothing left of that by the time this is all over."

"That so?"

"Hank, you ever wonder where species go when they become extinct?"

"What?"

"Just like the dinosaurs, man, we're gonna find out."

He's smiling.

"Help me understand. How did you fall in with this? I mean, Extinction Event? Murder Virus? What the fuck, Roy? Your mom raised you better than this."

"My mom denied me both her own heritage and that of my father. Doesn't matter now, though, truth will out."

"Thank you, Mr. Reznor."

Roy laughs at this. My levity isn't entirely out of place; Roy always appreciated my ability to make him laugh in the face of horror. When Danny died all those years ago, my gallows humor was the only thing that kept either of us from going over the edge.

"Before we bought the townhome, Marej and I stayed at this house in Bothell. Well, Marej was living there when I met him, and I ended up moving into his room. It was kind of a community in and of itself, that house.

"U of W campus?"

"More or less. The school didn't own the house; that was this guy Murph. He was older, had never left the comfortable surroundings of academic rebellion. If you catch my drift."

Finally. I knew I'd hear the name Murph again. In my head, I underline his entry in the little black book I lost running from the murder church.

"Murph, huh? Let me guess, yet another trust funder who graduated and didn't feel like trading up his status with the college population for starting over in the real world?"

"Hank for the win! Anyway, we were staying in the house, and Murph, he would talk all this weird shit. The end of the world kept coming up, but it wasn't preachy, and he didn't sound like a nut. He *knew* things. He was psychic, I think, and his dad, well, his dad had a special interest in this type of thing."

"What do you mean?"

"Murph's dad was ex-spook. He'd been something of a guru in the sixties, crashed and burned in the 70s, then got co-opted by the CIA. Black Ops, Project MK Ultra, all that fun stuff. Uncle Sam had him design a secret weapon."

The bomb goes off:

"Harvest. You're talking about fucking Abramelin Harvest!"

"Yeah, and guess what? Turns out, Harvest is my dad, too."

∽

J oseph overhears Roy's confession, and since I'm sitting there stunned, jaw on the floor, I can't react fast enough to stop him when he charges in and pulls Roy up by his arm.

"Hey! What the fuck, man?" Roy's indignation is lopped off at the knees as Joe punches him once in the face. Hard.

Stunned, I watch Joseph drag a ragdoll-Roy back through the bar and into the men's room. My shock dissolves, and I'm behind them by ten steps.

By the time I catch up, the commotion has Guinevere and Doug hot on my heels. I come through the men's room door like a comic book splash page, but I'm too late. Joseph already has Roy's left wrist handcuffed to the pipe that runs from the toilet through the wall, his right to the toilet paper dispenser. My former friend's face is distorted in anguish, as the position puts his shoulder and abdomen at odds with one another.

"You'll break his fucking arm!" I shout, and Joseph stops me in my tracks by swallowing the key. No bullshit.

"Aw, man, that's fucking disgusting!" Doug says.

"What makes you think I won't just cut you open and root around in your guts until I find the thing?"

You can tell by the look on Joseph's face he hadn't thought this through very well. He tries to look staunch and fearless; instead, he manages to reinforce his brash stupidity.

"This is for his own good as much as it is for ours."

An explosion from the front rocks the entire building, and in its aftermath, a more virulent sense of panic washes over the room. Things go into hyperspeed. I swallow hard and can taste the metallic grind of uninhibited fear.

"What's happening?" Joseph yells, turning his attention to the foyer, where Guinevere Speck has drawn a gun and started to fire in the direction of the front door.

"Listen to me! You can't shoot your way out of this! There's too many of them!"

"How many can there be?" I joke and immediately wish I hadn't. I look again to Roy; he's smiling. He mouths what I think is "One sec;" I wince when I hear the bones in his shoulder pop as he stands straight up, his right arm disappearing behind him in a spasming crooked snake.

"Aw shit," Doug exclaims and goes white as Roy dips beneath his limp arm, now close enough to Joseph to kick him in the head. Caught off guard, Joe goes down, and I stoop to pin him to the floor while Roy goes to work freeing himself. I wrangle the keys to the handcuffs off him, and Speck motions for me to throw them to her.

"This place is about to be compromised. I'll get our friend," she says over the sound of breaking metal. I turn and watch Roy free himself from the pipe he's chained to with two swift kicks. It bursts, then he does the same with the dispenser. A moment later, Roy is free and, the front door to the bowling alley bursts open, a wave of howling murderheads flooding the place.

"This way!" Speck yells, heading into the kitchen, Angela right behind her.

"Go! Go!" Douglas screams, waving us through behind them.

"Where the fuck are we going?" I scream, trailing just behind Roy. His mangled arm flaps after him like a loose scarf, but Roy gives no sign that he's in pain.

"The underground," he says, as we pass through a door at the back of the kitchen and into complete and total darkness.

CHAPTER 30

Once we're through the door, Doug hangs back to drag some boxes in front of it.

"This will slow 'em down, but it's not gonna stop 'em."

We're running, but it's so dark I can't see anything ahead of us beyond, say, ten feet. The walls are concrete, and I can hear loud reverberations of water dripping somewhere in the immediate distance.

"Where does this go?"

"I already told you, the underground."

Behind us, I can already hear the mob hurling themselves against the flimsy fiberglass door. Doug's right; it's not going to hold.

We pass through another doorway, and a small wave of relief slides over me as I spot a wall lined by beer kegs.

"Help me with these," Joseph hollers over the sound of the crowd shattering through the first barrier and stampeding our way. He drops the keg and throws his back against the door just as the first wave of crazies hits it. This door is steel, and when it jolts inward, it cracks Joseph in the jaw. For a second, I think he's going to drop, but incredibly, he holds his position.

I finish dragging the first keg towards him, Doug hot on my heels with the next. Two in place, I'm back for another, no help from the others, who stand by like they're watching the handyman fix their sink.

"A little fucking help, please?" I bark, the room illuminated for an instant as Speck lights a cigarette.

As I drag the next barrel from the wall, a large piece of sheet metal falls from where it had been pinned by the kegs. It hits the floor in a cacophony, and I get an idea.

"Help me with this instead," I say, stooping to try and lift one edge of the metal.

With Doug's help, we manage to get it up. The sheet is big enough to cover most of the entrance, but it's slicing into my fingers as we carry it, slipping from my hands. We're struggling.

"Help him!" Joseph yells at the others, the door continually smashing him in the back of the head.

"I would if I had two functioning arms. Guess you shouldn't have done that, eh?" Roy snarls.

Joseph screams in wordless frustration, ducks away from the door just long enough to help Doug and I carry the sheet the last few feet. In that brief instant, the top wedges open and a small, long-haired man slips through. Joseph sees him a moment too late, kicks out and hits the guy square in his back. The intruder splays onto his stomach just as Doug and I get the metal in place. Angela and Speck manage to roll another barrel in line. This should work perfectly, but there's no time to catch our breath. Joseph and I square off against the little guy, who is already back on his feet and brandishing a large piece of broken window as a blade.

I pick a rusty metal pipe off the ground and start swinging it at Tattoo. We dance in a circle for a moment, and

I'm outside myself, watching as I trade slashes with this psycho. It's all schoolyard flinches and hesitation on my part. I'm staring at this crazy fucker's hand where he's holding the glass, watching how it butchers his palm and fingers. I see no reaction from him to the pain.

Just like Roy and his arm, I think.

Behind us, Speck and Angela get another barrel in place. The door is now completely secure.

"C'mon you fucking maggot," I taunt. The little guy is all barks and grunts. He shimmies in and out of the shadows so that it's difficult for me to press the attack. There's an explosion, followed by a rush of air so close to my arm that I feel the fabric of my shirt separate.

I blink, and Mr. Psycho is lying on the stained tiles, a perfectly round hole about two inches circumference leaking dark, black blood in the center of his forehead.

I turn and see Guinevere Speck slipping a handgun back into the waistband of her pants.

"You almost took off my elbow, you crazy bitch!" I scream, my ears still ringing. The acoustics in the room are massive.

"Oh, stop being so melodramatic, okay? Should I have let him gut you?"

"Nice shot, boss," Doug says. He brushes dirt from a final keg he's stacked against the others, then wipes his hands on his pants like a ten-year-old.

"This should hold. Now, where the hell are we going?"

"Down," Roy says and turns to lead the way.

∼

"Look, I've taken the fucking Seattle underground tour - this is not that."

"Not the Seattle Underground that everyone knows

about. This tunnel leads below that. When the underground used to be the street, there were maintenance tunnels below that. Below that? Well, the natives had sacred catacombs. Shit the white man never knew about."

"Jesus."

"There's a whole network of tunnels like this, below the below. We're going into the Underground's Underground. You'll probably feel your ears pop at some point."

"It'd be easier if I could see where you are," Angela barks. Even in the dark, I can see she's walking lopsided.

"Broke a heel?" I ask, and she stops only a few inches in front of me and snaps the heel off of her good shoe, "You really are a great detective, you know that, Henry?"

"Fuck off."

CHAPTER 31

We walk on. It's slower going in the darkness. The feeling of impending doom has hit the ebb of its orbit as we leave the blood-thirsty mob behind. Their battering recedes into an all-encompassing silence as we press on, eventually disturbed only by our footsteps' echoes and the irregular rhythms of dripping water.

The floor slopes, and our visibility needle moves slightly out of null once thin beams of light flicker in via periodic slats in the walls. This isn't sunlight, as we are way below ground level. In these moments of illumination, I see that Angela is in front of me. Beyond her is Joseph. Roy's at the lead. That puts Guinevere and Doug behind me.

I'm lulled into a walking trance and accidentally step on the back of Angela's foot.

"OW! Goddamnit, watch where you're going."

"Sorry. Not so easy to see."

"Try harder."

I hear something in her voice... like she's crying on the inside, afraid, even if she's not showing it to us.

Inspired by her emotion, I move up closer to her as I walk.

"So, one of those people you gunned down the day you killed your partner? Luis Flores. His sister's the one who hired me to find you."

"Thanks for that. Was a lot easier to handle not knowing any names."

Hearing her say it like that, I realize infected or not, Angela still has all her faculties, including her conscience.

"I don't get it. If you're infected, how come you feel guilt? And why aren't you trying to kill us?"

"Maybe I'm just waiting for the right moment. Ever think of that?"

Touché. I back off a couple of steps again and leave Angela to stew in her juices.

CHAPTER 32

F inally, after what feels like forever, we come to a large, industrial space big and light enough that I feel safe catching my breath. There's a light switch, and miracle of miracles, it works. The ancient, flickering sodium vapes reveal the textures around us. Tiled walls and floor, all stained and chipped by long-dead machines and the passage of time. God only knows what this place would have been used for if it's buried this far underground.

"Doesn't look like Sacagwea's garage, I'll tell you that," Joseph says, "This is recent, probably turn of the last century."

"Bet you're great at antiquing," I say and smile when I hear Angela laugh.

"Jesus, are we below the harbor?"

"Not yet," Roy answers, "We're clear across town from the bowling alley. Marej first found out about these tunnels from the people he sells drugs for. They use these routes to move large amounts of product long distances safely. This is where he met Murph."

"Who uses them for totally different reasons, I'm guessing."

"Yeah," Roy says and stops. His arm still hangs limp, but there's no sign of pain on his face.

"You're infected, aren't you?"

"What?" he says, not defensive at all. Two to one, he's been waiting for me to catch up.

"You think you're not?" he asks.

"I don't know what the hell I think, but you don't see me running around killing every mother fucker in sight, do you? You either, so what gives?"

"Basic biology, brother. The Omega Virus is like any other virus; it affects different people in different ways. If it had done to you what it did to ninety-five percent of the population, you wouldn't be here with me."

"You say that as if this was all planned."

"Hank - it was. Jesus. For a psychic P.I., you're pretty slow these days."

"This is madness."

"No, it's not. *This* is the natural order of things. The human population of planet earth? *That's* madness."

"Stop bickering you two," Speck says, stepping in between us. For the first time, I get a very sexual vibe from this woman. It's disconcerting. She's hot, but her diminutive stature and business-like dress and demeanor contradict each other. The image she projects makes me think of someone I grew up with, a kid whose younger sister would dress up and pretend to be, of all things, the principal of the school."

"Oh bullshit," Speck says, and I turn quickly, startled.

"Did you just read my fucking mind?"

"Open book."

"Gimmie a cigarette, would you?" Joseph asks her.

"Fuck off, stupid. You want to blow us all up?"

"What?"

"We're far enough underground that there's natural gas. Boom Boom. You know."

"Goddamnit. Well then, when the hell do we get to this 'Paradise?' We've been walking for the better part of an hour."

"Can't handle it, bro?" Doug asks, and the tension between the two feels like *it* might ignite the gas.

"Not much farther," Roy says and points into the distance. Ahead, the room narrows into a corridor, out of which drifts what looks like fog.

"What is that?"

"A short tunnel that will lead us beneath the foundation of a local bookstore."

Angela, Joseph, and I all look to one another, stunned.

"Charters?"

Roy smiles devilishly: "Who *have* you been talking to?"

CHAPTER 33

When I was five, my mom moved us out of the one-bedroom apartment where I'd spent the first years of my life and into a house. A 'fixer-upper' for sure, our new digs proved to be an old converted summer home from the twenties. It sat in the middle of a small 'experimental' community in the middle of a forest preserve. Looking back on it, the house, which, if you listened close you could hear begging for a new coat of paint and perhaps an addition or two, became the prototype by which I would judge all subsequent residences. Not to say it was particularly grand. It was not. That house, however, was *ours*.

We're talking about old, weathered drywall, cracked tiles in the kitchen, and ancient carpet. At first glance, the unfinished basement looked like a dungeon: stone walls, stone floor, and none of the accruements ordinarily associated with modern suburban, middle-class housing. I realized later my mother chose the house not only because it was all we could afford at the time but as something she could spend her free time improving. An ongoing project. That's what she wanted, more than anything else. That's what we all want -

something to winnow away the hours, distracting us from the fact that none of this dog and pony show means spit. Death lurks just behind some inevitable corner, waiting to dash everything we've built to kindling.

I loved that house.

I spent some of the most formative hours of my life in that basement. It's where I began to establish a sense of self. It was there that I felt the onset of my talents, there that I first stared into a mirror and contacted something else, something that made my world-view what it is today.

I used to have this painting I did of a room made entirely of stone, suspended in space and time. My interpretation of that space beneath the house transposed onto a cosmic map, a geometrical cube smack-dab in the middle of a star-infused void. That painting hung on my wall until I moved out. I haven't thought about it in years. Now I find that conjuring of my pre-pubescent imagination stands revealed as a portal to this exact moment in my life, because the room below Charter's is more like that basement than I can believe. Same stone walls and floor, same feeling of suspension.

I'd known this was coming all along. That's the problem with the aether and seeing the future. There's never any context for what you see. So what if you see your own death? If you can't make heads or tails of the specifics, it's just another vague imagining until it's too late and it's right in front of you. Recognizing this place now, I realize there's a good chance this will be the last room I see.

Luckily, I've been wrong before. I just usually don't let on that I'm wrong. This time, I'm fucking counting on it.

As we comb the place, Angela and Joseph bring me up to speed on its significance to Tony Tod and our current predicament. That's another problem with being psychic; often, you're the last to know what you've told everyone else.

Something catches my eye — a hard, smooth black

surface slopes down one wall from a hole in the ceiling. Around the anthracite's base, what looks like a machine protrudes just enough that I can read the decal on its side. Zoeller. Zoeller makes sump-pumps. I know because we had one in that basement.

"This place keeps popping up," Angela reflects out loud, "It must have more significance than just the store where all these people worked."

I hear snickering and spy the big smile on Roy's puss. He's enjoying this a little more than I would like.

I step beneath the opening and stare up, around the sludge. There are a few inches of open space, and I have a strong urge to try to reach inside.

So I do.

Roy's snickers increase, and perhaps reciprocally, everyone else takes a step away from me. I have to go up on my tippy toes, but soon my fingers break some of the black shit off the trunk. It doesn't smell good, but it doesn't smell like excrement, so there's that. Gritting my teeth against the repulsion that touching slimy surfaces inspires, I slip my fingers through. With surprisingly little effort, my hand, wrist, and then arm follows. Watching this happen triggers a strong feeling of déjà vu, where I remember something I know didn't happen to me. A switch in my head flips, and I start to cough uncontrollably, almost to the point of vomiting. Despite this, or perhaps because of it, I keep reaching.

With my ear against this atrocious black funk and all my attention focused on the task, I become so inexplicably driven that I start to hear things. It's like having your ear in a sea shell; distant, ambiguous voices occur to me. They whisper things to me, things about myself, about the others. Maybe it's my inability to tell where these voices originate that puts them so close inside my head, but the result is a disorientation that bleeds into the physical world. The sensation causes me to stumble, and then something amazing happens.

I fall. Up.

My head goes light, and everything swims for a minute. When my vision returns, I have this realization where I remember what it felt like to fall up.

"What the fuck was that?" I can hear Angela ask from below.

Or is it above?

The disorientation peels back a layer. I sit up and look around. The room is dark, but I can see enough to know it is more developed than the one I just left. The floor is concrete, and there's garbage everywhere: fast-food wrappers, empty plastic bottles from soft drinks, milk, and beer cans. A lot of beer cans. Also, a small mirror and a sack of white powder next to it. I move toward that, dipping one wet finger into the bag and rubbing the resultant paste on my upper gums. Whoah.

"Same stuff Marej had," I say out loud. I'm about to take another dip when a gunshot rings out from below, followed by the rising strains of panic.

Shit.

~

"Gerald, hurry!"

Angela's voice ripples with fear, and for a moment, I can't believe it's her at all. She's shown so little emotion thus far and definitely no weakness or need. Her pleas suggest something substantially bad is about to happen. For a moment, I think about leaving them down there, heading out on my own. I can't do it, though. Someone once told me my altruism would one day be the death of me. Fuck it. I push all differences aside and extend my hand to her.

"Take my hand," I yell, dread creeping into my voice. What's down there? As I do this, several things happen at once.

First, I feel Angela's hand grasp mine and I start to pull. Roy screams, and all the hairs on the back of my neck stand up as I see someone move toward me out of the corner of my eye. In the room below, there's a gunshot as Angela's head crowns through the small passage.

"Jesus Christ – where did they all come from?" she says, out of breath.

Two more gunshots, but I hear them from a distance as my mind falls back into that spooky this-never-fucking-happened déjà vu moment. Not me. No. A huge chunk of my recent channeling floats to the top of my brain, and I realize I'm remembering Tony Tod's experiences in this room. Is that who's in here with us?

Something clatters to the floor in the far corner, and I feel Angela straighten up at the sound.

"What was that? Is someone there?"

"I don't know," I answer, wishing it was true. I turn away from the hole for just a second and stare into the darkness. I can tell Angela senses him too. We scan the room. Nothing.

"Hurry!" someone screams from below. I return to the task at hand.

Next up is Guinevere. She has to jump to catch my hand, and I'm not ready for it, almost fall back through. We balance out, and I pull. As I do, my eyes lock on the far corner again. This time, someone is definitely standing there.

"Do you see him?" I ask Angela.

"Who?" she asks, following my eyes, "There's no one there."

"Yes, there is," I say. I'm not even sure how I know it's Tony Tod, but I know.

Unlike Angela, Guinevere's letting me do all the work.

When I see the figure move toward me, I almost drop her. We maintain, and the scare gets her moving. She literally starts clawing her way up my arm and through the slime around the hole's edges. Contact with our body temperature has begun to melt the stuff. Its petrified marble-like surface is becoming slick. Once through, Guinevere walks off into the room, and I know she sees Tod, too.

Meanwhile, I reach back in for the next happy camper. When they grab hold, I haven't quite recalibrated my expectations for the extra weight, and they almost pull me onto my face. My head slams into the black shit and some of it breaks off into my ear, smears along my face. The voices swell again, and before I can finish pulling Joseph through, I can hear someone talking to me as if from a great distance.

'*Kill them.*'

Is there no originality left?

The apparition catches my attention again. This time, Tod stands in front of the large door at the far end of the room. Broken locks hang from the outside. The hinges are damaged, dangling by a screw in one spot, and what looks like fingernail scratches mar the wood grain on the inside.

"Hey! Wake the fuck up and help me!" Joseph says, fighting to make it up amidst the turmoil below. I snap out of my trance and pull him through in a burst of adrenaline. This time, I collapse to the floor.

"Your turn," I say.

"Fuck that. Leave those two."

"I don't think so," Guinevere Speck says, leveling her gun at him.

Joe curses her but leans through the hole to grab whoever's next. I remain on the floor, the cool Earth seeping in through my already sweat-drenched shirt. I turn back toward the doorway. Is it my imagination, or is that someone lying dead on their back in the corridor outside, their feet pointing up like the Wicked Witch of the West?

"We've got a body," Angela says as Doug emerges from the opening amidst a virtual onslaught of screams and gunshots.

"You left the guy with one good arm to fend for himself?" I ask, exasperated.

Joseph gets right up in my face.

"I'm only going to say this once. Fuck your friend."

That does it. Long time coming, I shove Joseph backward. Hard. He goes for his gun but stumbles, and I charge, haul off and slug him as hard as I can in the face. He goes down on his back, and I return one last time to the hole. A lot of the black stuff has rubbed off on everyone coming up, so now I can actually see clearly into the lower level. Roy is directly beneath me, his face contorted in horror, his good arm waving with panicked gesticulations of the purest terror.

"Hank! Help! Get me out of here! Hank!"

Someone hits me in the back of the head, and the last thing I see before the world goes dark is half a dozen hands dragging Roy to the ground.

CHAPTER 34

When I come to, we're no longer in the room with the hole. Instead, we're in what I would describe as your typical corporate office. Ten feet and a left turn before the first door I see is a small employee break room, LCD flatscreen mounted on the wall. Nothing in the fridge. Which sucks because I'm starving.

"Communication," Angela says, making it sound like the name of a long lost lover.

I remember the final frame of the last reel and pop onto my feet faster than I would have thought possible, considering the throb in my skull.

I go straight for Joseph.

"You fucking piece of shit!" I yell as he stands to confront my onslaught. I outmaneuver his defense by faking like I'm about to shove him with both hands to the chest. When his arms come up, I reach past them, lock my fingers behind his head and pull his face forward into my knee, which I bring up with so much momentum I swear I feel it leave an apple-sized dent in his skull. Joseph goes down; it's his turn to take a nap.

Without saying a word to the stunned onlookers, I stalk out of the room and into the corridor. At the end, I find the door to the room with the hole. It's been barricaded with everything one would expect to see an office barricade made of: a heavy metal filing cabinet, a large wastebasket, probably from a bathroom. Part of a desk, a large copy machine/printer, and a stack of boxes that contain... porno magazines?

Behind me, Guinevere approaches cautiously. I know without having to see that she has one hand on her gun.

"We're not any happier about losing Roy than you, but trust me. You don't want to open that door."

"Oh yeah? Why? What's behind it?"

"A lot of murder happy bastards, all jonesing to play in our blood."

"Roy?"

"I doubt there's any way he could have survived. That bastard Joseph fucked him good."

"Then let's fucking kill Joseph."

"Oh, I intend to. But my instructions are to bring all of you."

"Instructions? Whose instructions?"

"Soon enough, buddy. Soon enough."

I follow Guinevere back into the break room. Angela is eating a pack of Maruchan dry, a solid brick of noodles. Tiny bits fall from around her mouth as she chomps down, oblivious or uncaring.

"What's the plan?"

"We have to get out of here, down the block, and around the corner."

"I thought outside was bad. Isn't that why we just walked through about a hundred miles of tunnels?"

This idea sounds so insane that I completely forget my anger and grief at losing Roy.

"It's through a warehouse, couple of blocks over."

"You gotta be fucking kidding me..."

You'd think at this point, I'd be so tired I would give up. At least that's what I'd think. Not the case. Somewhere inside me, an emergency flare of energy and can-do spirit light up. Must have been my three months in the Scouts as a kid, before they kicked me out for setting up a pyramid scheme to get other kids' badges.

"Okay, let's look around and see if there's anything that might help. Weapons and the like."

"Weapons? In a book store?"

"A book store where half the fucking staff was infected with a murder virus."

"Good point."

CHAPTER 35

The first thing any movie about the apocalypse will tell you is to check all broadcasting destinations. In *Night of the Living Dead*, television news served as the lifeline for the characters to receive information about the world outside. By *Dawn of the Dead*, the last of the television stations were overrun and off the air. Luckily, things are different in the modern, digital world. As long as the satellites and towers function, there's a channel for information to flow through. Even better, everyone has a receiver/broadcast tool in their pocket.

"Anyone's phone have juice? Mine's dead," I lie, seeing Angela has hers in her hands already.

"Check youtube."

"Way ahead of you," she says and holds up her phone so I can see the screen.

We all huddle around her, but it's hard to see. Plus, there's a halitosis crisis at the end of the world, and it ain't pretty. I step back and spot the remote for the tv on the table, next to a Mr. Coffee and a mug filled with sweetener packets. The mug's design features a dog with five o'clock shadow adding the contents of a flask to his coffee. The caption says, "F*ck Mondays."

I flip the tv on and select the youtube icon. Angela's already on my wavelength. She uses Bluetooth to cast the images from her phone to the tv. Her personalized landing page appears big enough for all of us to see comfortably.

"What the fuck is Christian Fisting?" Guinevere asks in mock outrage, the first smile I've seen on her face since meeting her. I move closer to the screen to inspect the image, a fist holding a crucifix in a vaguely threatening manner.

"Band," I say, laughing. I swear a look of disappointment flashes across Guinevere's face.

Angela scrolls down to where the Emergency Feed runs along the bottom of her curated content. She clicks a thumbnail with the caption, "Mayor Arlington Grimoldi Gives Update on MV-20."

"This oughta be good. Guy's a cunt," Guinevere says. On the screen, a man so tanned he looks like talking jerky addresses the press from behind a podium. He wears what looks like a two thousand dollar suit, a sharp contrast to the dark brown blouse and wrinkled Khakis of the sign language translator who stands beside him, gesticulating his every word. The tv's volume is set to off, so I manually turn it up.

"... With Stay at Home orders from the President being all but ignored, the State had no choice but to call in Military support. Unfortunately, it does not appear at this time that support will make it here intact. The National situation has eclipsed Eastern Europe for casualties, so I am personally asking every citizen who has not already succumbed to MV-20 to stay in their homes. Protect yourselves and your families. As your elected representative, I have met with considerable resistance in the "Your Own Home" initiative, however, in areas of the country such as New York and Chicago, YOH has been the deciding factor in-"

"What the hell is this YOH shit?" I ask, feeling incredibly out of touch. How long did they have me in that Bowling Alley?

"They're telling people to cut ties with everyone except those under the same roof. To minimize infection rates."

"Makes sense," Joseph says from behind me, where he sits handcuffed to the back of his chair. I throw him a look that firmly establishes my intentions for him should he continue to speak. From over my shoulder, the Mayor continues to address tv land.

"...If you need supplies, the number on the bottom of the screen has been set up to take requests; however, we are dangerously short-handed on volunteers and-"

The signal clicks off. We all look to Angela, who has pocketed her phone.

"Fuck this. We need to move, not sit here watching someone tell us what we already know."

"It'd be nice to know what the rest of the world looks like."

"Seems to me we already know," I say, "Let me ask you all something. Any of you feel motivated by what we just saw? I know I don't. Hearing that just made me want to put a gun in my mouth."

"Why don't you?" Joseph says from his chair. I kick him in the shin. Hard. He winces in pain. Petty? Yeah. So what?

Angela continues.

"Time for my pep talk, I guess. Here goes. The US government sprung me from a maximum-security prison and sent me here because they traced the origin of Harvest's Manuscript to Seattle, Washington. Gerald proved a lucky find because, despite all my doubts, his abilities have helped us narrow the path of first-contact to within a twenty-five-mile radius. Guinevere's arrival just cinched my suspicion that we are close. Now, I've let you fuckers pull the strings up to this point because it suited me to let you think you were in charge. That is no longer the case."

"Oh, so this is what, a mutiny?" Doug says, squaring up to her.

"Douglas, don't-" Guinevere is cut-off as Angela's gun comes up so fast I don't have time to cover my ears. The shot rings out, my world turns into a high-pitched drone, and Dougie's head explodes all over his boss.

"Now, we are following Guinevere here to Paradise, end of story. We are not doing this because she was told to bring us. We are doing it because I intend to fight my way to the exact origin of this event, find those responsible, and kill them. End of fucking story. Any questions, comments, threats, or observations?"

Silence.

"I thought not. Ms. Speck? Without further adieu, if you please?"

"No problem, Angela."

"Detective Miller."

"No problem, Detective Miller."

Guinevere says this in a tone that establishes that, without her goon, she's fucked. This is the first sign of weakness she has shown, her otherwise ruthless and cynical demeanor now as useless as her lap dog's braincase, which lays hollow and smoking on the floor.

CHAPTER 36

The store's lights are all on, which just serves to make the place even spookier than it already is.

"Something about abandoned retail environments always gives me the creeps," I say, close behind Angela. Before leaving the break room, she confiscated Speck's handgun and entrusted it to me.

"Yeah. My partner and I, well, my former partner, we worked a case once that led to a shoot-out in an abandoned shopping mall. Creepiest fucking place I have ever been."

We emerge from the back offices into a stock room. It's a large space filled with human implements, everything powered-up, and no one to use any of it. I feel like I'm stuck in the leading role of a George A. Romero zombie movie; what's around this corner? What's around that one?

A bank of computer monitors lines the far wall. There's a surveillance camera in the corner of the room.

"Someone watching us?" Joseph asks.

"Maybe."

"One more reason to let me out of these fucking handcuffs."

"Oh yeah? Why, exactly?"

"D'uh, if someone's watching us, chances are they're waiting for the right moment to attack. You're going to need all the help you can get."

Angela shoots me a look that tells me she now sees me as her equal, no longer her captive or some stupid bastard she has to babysit.

"He's right," she says.

"He is," I say, and get up in Joseph's face, "If she takes those handcuffs off and you even look at me funny, you're dead. Capiche?"

"Fuck you."

"Don't make me change my mind," she threatens, and Joseph acquiesces.

The handcuffs come off.

"He's right. CCTV."

"Security cameras?"

I hunt around on the small console nearby, flipping switches until all screens light up. Images follow a moment later.

"Is that outside?"

"These first couple appear to be outside. The rest face the sales floor. Those last two are back here. Look."

I point at a screen on the far left, where you can see the backs of our heads.

"Is that… are those people in the magazine section? Really?" Guinevere asks.

"You ever see *Dawn of the Dead*? People return to what they know on impulse, regardless of their state of mind. It's one of the reasons Amazon couldn't completely kill off the brick-and-mortar bookstore. Cultural landmark."

"Back in the 90s," Speck starts, "a friend of mine worked at the Charters in Hollywood. He told me this story once.

Their GM got a call bright and early on Thanksgiving one year. The store was closed, but the regular customers pulled the front door open and went inside. Oblivious to the alarm, they stood around reading magazines like nothing was wrong. Police arrived, said most of the customers didn't even realize the store was closed, you know, for the fucking holiday. My friend said Corporate was fielding complaints for weeks."

"Sounds about right."

"Makes me think we deserve this," I say and mean it. Hard not to while juxtaposing the monitor image of a crowd of people beating a man to death outside the building with others thumbing through Dwell and Interior Design a few hundred feet away.

"Enough storytime. We need to get out of this store and down the street."

Something's been bothering me about this suicide mission Angela has us gearing up for. I've been reticent to say anything since she's A) infected and B) holding a firearm. But it's now or never.

"Count me out."

"Excuse me? I believe I made myself quite clear when I took over," she says, turning on me with a bloodthirsty look in her eyes.

"Look, my only stake in any of this was Roy. I came to Seattle because I thought he was dead and needed to find out what happened to him. Now that I know he's an asshole, well, let's just say this is where I leave you and leave it at that?

"And where would you go? Exactly?"

There's a quick glitch that runs through all the screens, then the images return. One, in particular, catches everyone's attention.

Focus on a mob of people outside the front door. They're

fighting one another, blood and guts rendered in black and white, so none of it looks real. What does look real, however, is the effete man-child standing perfectly still, staring up at the camera smiling. His face is covered in what I can only assume is blood.

"Shit."

"What?" Angela and Guinevere ask in accidental unison.

"I know that guy."

On the screen, Marej leers directly into my soul.

We're running through the book store's lower level, through the literature section, to be exact. Welsh, Wallace, Thompson - names that fly by amid smears of blood and gore. I glimpse a piece of skull lying on the floor.

"Somebody went fucking crazy in here."

We stop in our tracks when we see the cash registers ahead; the magazines are just beyond.

So is the entrance.

I count five registers, a convoluted retail cue of tack board and POP displays, and beyond that, freedom. Well, Marej, then freedom.

"There couldn't have been more than three people in the magazine section. We can take them."

"Makes sense. But if the infected are already inside, why isn't the front door wide open? Something's wrong with this whole thing."

"What would you have us do, Gerald?" Angela asks. I can tell she's hoping I have a better idea. I don't. Not really.

"Fire exit? Or, how about the loading bay?"

My words come out confident, however, I'm anything but. My body feels too heavy to move. I pop my head around the corner of the aisle we've taken cover in; authors D through H. Don Delillo's *White Noise* catches my eye, and I linger on its spine. I love this book, but it's suddenly hard to remember a world where I had the environment to allow reading. What the fuck happened to the reality I knew only a few days ago?

I'm not paying attention when someone races by me in the outside aisle. I do a double-take - it's a little boy. He can't be more than eight years old. I shiver for a moment, realizing how close I came to stepping out in front of him. Watching the boy now, I can tell he didn't see us, he's too busy running from something...

"Back!" I whisper-yell at the others, throwing myself at them to force everyone into the alcove at the rear of the aisle. A moment later, a woman runs by, also oblivious to us. I wait a beat, then inch back out to see what's happening. On the main floor, I see the eight-year-old swing a bicycle chain and catch the woman in the throat with it. The chain wraps tight around her neck, the kid pulls, and I can literally see the spot where her throat collapses. I gag as blood bursts from the woman's nose, mouth, and eyes, splattering a *Goodnight Moon* cardboard dump.

"There are definitely more than three hostiles in here with us," I say, wondering where Marej went. Is he in here? There's an explosion, and automatic gunfire saws through the glass windows by the magazines—chunks of glass rain across the front of the store like hail.

"Down! Down!" I yell. Everyone drops, and we start crawling toward the back of the store on our bellies. We're about halfway to the offices again when from somewhere nearby, I hear maniacal laughter. I grip my gun and pop up, itching to kill something to relieve the suspense of what feels like an inevitable game of cat-and-mouse.

"Don't shoot!" Someone says from behind me. I turn, face-to-face with Marej. He is surrounded by a group of people who look like they should be sitting in a coffee house listening to Phish. The stink of Patchouli fills my nose and makes my hatred surge.

"Kill them," he says, a moment before I blow a hole in his face the size of a silver dollar.

CHAPTER 37

Watching Marej's face explode kicks my adrenaline into overdrive, but my hands stay steady. Something moves to my left; I turn and shoot another hippie in the face, then swivel back to twelve O'clock only to have the gun swatted from my hand. A knee hits my groin and I double over. Through the searing pain, I see Joseph recover my gun and unload two rounds into my assailant before taking a fist to the back of his head. Angela is a few feet ahead of us. She's firing staccato, semi-auto rounds that each drop a body. I suck in my breath and snatch the chain from around the dead woman's neck just in time to turn and catch the eight-year-old in the face with it. I see his right eye explode in what looks like a squib of mayonnaise, but he keeps coming, diving into my abdomen like a ferocious poodle. We fall backward, and I land on one of the hippies' guns. A moment later, I'm covered in the vestiges of a third-grade education. I watch Angela reload and kill her way through the rest of Marej's friends while Joseph and I catch our breaths. My balls feel like someone superglued them to the inside of my ass.

"Where the fuck is Guinevere?"

"Right here," she says, and we all turn to see her sitting in a comfy chair, apparently enjoying the show. For the first time, I notice the elegance of Guinevere's cheekbones and imagine what they would feel like caving in beneath my knuckles. My first taste of the infection, or a sane response to this insane woman's audacity? No time to decide, as from the front of the store, a fresh wave of killdos charge into the store.

I fire two shots into the onrushing horde, then the gun clicks empty. Angela and Joseph pick up the slack as I toss the gun at the closest oncoming head but miss, then snag the first thing within reach and slam it into their chest. Lucky for me, that first thing is a corkscrew. I'm just able to see the foil-embossed font for a celebrity chef's line of cookbooks on the handle before they drop. I've bought myself a chance to find another, hopefully, reusable weapon.

Lookee lookee. Some irresponsible stock room employee has left a box cutter by one of the store's computer terminals. I grab it and turn with a wide slash, cut two throats for the price of one. Two more flannel-wearing middle-agers fall to the floor, gurgling blood instead of air.

The sight gives me pause. Big mistake. A Jerry Garcia look-alike comes at me from the left with a pipe he must have pulled off the urinal in the bathroom. He swings, I barely dodge, then lurch forward and bury the cutter in his esophagus.

"Henry - behind you!" someone screams. I pull the box cutter free and turn, blindly hitting home with another slash. A blonde hippie chick's face opens like a cheap bag of meat, muscle, and nasal sinew gushing from the wound like sausage from casing. She drops a knife, and I instantly trade up for the better weapon, though I must say, the box cutter served me well.

I turn back to where Angela grapples with a woman who looks like my high school principal. I move in to help, but a ball-peen hammer crashes down on my left shoulder. I crumple under the blow, but even as I hit the floor, I reach out and grab my assailant by her Birkenstock-clad foot and rip those chalk-white legs out from under her. Joanie Mitchell comes down on top of my back, where the hammer's dull, flat side hits me again, this time in the ass. This leaves the teeth face-up, so when I pull her up by her shitty, Kimono-like dress and then slam her face-first into the floor, those teeth meet her windpipe.

Gurgling refrain.

Despite the howling pain in my shoulder and bum, I wriggle out from under the dead chick in time to see Joe wrestle a revolver away from a pimple-faced teenager. He opens fire and wipes away all the remaining attackers except two. One charges me, wailing like an enraged banshee. Only the wail turns to a gurgle as both Angela and Joseph unload three rounds a piece into her just inches before she would have overtaken me. The force of the bullets doesn't so much stop her as push her back in jagged convulsions. The last of these sends her head-over-heels backward to the floor. Her many new holes enthusiastically leak her essence out onto the tile. That leaves just one hot-head little hippie chick, blood all over her face and dress.

"Wait!" I scream. Idea.

"What?"

"Let me see if I can, uh, get something from her."

"I thought they had to be dead for you to talk to?"

"I didn't say I didn't want you to kill her; I just wanted to be ready."

"Oh, okay," Angela says, and she and Joseph drop the hippie chick with a bullet each, one under each eye. The exit wounds open the back of her head like a convertible. She's so

177

close to me that I get a fresh coat of brain-paint, which causes me to laugh despite the horror of it all.

"Effective," I say, stooping down to try and focus on the light I see receding from the girl's eyes. If I can just follow that light...

CHAPTER 38

CARLY BARRETT

There's really no way to deal with the disappointment. I mean, I've tried my whole life to be a good person. It hasn't been easy, and the temptation has always lurked just below the surface, to lose my shit and just be a bastard.

But again, I tried.

My mom died when I was fifteen and my dad, well, he's a fucking jerk, so let's not even go there. I went to live with my mom's sister Ellen after I realized I wasn't going to be able to handle dad anymore. That was the best living situation I had as far as family was concerned. Not perfect, but I loved my aunt, and she loved me.

By that point, college was only a couple years away. My plan was to work my ass off and graduate a year early so I could move to Berkley six full months before turning eighteen. In the interim, aunt Ellen was happy to have me. The only problem was moving so far out of the way, from Frisco to Portland, just to stay with her. I checked with the high school there and found everything I'd taken, gen eds, and stuff would transfer. Still, relocating in the middle of the tenth grade was not easy. I didn't really have a choice, though, so I put my head down and plowed ahead.

I lived with Ellen for almost a year before she got sick. It happened so fast, and I can't help but worry that with both mom and her sister getting cancer before they turned forty, that shit is just waiting for me, ya know?

Over the next few months, I did what I could to help Ellen. I had all honors classes, though, so school was pretty intense. It was all I could do to balance studying with taking her back and forth to the hospital and all the various doctor visits and stuff. Ellen underwent test after test, but nothing helped. Between her and school, eventually, I found myself struggling to keep my head above water.

In hindsight, there were probably still a lot of issues bubbling around inside my head from mom's death. After she died, I had so much other stuff going on that I never really had a chance to cry. Then there I was going through it all again so soon after. Talk about sticking it in and breaking it off, right?

Aunt Ellen died five months later, and I faced a hard decision. I still had six months before I could finish school, but now I had nowhere to live. Ellen's townhome was a rental, and the landlord made no small deal about the fact that she wasn't going to give me a break just because Ellen had lived there for so long.

Business, that's what she said.

It was about then that I met Murphy.

I was visiting my friend Carrie in Seattle; Murphy was hanging out in Pioneer Square with a mutual acquaintance. We took to one another from the jump. He invited me to a party the next night, so I talked Carrie into going.

Murphy was a student, but he was like thirty-something years old. See, his parents died when he was younger and left him all this money, so he was pretty much independently wealthy. Way he tells it, after a year of traveling the world, he wanted to go back to school for something he truly loved.

Sociology.

Yeah, that surprised me, too. I mean, who loves Sociology? Murphy, that's who. Apparently, his father had been a sociologist and something of a social engineer to boot. He'd instilled some pretty crazy ideas in Murphy's head from a young age. Those ideas defined Murphy. Later, they came to define me, too.

With his money, Murphy was free to buy a house off the University's campus. He was a socialite, so it wasn't hard for him to find a shitload of roommates and pretty much stage the best possible reinvention of his twenties he could manage. This included hosting weekly parties, donating money to the campus bar to build an addition for live music, and fucking as many college girls as possible.

I was one of those girls.

Thing was, I really thought Murph and I had a connection, so when he offered to let me move into his place, I figured maybe I could change him.

Well, *that* didn't happen.

What did happen was I became part of the 'cult of Murph' as some of the girls around campus called it. There was something about this guy... so confident and charismatic. I knew he was fucking every girl who came into that house, but that didn't make me want to stop. It was weird, but words don't do the feelings he inspired justice, so let's just say there were about half a dozen of us that ended up making peace with the idea of sharing him. I mean, I'm no angel, it wouldn't be the first time I'd shared someone, but with Murph, it wasn't the physical that ate at me. It was the mental.

So I moved in along with the others, and that's when I began seeing their little group's inner workings. Murph was different – he'd been around, ya know? In that time, he'd kinda read between the lines of life and come up with some pretty radical philosophies. Part of that manifested as something that more than a little resembled the inner workings of Operation: Mayhem from *Fight Club*. Except Murph and his people didn't want to fight anyone, they wanted to kill them.

~

With my increasing proximity to Murphy, it wasn't long before I became involved with the group. They called themselves 'The Omega Council,' or OC. For short. This was primarily a gag, but it stuck.

The OC talked about how the human race reproduced so fast, we were choking the life out of the Earth. Our unchecked propagation caused irreparable harm to every living thing we shared the planet with. It'd been like this for a long time, Murph said, at least since the Industrial Revolution. That's when humanity began to perfect how to take everything for ourselves, leaving nothing for the rest of the planet. Ordinarily, Murphy said, the Earth has ways of dealing with unchecked population growth. In our case, technology had given us an edge, so the planet was having a hard time instituting an 'Event' to balance the scales again.

At first, OC meetings were weird. I mean, I'd been in a couple of fights when I was a kid, but this was different. This was full-on killing that Murphy talked about. He told me later that he'd had his doubts about whether I would be up for the job until he saw me shoot. Teaching me how to shoot was the one good thing my dad did for me. He had me at the gun range every weekend from the age of eleven until we parted ways.

"Practice makes perfect," Dad always said.

In keeping with my specialty, I became the OC's sniper. Periodically, we'd do random tactical maneuvers in areas outside the city, never too close together to create a pattern for anybody to follow. One of our best tricks was to put snipers, usually me and this other guy Roy, out in public places in surrounding small towns. We wouldn't do the Whitman and pick hyper-populated areas. Instead, we'd find smaller country roads or more rural areas and pick people off far from prying eyes. Often, this MO meant we'd be able to kill entire families - carloads of people in a single strike. Remember those rumors of Muslim Terrorist Cells operating in rural Pacific Northwest? Yeah, well, I like my bacon on Sunday morning just fine.

Murph loved this strategy. Sometimes we'd kill dozens of people in a weekend sometimes, and he applauded it as the easiest way to take chunks out of what he called the 'Population Force.'

See, humanity's growth was beyond what you could classify as rationally exponential. Find a population tracker online and just sit and watch the thing. It's terrifying, but you'll start to understand what we're dealing with. I was happy to do my part, and every time I took aim and used what dad taught me out on the field, I always imagined it was him I was killing. The rest came naturally.

After some time, Murph got sick. He explained this to me, said his father - the late, great Acid Guru Abramelin Harvest - had given him this gift, this message to spread to make the world a better place. The thing was, a mission like that took its toll. Murph said the chosen always die young because of warring DNA codes emerging within the human genome – I never really understood all his science shit. All I knew was I loved him, and I loved killing for him. So much so that it had begun to define me. I mean, when the keys to greatness are dropped in your lap, how can you go back to writing papers about statistics and sociological trends?

The only trend I was interested in now was a downward one.

Not long after he became sick, Murph disappeared. Just like that. We didn't know what happened but assumed the worst. For closure, we buried an empty coffin.

Another funeral, just like mom and Aunt Ellen.

I stayed on at his house, along with the rest of the OC. To the outside world, it looked like any other college party house. Only we weren't sitting around listening to Dubstep and smoking pot – we were bound for greatness.

Roy and I began to handle most of the organization. We'd been the primary killers up 'til then, and by the time Murph's father's 'Representatives' showed up, we were running an almost military-style operation. Three shifts, twice a week, fanning out from safe houses in Fall City, Portland, La Grande, Boise, Casper. Our agents would travel for days sometimes, hitting the major arteries of the Western United States. Places like La Grande, areas big enough to make a dent but not big enough to really suggest a pattern. We'd coordinate attacks between multiple groups sent to places far enough away to look unconnected, places like El Cajon or Otay Mesa.

It also helped that, by this time, we had outgrown Murphy's single home. There were seven 'chapters' located all over the western half of the country. What's more, Murphy's Trust financed a publishing company that put his father's works in print. The world was fucked, and we had the solution. Word had begun to spread, and we had recruits showing up in droves. More extensive operations were easier to arrange by the day. Quite literally, we were legion, and that meant we could now cover a hell of a lot more ground than when there were just twelve of us.

When I finally met Marej, Roy was on his way out. There was a small group going to the desert on some sort of vision quest. One of those new-age techno Temporary Autonomous Zones. Black Rock City part two, or whatever. This left me back at the old Murph hut to run an increasingly delicate operation around the Pacific Northwest. I made no bones about doing it alone. I'd earned my place among the elite, and I would be a part of history.

When the woman from Jonestown Books showed up with a carton of the new book, it felt like the final affirmation of everything my life had become. Abramelin Harvest: *An Exploration of Macrocosmic Surgical Techniques to Rid the World of the Human Disease.* What a title, right! I burned through it in a day. In its pages, the words and sentences, paragraphs, and chapter titles, I saw echoes of everyone and everything in my life that mattered.

Age twelve: My father holds my shoulders as I take aim at a far-off stray dog and says: 'Lying in the middle of the road will get you nowhere. Stand up. Point. Shoot.'

Age Sixteen: I bury my mother. While going through her stuff with Aunt Ellen, I find a cache of papers that had belonged to her father, my grandpa W, two lifetimes ago. It read:

In a world that otherwise holds us helpless, we obsess over the ability to inflict ourselves on our environment in any way possible. To affect those defiant forces of nature that can crush us like flies, that can remove everything we are, everything we have ever accomplished.

Moments after Murphy and I first make love, he says to me: "Killing one human being will not do ANYTHING. Killing two is better. However, working on an exponential algorithm, a person can unlock a tidal wave of extinction energy that, much like the wave a skilled surfer rides, continues long after the passenger has crested and fallen."

I read Murphy's father's book, and I realized my entire

world, my entire life, has been written from the start on pages of skin penned in the blood of man.

I Kill, Therefore I Am.

CHAPTER 39

When I open my eyes this time, I feel filthy. Physically, emotionally, spiritually. Like I've been raped by a demon.

Angela's in the comfy chair, while Guinevere lays unconscious on the ground beside her. Joseph is flipping through yesterday's newspaper, apparently unimpressed with me.

"What'd she say?" I ask.

"Trust me, you don't want to know," Angela answers.

"Shit."

Angela nods. The hostility between us is gone, irrelevant in the escalating state of hopelessness that has come to define our reality. I'm not sure I can say the same about Joseph and me, but he did save my ass in the melee, so I'm willing to draw the peace card for now.

"Still thinking about going your own way?"

"Yeah, ah, about that. I think I've grown rather attached to you guys…"

Angela nods, "Come on then. We have to get to that tunnel."

With no avenue for salvation, the idea of head-on conflict

– revenge really, in all its juicy, nasty glory - becomes the only thing to live for. It's a hard pill to swallow. I know the world outside is irreparably gone, not coming back, but I can't help think how much I'd rather just leave town, put my feet up at a bar, and drink for about a year straight. Maybe that's what Paradise will be.

I doubt it, though.

We race toward the back offices again. Remembering my hallucination from earlier, I stop us at the door to Tony's office. I half expect to find him waiting for us. Instead, when I kick the locked door down, we see a stockpile of weapons that would make a gun lobbyist blush.

Cue obligatory weapons choosing montage, a cinematic staple.

Joseph sees my choices, all handguns, and scoffs, "You might want something with a little more bang for your buck. Look at all this stuff."

"Nope. I'm familiar with handguns, so that's what I take. Anything bigger, I'd be just as likely to kill one of you on accident."

"Oh, how nice. You hear that, honey? Junior doesn't want to kill us anymore."

"Whatever. I'm going to the little girls' room. Don't kill anything without me. Toodles."

Angela walks off, and Joseph turns back to me.

"You sure you don't want me to show you how to use one of these? UZIs are fun as hell."

"No thanks. So, where'd you get the Rambo training?"

"LRRP in Afghanistan, two tours. That's why I got into this business: I'm pretty damn good at killing people, especially quietly and from a distance."

"That what the Agency is looking for in their recruits?"

He goes silent, and the camaraderie appears to be over.

While I ponder how little I know about my two accomplices in this apocalyptic moment, I work on how many weapons I can carry. I've got a Luger in my waistband, but I can already tell it's going to rub against my torso and drive me crazy, so I decide to take that in hand. I grab two smaller handguns; one gets taped to my ankle cop-show style, the other goes in my waistband: less weight, less rub. Finally, a small machete hangs off my belt opposite the gun.

After a few more moments pass in uncomfortable silence, Angela returns. She shows us Guinevere's phone, the GPS map to where we're headed.

"I don't know about you two, but I plan on killing everything between us and our destination."

"What about Speck?"

"That bitch? Leave her."

CHAPTER 40

We exit the store by way of the loading dock. In the distance, I can see a group of murder heads. They're occupying themselves by taking turns beating on a couple of cops unfortunate enough to have happened on the mob.

"Two blocks up, we go left; the warehouse will be on our right," Angela reads from Guinevere's phone.

"Stay low," I say. The three of us are running bent over, like the images I remember from the TV show MASH's opening credits. Not sure why we think this will camouflage us, as there's no cover of any kind until we make it to the street. Once in the open, I'm hoping the intermittent burning cars will conceal our escape. To my surprise, it works. We make it to the left turn and round the corner at full speed, only to stop on a dime.

"Oh shit."

We emerge into what I can only describe as a Bosch-like nightmarescape. Flesh-detritus everywhere. Fires burning, people fighting, and bodies. My god, the bodies. This is death on a scale not seen in the mainland United States since... well since the white man came in and took it from the my people and the other tribes that lived here for so long before Europeans arrived.

Pioneer Square looks like the historical photos I've seen of Auschwitz.

"Guys..." I don't have time to finish my thought before the mob sees us.

"Come and get it," Joseph screams, opening up with an UZI in each hand. This act singlehandedly completes our reality's transformation into an 80s action/horror film. I play along by shooting at the legs of the six or so people in the lead. Several of them fall, tripping up the others behind them, creating a kind of rolling avalanche effect.

It's not enough. A moment later, I feel someone cut into my left side with a thankfully ill-timed machete swipe. Double fisting it, my left hand fires into the crowd with the Luger, while my right brings the butt of the other gun down on machete guy's nose. The feeling of cartilage shattering beneath my blow eases the fire in my side. When Machete Guy drops, I put a round through his face just for fun. They're still coming, but I manage to retreat while someone with a machine gun perforates people around me with frenzied, unaimed fire.

"We're almost clear of them!" Joseph yells, his voice drowned out by the sound of a loud motor. I smell gas and lurch toward him just in time to slam my body into a blood-soaked cheerleader brandishing a petite chainsaw. Buffy falls on her own blade and spasms in a bloody routine of flailing and screaming. I think of Misty Humbucker, the cheerleader who had her boyfriend Todd kick my ass Freshman year. Satisfaction washes over me as Joey and I turn our backs on the crowd and see Angela is already ten steps from reaching the door.

We catch up, and it dawns on me that none of the buildings are on fire. Meanwhile, on all sides, piles of bodies burn.

Black smoke rises into the breeze, casting a horrible shadow over the entire scene. Seattle doesn't look like a modern city anymore. Now, it's a biblical tableau of wrath.

We run to catch Angela as she opens the door. Behind us, the wheels of the virus continue undaunted by our valiant efforts.

We reach her just in time to pass through a rusted metal door. Once inside, Joey and I start dragging shit in front of it. The room is filled with pallets of boxes and large wooden crates, and in hardly no time, we have a massive barricade in place.

Safe. For now.

"That won't hold for very long. Plus, lots of windows," Angela says over the sound of dozens of people beating on the iron door.

"Took you long enough," I hear the voice but can't believe it; Roy, alive and well.

"What'dya have nine lives or something?" Joseph spits, training his gun on Roy.

"C'mon, it's safer further on."

Confused, we follow.

The warehouse is an open two levels. The ground floor is filled with boxes, pallets, and empty metal shelving choked with cobwebs. The second is an open walkway with offices built-in along the walls. A double-tier, open metal staircase divides the two.

Looking at the boxes and pallets, I see they all have the Charters logo stenciled onto them - an open book above what looks like a smile.

"Why is their warehouse two blocks from their store?"

"I think it was a temporary solution. Land is at a premium in this town since Amazon moved in."

"Doesn't matter now, does it?" Roy asks, leading us toward the back of the room. At the far end, there's an alcove with two uni-sex bathrooms, a water fountain, and another doorway. Inside? You guessed it: more stairs going down.

"I'd kill to have to investigate a treehouse about now," Angela says.

I count fifteen stairs before we come out in another underground corridor. This one is more akin to what you see when you do the typical Seattle Underground Tours. There's makeshift lighting by way of intermittent auto shop lamps strung from the exposed crossbeams where there used to be walls.

"This is the Seattle that was," Roy says with a spooky, Vincent Price-lilt to his voice.

"You know Roy, I'm not sure I like this new you. I find myself thinking I was a lot better off when I thought you were dead."

"Which time you thought I was dead?"

"The first time. Before I showed up and discovered what an asshole you've become."

"*I* didn't leave *you* to be torn apart by a swarm of murder drones."

"I didn't leave you, either. I didn't get to make a choice," I say, shooting daggers at Joseph.

"It doesn't matter, anyway. I forgive all of you."

"And just how did you survive back there?" Angela asks. Roy doesn't answer, and before anyone can press the question, our path grows dark and narrow. Everyone's hackles come up.

The lamps become infrequent as we walk, and the corridor tapers to a sightless funnel. There's no end in sight, no doors, and nowhere to go but forward. These handicaps transform our journey into a beast of its own momentum. This internal propulsion system pushes me forward into the darkness, inspiring thoughts of violence toward, well, pretty much toward everyone.

Maybe we are all infected. If not, infection feels inevitable at this point. Next chance I get, I want to try and get a WIFI signal somewhere, see what news might have surfaced about other cities, states, and countries. This can't really be everywhere, can it?

I think about the hippie chick I channeled back at Charters. Angela described her as logical and astute, while most of the infected we've physically encountered have been seething, animalistic killbots. Could the virus be degenerative? Maybe I *am* in a zombie movie; only this one is real. I find myself checking for cameras. George, are you with us? Sure feels like it, as our small band of survivors seek shelter amidst a landscape of death and dismemberment.

"One thing I'd like to know," Joseph says as we walk, "The black stuff we found in the room below the store. What the fuck was that?"

"It's not feces if that's what you're worried about," Angela says, "it's... something else. Some kind of excretion. I saw it once before-"

"Newark?" Joseph's lightbulb moment.

"Yeah. I told you, that warehouse by the river? There were deposits of that shit everywhere. I think the infected take some kind of energy from the people they kill. Like a vampire, only in that, it's a kind of power transfer."

"Vampires. Pfft," Roy scoffs under his breath. Angela either doesn't hear or ignores him.

"What happened in Newark?" I ask, intrigued. Apparently, I was wrong to assume Joseph had brought Angela straight to Seattle after springing her.

"Let's just say it was a bloodbath and leave it at that, shall we?" Angela retorts and then changes the subject, "Maybe the virus is forcing some kind of makeshift evolution – empowering those it deems best suited to carry out its vision?"

"Homicidal Darwinism," I say, suddenly convinced she might be on to something.

"The best kind," Roy says as we come to an open double door that's been torn from its hinges. Beyond the threshold, we enter an enormous, drafty room. It's so massive that fog obscures the corners on all sides, seeping out from between more rows of large, wooden crates that stretch back as far as the eye can see.

"You got the arc of the covenant in here?" Joseph chuckles at the sound of his own voice, but I'm not laughing, and neither is Angela. From somewhere, I hear music.

"Is that... the same song as before?"

I strain my ears, but the song's cut off by the louder, more localized sound of an industrial-grade HVAC system.

Climate control?

Something occurs to me. I walk to one of the crates and pull at the corner of the lid. It's not on tight.

"Does Charters really sell this many books? And why are these underground?"

"Donation center. It was their aggressive donation program that really helped Charters stay in business through the proliferation of internet shopping."

I dig into the crate and pull out a handful of paperbacks— none of them written by Harvest. I realize something.

"The virus. It's no longer just in Harvest's book, is it?"

Roy smiles like he did the night he lost his virginity, Junior year in High School.

Now everything makes sense. The way the book kept showing up, expanding. It was printed into other books, arranged beneath the ordinary layers of entertainment we've become so accustomed to consuming, dependent on, really.

"Then it's everywhere now, isn't it?"

Roy nods. He's so pleased with himself; it's all I can do not to lunge for his throat.

"The actual virus has been in place for years; it was just a matter of building the beaker around the experiment, so to speak. It only took one thing to set off this final, omnipresent wave."

That thing, I knew without him telling me, was the PSA.

The sound of Angela's gun cocking sends my epiphany spiraling into the aether, just another terrible fact in a day of death and madness.

"You know what, Roy? Gerald may have some long-standing loyalty to you, but me? I just met you tonight. When the US government pulled me out of my cell and offered me a chance to help find the source of this pandemic, I said yes. Not because I wanted to stop the virus, but because I intend on killing the person responsible for it. That might not be you, but for my money, you're pretty fucking close."

"Well then, I guess you should kill me. Frankly, I don't think-"

Roy doesn't finish. Angela drops him with one bullet placed perfectly between his eyes. My past is dead, now I'm free to accept the future.

~

The moment Roy hits the ground, I pull the machete from my belt and begin hacking at his neck with frantic blows.

"What the hell are you doing?" Angela screams at me.

"Making sure he's dead this time."

"Ha! No more fooling around, huh Henry?"

Joseph's sarcasm should bother me, but it doesn't. Fuck Roy. This isn't grief; this is practical survival: I don't want him popping back up somewhere down the road, as after this, Roy's liable to kill me first.

I kneel next to the headless corpse. I grasp the head by the hair, intending to throw it against the wall for good measure. When I touch it, the last electrical impulses firing in his brain pull me in and show me a side of Roy I've never seen before.

CHAPTER 41

ROY

I had a dream. In it, my friend Danny came to me and told me that death is the most beautiful feeling. He said he felt the warmest, most amazing high settle over him when he died, like a slow buzz on a lazy summer afternoon.

His words, not mine.

Danny also said that, as violent as his death was, the pain only lasted for a second before the sensation blotted it out.

He said he couldn't wait for me to have this experience. He knew I would love it.

I started to obsess about this 'Death Buzz.' Was there some way to know this feeling without actually dying? Was there a way to replicate it? Imagine the money you could make if you could put *that* in a pill.

After that first dream, Danny didn't return. This made me sad and frustrated. Eventually, I gave up thinking about it. Years went by. Then, I met Murph. He told me about how his father had predicted the need for what he called an "Extinction Event." He described how he'd taken up the mantle of helping cleanse the planet and how killing made him feel what Murph also called a Death Buzz. Danny and Murphy never had a chance to meet one another. They're both from different eras of my life, and I hadn't told Murphy about the Danny dream. That meant the Danny dream was real, and I'd finally found a way to experience the Death Buzz without dying. To do it, though, I would have to kill someone.

At first, I thought Murph was a psycho. Here's the thing, though: psychos turn me on. Probably anyone else would have run right the fuck away from him and not looked back, maybe gone to the cops. Not me. I couldn't get his words out of my head. There was something about him...

A couple of days passed before I broke down and called him. He said if I wasn't ready to talk about that stuff, we didn't have to. We hung out the next night, and he gave me this book. It was homemade, a print-out of a pdf or something, with construction paper for the covers. When I took it from him, something happened—something I could never have expected.

Holding the book in my hands, I felt the buzz immediately. Could hear it, too. What did it sound like? Well, hard to describe. For whatever reason, I equate the sound from the book to the electrical buzz you hear in large, wide-open fields in the Midwest, where power lines are present. More of a feeling than a sound. Later, after I started reading the thing, I learned the buzzing was inside me, not the book. The author - Murph's dad - called this phenomenon an 'Extinction Alert.'

I was curious, so I tentatively opened the book and started to read. Hardly four hours later, I'd read the entire thing. When I finished, I flipped back to the beginning and started again. I must have read that thing ten times at least that day, and when I was done, I realized every reading was different.

The next day, I told Murphy I wanted to try it. You know, killing someone. I had the perfect person in mind.

There was this cop, a real piece of shit who liked to harass anyone he felt was different. Gay, black, whatever. If you weren't Caucasian, all-American hetero-whatever, this guy would fuck with you. Earlier that year, right before I met Murphy, this cop arrested me for drunken disorderly. Sure, I was fucked up, but I was walking home, totally minding my own business. He pulled up alongside me, asked me where I was coming from. When he heard the name "Alexander's," that's what did it. Alexander's is a gay club, so he had me. He handcuffed me, brought me into the station, and locked me up. No phone call, nothing. It was a holiday weekend, and he just left me there for three days. It was crazy. When they finally got me out, I had to be hospitalized for dehydration. Afterward, I talked to a lawyer about suing the department, but the cop found me, basically told me if I proceeded, he'd make me disappear.

So you can see how, even though the idea of killing someone was tough to comprehend, the person I chose to break my cherry ended up making it pretty easy to do. Murph even helped me dump the body, and I guess this cop had fucked with so many people that without evidence, there were too many suspects. The investigating officers couldn't narrow it down or make a case against anyone.

When I killed him, it was with a rifle from a distance. Growing up, I didn't have a father. My mom's brother Ben was my male role model. Ben was in the military, trained as a sharp-shooter. I was an angry kid interested in guns, so Ben thought if he taught me to use weapons responsibly, it might keep me from joining a gang or something. The first time he took me to a rifle range, we were both surprised to discover my talent. Marksmanship must run in our blood.

Anyway, I shot the cop's kneecap out from five hundred meters. He was off duty, out to pick up a hamburger or something. Alone. Murph helped me follow him for a few weeks, so we could suss out his routines and habits. On Thursdays, he always walked three blocks from his apartment to this hole in the wall burger joint, Rory's, and he always cut through the alley behind his apartment. That's where I got him.

Once his knee was out, Murph was waiting nearby in the bushes with a gag. He stopped the bastard from screaming and attracting more attention until I could climb out of my nest and make it down there. That's when Murph handed me the Bowie knife. I took it and staring right into that son of a bitch's eyes, I cut his fucking throat from ear to ear. At first, the sounds he made as his breath gurgled out of the wound made me want to puke. But then a funny thing happened. What I can only describe as a vibrant epiphany washed over me, making my entire body feel warm and charged with this... I don't know, I'm tempted to call it energy, but that doesn't feel quite right. Energy doesn't give the sensation justice.

This was the Death Buzz Danny had come to me about. I was sure of it.

Once the cop was dead, we rolled him in a rubber tarp Murph brought, pulled the van up, and drove the body out to Lake Pleasant. There we waited for dark, then sunk the fucker by handcuffing a manhole cover to each ankle and stuffing rocks into the gash I'd cut in his throat. Then we went and got drunk, and I woke up the next morning in Murph's bed.

At the time, I thought I was in love.

I ended up moving in with Murphy. He had this house, just off the U of W campus in Bothell. Lots of people lived there, and they had a kind of secret organization they called the OC. After seeing how good I was with a rifle, Murph wanted me to join. I'd become something of a confidante to him.

The next life I took was more difficult because it was a random person. With this one, I puked my guts out before the buzz came on. Murder is a huge social more to break, especially when it's not motivated by anything personal. But right after I was sick, I felt the rush come up from inside me again, and I mean, fuuuaaahhhkk! It felt like a five megaton bomb of LSD going off in my cerebral cortex. Not a bad feeling, but a strong one.

After that, though, the feeling became diluted, so that I began to actually enjoy the effects. It reminded me of back when I first started smoking pot in high school. My friend Hank and I would sneak out behind C-Building at school and smoke tin foil bowls of ditch weed. That first time you feel marijuana's effects, you just want it more and more. Same here.

I saw how the Death Buzz affected others in the OC in a more detrimental way. One guy, Sherman, he started acting like an animal. I ended up shooting him when he tried to kill one of our other members, and Murphy explained to us how not everyone would be able to handle the effects. He said the Buzz would turn most people into slathering monsters, unable to think beyond the rush of their next kill.

The book was a living thing in its own right. It was changing. Growing. Just like the OC. Murphy said an independent publisher would soon be mass-producing it. He'd also taken steps to contact some old friends of his father's, big-time Hollywood types. The goal, he said, was to spread the message as far and wide as possible. The grand design was nothing less than the eventual extinction of the human race. Something about this sounded familiar, and I began to go back to journals my father had kept, that he'd left with my mom before he'd skipped out on us. My mom had saved them all these years. She was pure Algonquin blood, and she'd met my father while he was staying with her family, researching their folklore. I found detailed notes about the Wendigo myth in the journals and how it might be converted into a modern form. I took the journals to Murphy, and he was shocked. He didn't say why, but after that, he decided I should go to Seattle and start my own chapter of our organization. Our numbers were increasing on an almost daily basis, and as we expanded, I knew we needed to have a presence in the closest major city.

A few weeks later, I got a call that Murphy died. I was heartbroken, but his death didn't matter in terms of our cause; things were already in place and had their own momentum. I met someone in Seattle who I fell in love with. Things were good. Not long after that, people who claimed to be representatives of Murphy's father approached me. They told me they needed to take me somewhere to oversee 'the final stages.' I didn't understand until they dropped a bomb on me: my father was Abramelin Harvest, the same man who was Murphy's father.

Yeah, I'd been fucking my brother. You can imagine that messed me up for a while.

In the end, they told me that as the last of Harvest's bloodline 'on the surface world,' they needed me to act as liaison with "Paradise." I had no idea what the fuck they were talking about until they took me there - a massive city built in the center of the Earth. Here, dozens of people hand-picked by my father worked to prepare the final steps in the Extinction Agenda.

It was real, all of it. The Wendigo, the virus, the city built from refuse. And it was all mine to inherit. I would help bring about the end of the world.

Excited, I made my preparations.

The cloud of cordite is still fresh in my nostrils as Angela shakes me out of Roy's final reverie. My knees feel weak; not the most opportune moment for hearing what I can only describe as the sound of hell pouring into our world. The air around us begins to boil with a lacerating wail that short-circuits my ability to react.

"What the fuck is that?" I scream, knowing no one hears me. There's a rumbling, and then, once again, we're running into the darkness, pursued by a mob of rabid murder junkies.

CHAPTER 42

As I run, I can feel Angela's arms pumping out behind me like an Olympic sprinter. The only sound in my ears louder than her breathing is my own. I regret the beer-and-pizza lifestyle my Chicago childhood instilled in me.

Behind her, I hear Joseph turn to fire off a few rounds every couple of seconds. The reverberations from his gun are a welcome respite to the unholy shriek from dozens of murderous bastards hot on our heels.

The corridor we're in feels like it's tapering, the walls now so close together I can't help but bounce my shoulders off them every few steps. They're covered in a kind of dank, globular slime that reminds me of the snot Roy used to smear on the wall of his closet when we were kids.

There's a hiccup in Joseph's steps and a beat later, all three of us are careening headfirst into the dirt that clogs the floor.

"We need to keep moving," he says, panicked, scrambling to regain his feet. He's barely able to get the words out.

I stand, but it takes me a few seconds to find my sea legs. Joseph's in much better shape than I would have previously

205

given him credit for. I'm probably lucky he didn't kick my ass earlier.

"I'm winded," I say, panting.

"Fuck that," he says, but a few steps later, the tunnel slows us even more when the ceiling drops sharp and low, forcing us to walk hunched over, our backs perpendicular to our legs. After only a half-dozen steps, the strain on my body becomes indescribable.

Joseph's leading. I see him turn left ahead, and I follow, Angela still behind me. The path slopes downward at a steep grade. My ears pop. Now we're forced onto our hands and knees. The shriek has grown distant; our panic has not.

Ahead, Joseph comes to a stop. Angela flips on her phone's flashlight. It shows a rise in the floor where the corridor opens up again. We have to slither over the dirt on our bellies, but once cleared, we're able to get back up on our feet. A moment later, we're standing in a vast drainage chamber.

A natural room, almost like a cave, the circumference has to be the size of a football field. At least. The ceiling of the passage towers above us. Stepping clear of the outcropping, I see scores of large drainage pipes leaking strange black fluid from above us, the wet sound of run-off trickling down the slime-covered walls. All of this drains downward into a collective pool that lies about two stories below. It's a scene I relate to the cover art from old 60's SciFi paperback novels. Staring at that sinister ooze, a terrible feeling passes over me. The primordial pit's surface agitates as the release of ancient gases spurs periodic bubblings. Likewise, every drop that falls from the pipes above us reverberates on the face of that hidden lake—the cavern amplifying the sonic textures of water torture one-thousand percent.

"Where the fuck are we?" Joseph says as the shrieking behind us builds in intensity. We're about to have company.

"Some kind of massive drainage room?"

"Many modern buildings have been constructed with the Event in mind. Added floors, made to be forgotten, hidden behind and beneath the functional areas of the buildings can be found, if one has the right compass, the right ideas to point to them," I recite, my flawless familiarity with Harvest's text the final proof that yes, I am infected. I haven't even read the fucking thing.

"The violence is changing the city. It's… cocooning, gathering nutrients from the dead. The infected are literally *taking lives*, shitting and pissing and puking out bits of psychic energy it can't digest."

"All the run-off is congealing right here."

The sound of frenzied madness explodes from the tunnel. With nowhere else to go, the only thing we can do before we're overrun by dozens of murder drones is…

"JUMP!"

PART IV
PARADISE

CHAPTER 43

SET ADRIFT ON MEMORY BLISS

The fall isn't so bad, but it knocks the wind straight out of my chest and it takes me a few moments to recover. When I do, I sit up and see we're floating on a massive raft of some kind. Bone white and slightly powdery to the touch.

No one's talking. To my left, Angela silently searches the encroaching darkness for a horizon that isn't there. Joseph's lying on his back, silent and unmoving.

I try to speak, but no words come. There's a vast, cosmic chill in the air; it eats the words from my brain before they hit my tongue.

We drift…

These caverns, endless as they seem, inspire hopelessness that transcends even the idea of the surface world caught in the throes of an apocalypse. It makes me feel delirious. So much so, I begin to think I can hear someone talking to me. Not Joseph or Angela. Someone else. It's not a voice, exactly, more like a low-end throb that runs parallel to my thoughts, interpolating them from time to time. If it is a voice - and why am I even entertaining such a ludicrous idea? - it's speaking in a language unlike anything I've ever heard before. I suppose this proves I've lost my mind once and for all because it's not just that I hear this voice. I can understand it, too.

What's it saying? Why it's quoting what I inexplicably recognize as passages from Harvest's book:

Some ideas are self-propagating. I am an idea, a story, that has been deputized by the planet, highly evolved into a form resistant, tenacious, and ruthless enough to eradicate the disease choking this world to death. The infection is humanity, and murder is the cure...

The words dip back into that underlying stream of secondary consciousness that now runs parallel to my own. White noise interweaves with my comprehension until I suddenly understand the hard, white material beneath us isn't a raft at all.

Terror electrifies my entire skeleton, lighting up the neural highway from the seat of my spine through to my brain stem. A million years of imagery runs through me in a shot, reality compressed into a single pinprick that annihilates everything I have learned to call "me." Everything but the need to get off this fucking monstrosity.

"Guys," I say, so quiet I'm not entirely sure I've actually spoken until both Angela and Joseph turn. They stare expectantly, as if what I'm about to say might be good news.

A hot breeze blows in from the darkness ahead. Or behind. Direction, like time, has faded to an irrelevancy. The feel of the stagnant, stygian breath of the unknown across my face makes me feel so much worse about everything. Whose breath is that? I look over the side of the 'raft' and see a continuous bubbling.

"This isn't a raft."

I look down at the massive, off-white thing beneath my

feet. My eyes trace its shape, the curves of its surface, the granulated texture I can feel through my clothes. The image is fleeting and indistinct, but I get it regardless.

"It's a fucking floating boulder," Joseph says, turning back around as if he's just solved all our problems with a thanky-ouverymuch mic-drop.

"No. This isn't a rock."

"Then what the hell is it?"

"I don't know, but whatever it is, it's alive."

We go back to being quiet, but there's a hostility at the heart of the silence now. An expectant tone of terror that whatever this is could rear up at any moment, send us all sprawling into the sludge, rending our bodies limb from limb.

"Shut the fuck up, man," Joseph says, even though I haven't spoken for the last ten minutes. I couldn't talk right now if prompted; all my mind can focus on is the fact that we're drifting on the back of a monster. I am literally para-lyzed by these thoughts as I stare out across a vague and threatening horizon.

After an interval that could be an eternity, I hear Joseph begin sobbing.

To say this takes me by surprise is an understatement. Angela's response, mean as it is, brings with it a sense of normalcy.

"Are you fucking serious? What happened to the hardass who smacked my head off the wall in the interrogation room? The ruthless son of a bitch who told me he'd fucking kill me if I so much as looked at him wrong?"

Joseph doesn't answer. He lays on his back, eyes closed, sobs pushing fresh tears across his face. Unable to rouse a response from him, Angela turns her venomous frustration on me.

"Look, I don't care what Mr. Fucking Psychic says, whatever this thing is, it's not a monster. There's no such thing as monsters."

"Keep telling yourself that," Joseph says, quietly. Not a rebuttal so much as a correction, "I've seen things. I've seen monsters."

A deep rumble passes beneath us.

"What was that?" Angela asks, a tremor in her voice.

"Nothing," I say, lying. I know what it is, or at least what it sounds like. Laughter.

~

We drift.

The horizon remains empty in every direction, nothing but the same oily black ocean, intermittent bubbling, and an inexplicable momentum that pulls us slowly along like an invisible current.

Time takes on a soupy, elastic quality. It bends my fear until it is unrecognizable as an emotion, becoming something more akin to an altered state. Condensation settles on us; I can feel it on my arms and face. My shirt is sopping rags, and my shoes are moist and squishy. For a moment, I remember the black sludge from the room below Charters, what it was like to reach through it. Now, the black sludge surrounds us, an ocean of the unknown.

Is this some kind of clue? It feels like it because, with the memory, an entire personality opens to my inner scrutiny. It is a man, a man I know. It takes me a moment to realize, but it's Tony.

Tony's final days blossom in high speed, time-lapse photography across the canvas behind my eyes. I see him in a place where the walls are covered with the words of the book. I can actually read them, some strange synesthesia converting the feeling to an image, a window into another life and time. The words build a bridge from Tony's brain to mine, initiating an unceasing circuit within my gray matter. I feel what he feels. The sensations of murder in the tips of my fingers as he pounces onto a man and tears his neck apart with his fingers, an uncontrollable frenzy of images spinning quickly through his head, completing outdated neural pathways hidden by evolution.

Evolution from a time when murder was a cultural trait, a time when if nature didn't take you out, then another human did.

Hunting.

Gathering.

Is this where we're headed? Those of us who have the 'less severe' version of this virus? A return to the time when food and land are day-to-day necessities, and there's nothing you can do to buffer your existence from the harsh need to take or be taken, kill or be killed? A time when there is no need to smoke strange herbs or drink poisonous liquids for recreation. Instead, recreational highs are achieved by way of the Death Buzz, humanity's built-in status quo maintenance.

Does any of this help me? Does any of it offer solace to our current predicament? No.

And still, we drift.

It takes a while, but eventually, hunger sets in. I think of the zombie movie comparisons again, how ours has become more like some weird offshoot, Donner-party version. A settler-era zombie flick. Has anyone done that? I bet George would have made a good one. Lucky bastard checked out before the real horror took over.

Those old Tom and Jerry cartoons come to mind. I feel like I'm going to look at Angela's head and see it replaced by a turkey leg.

I might be losing it.

CHAPTER 44

CONVERSATIONS AT THE END OF
YOUR LIFE

A loud, wet sound startles me out of a sleep-like hypnogogic state. I'm terrified before I even remember where I am and who I'm with.

"What the hell was that?" Joseph asks. Angela's eyes are open about twice normal size, so even her granite composure is stressed to the point of breaking.

"I saw..." she starts but doesn't finish, just continues to stare toward the back of the 'raft' with that wide-eyed, glassy look.

"You saw what? Hello?"

"I saw bubbles."

I plop back down on my back—no big deal.

"Monster flatulence," I say and laugh at my own joke.

"What?" My fellow castaways ask in unison.

"Probably a release of air or gas. I'd imagine regardless of whatever genus or species this thing is, gas is universal. "

"Drop the monster shit, dude. Not funny."

"Well gee, Joey, that's good because I certainly didn't mean for it to be funny. I thought you'd seen monsters?"

"Fucking asshole," he says, dismissing me. The straw that breaks this camel's back. I sit up again.

"Okay, you guys don't like my theory? Let's hear yours."

Silence. As I expected.

"Why do we need to have a theory?" Angela asks, annoyed.

"It seems to me that to be so sure my theory is wrong, you would need to have one of your own."

"Or maybe we just don't believe in fucking monsters," she says.

"Well?"

"Well what?"

"Care to offer an opinion? Theory? Question, comment, observation? We've had nothing but time to sit here and think, so tell uncle Gerry what's been rolling around inside that pretty little head of yours?"

"You're losing it."

"Confirmation of a suspicion. Newsflash: We're all losing it. When was the last time either of you ate? Drank water? We're all in this together, so c'mon. Pretend it's a game. Where are we? You can even make something up if you like."

Blank. Fucking. Stares.

"Fine. Don't blame me when Cthulhu here rears up and swallows us all whole, to be painfully digested in his guts for thousands of years."

"What is it with you, anyway, Gerald? How does one get to be 'psychic?'"

"Well, Joseph, you want the long version or the short version?"

"Forget I asked."

"Long version it is. When I was a kid, my grandfather told me about ghosts. We had one in the house where I grew up. It would frighten my sister and me in the middle of the night.

From about the age of six, this ghost shit got worse and worse, escalating every few months. One night, I went to bed tired. I don't mean tired like we know it as adults. I'm talking about kid-tired. You know, that tired you used to get after days of playing outside in late August, heat beating down on you while you run around and whatnot. Kid-tired isn't like adult tired. You can set it aside, keep going as long as you want. It only catches up with you *after* you close your eyes, not before. I think that's why I can still remember waking up so vividly because I don't remember falling asleep. My mother told me later that I konked out in the treehouse, and Grandfather carried me in. I woke up sweating, but when I tried to push the covers off, I couldn't. My hands worked up from beneath the pillow to where the top of the sheets should have been. Instead, there were just more and more covers, like I was drowning in them. As the sleep came off me and my disorientation grew, I started to freak out. I clawed faster and faster at the layers of cloth until finally, I started screaming and crying. It felt like forever before my mom and grandfather came running."

"What the hell happened?"

"My grandfather said that while I slept, the ghost took every blanket, every towel, every single piece of clothing in the house not being worn by someone and piled it all on top of me. After they pulled me out, my mother walked the entirety of the house. She found every closet, drawer, and laundry basket empty."

"Jesus..." Joseph says, his cool veneer of disinterest and skepticism dissipating in the wake of my story.

"After that, my grandfather must have figured he was going to have to explain a few things to me if I was ever going to be able to sleep in that house again. He sat me down the next day and told me how, when people die, they leave a residue in the places they inhabited most. He explained that residue is invisible to most people but that a few - himself included - could see and interpret it.

"He also told me that I was at the age where I had become like him.

"My father died when I was very young. He was Native American, Sioux, and his father helped my mom raise us. My grandfather worked for the United States Government. He never talked about his job, but because his career started during World War Two, I've always assumed he was a code breaker."

"The Government used Native languages used as code for military transmissions."

"Exactly. Now, what the hell linguistic code has to do with ghosts, I never understood. Later, I came to suspect that whatever capacity my grandfather continued to work for Uncle Sam in after the war most likely pertained to the weird, Cold War super-secret spook shit. MK-Ultra and the men who stare at goats. On the day in question, though, after my experience with Casper's laundry fetish, my grandfather let me in on something that has trailed me the rest of my life. It's all real. Ghosts, psychic powers, hell, even monsters."

"Enough with the monster shit."

"Angela, are you telling me that Johnson Hughs doesn't qualify as a monster? How about Roy?"

"You know what I mean."

"No. I don't. In fact, through this entire ordeal, I'm convinced that all this shit I'm seeing, that we're experiencing, this is all stuff my grandfather probably knew about for most of his life."

"This is fascinating, but I still don't understand what ghosts have to do with being a private detective."

"Where do you think psychic insights come from? Spirits tell me things. Things other people could never know."

"Can you get one to tell you where we are?"

"I already did; you just don't want to listen."

"Great. What now then?" Angela asks.

"Looks like we're about to find out. There's something just up ahead."

CHAPTER 45

Only a dozen or so yards from where we come to rest on a beach of black sand, a group of six people wait for us. There are five bearded men and one woman; she is a short, round blonde with eyes so green I can see their color even from this distance.

They approach us, their intentions unknown.

"Anyone have any bullets left?" I ask under my breath. Neither Joseph nor Angela answers me, a fact I take as a bad sign. About a hundred yards beyond the welcome committee, the beach ends in thick, dark vegetation. It looks like the setting for an 80s 'Nam movie from the 80s.

"Welcome, friends! Welcome to the shores of Paradise! Please, allow us to assist you."

How insane is it that after everything we've been through, we would encounter people who welcome us with friendship instead of murder-happy glee?

"Murph! Ease into it, man," one of the men says, his lumberjack beard disguising the movement of his mouth, "These folks have been topside through all this. They're not used to people doing anything but trying to kill them."

"Of course! Of course! I apologize. We've been down here so long, it's easy to forget what's happening up top."

"Murph? Murphy Harvest?"

"Yes. Hello, Detective Miller."

"We were lead to believe you were dead."

"I apologize for the misleading information; however, my subterfuge was indeed necessary at the time of its inception."

"Where are we?" I can hear the fatigue in Joseph's voice. It rivals my own. There's a lack of caution, almost like he's looking to pick a fight and lose.

"Paradise."

"You said. Where's that?"

"You have arrived at the calm in the center of the storm, Agent Killacky. You are, in a word, safe."

The three of us trade looks. I'm tired. If these people are going to kill me, I'd prefer they just get it over with.

Stepping onto the beach, the thing we have been riding shakes slightly then begins to float back the way we came. Joseph, Angela, and I watch it suspiciously as it drifts to about a hundred yards out, then stays perfectly still. Several feet to its left, a tiny cluster of bubbles appears every few seconds. A chill passes through me, and I turn to assess what's in front of me and see the look on Angela's face.

"Breathing. It's breathing."

"Told ya."

I realize there's no sand here, but rather a layer of marbled, obsidian glass so black I can see granulated reflections of myself as I walk. Likewise, what I first took to be vegetation in the distance is the farthest thing from living plant life imaginable. The strange, dark trees are actually towers of sculpted junk, piled high and fashioned into complicated, twisted shapes: a hub cap here, part of a mangled shopping cart there. In fact, the only actual vegetation present is old, dilapidated fake plants occasionally twisted into the mix. The overall effect is alien, a beach of sheer black glass surrounded by a jungle of extraterrestrial plants.

"It's all recycled waste from the world upstairs. Garbage that makes its way here, further down the line."

Murph is tall and thin, with large white teeth and a pointy red beard that makes him look like his name should be Lucifer. Knowing that he's the progeny of the man who created this nightmare, I'd say he's pretty close.

"Indeed, my father would have appreciated the comparison, Mr. Henry. The Lightbringer, introducer of knowledge to primitive humanity. May I call you Gerald? Or Hank? That is how Roy always referred to you."

"Gerald's fine."

Murphy makes it a point to illustrate beyond a shadow of a doubt that he can 'hear' my thoughts. In fact, as soon as I think this, he gives me a wink. The man's a reader, and what's more, so skilled at the art that I don't even feel it when he slips into my mind.

"Years of practice, Gerald. Also, yes. I have the birthmark."

Conversely, his etiquette feels almost malevolent.

"You're the one who started the Omega Club, the one that organized all of this. Is that correct?"

"Guilty, as charged Detective Miller. However, that part of my life is, thankfully, now over."

"Murph," the round woman chides, "introductions, please."

"Where *are* my manners? Gerald Henry. Detective Angela Miller. Special Agent Joseph Killacky. I present to you the Paradise Executive Team: Mary Worthington, Preston Thoreau, Ralston Fenget, Parker Hearst, and the younger fellow behind me is Jeffrey Franklin Faust."

"Faust," Angela says, "You're the CEO of Lindsey Corp, the parent company that owns Jonestown Books."

"You've done your homework. Bravo."

Faust smiles. So does Murphy. There are gallons of blood reflected in his eyes.

"Now, I'm afraid we've no time for introductions to the rest of the camp. No doubt people will introduce themselves as you encounter them. We're all very socially motivated here, in Paradise, because, well, we have to be. This is it, after all."

"This is what?" I ask.

"Why Gerald, this is the final respite of the Human Race."

~

"So Murph, why exactly do you call this place Paradise?"

"Detective Miller. May I call you Angela?"

She nods, and Murph bows slightly before continuing, "We are the chosen few, the people Abramelin Harvest hand-picked to survive the great culling. This makes us the Midwives of the next epoch. Thus, for our efforts, we have been rewarded with Paradise."

"I guess that'll teach you to talk to crazy folks and expect to get a straight answer."

"Gerald, your humor will be a welcome addition to our little outpost here, on the edge of forever. I can tell you that everyone is looking forward to meeting you."

"Let me get this straight. Nobody here is infected?"

"We are all infected. However," Murphy makes a grand, sweeping gesture with his arm as he continues, "Where there is no death, there is only life! And without death, life can be as fulfilling as we wish."

"What the fuck does that even mean?"

"It means, Agent Killacky, that as several others have

attempted to impart to you this very eve, the Omega Virus affects different people in different ways. The virus turns most of the population into mindless, proletariat murders. These are the worker bees, toiling in restless abandon at the blood mills the infection has made of our cities. Others, like those you will meet in Paradise, are better suited as Management. We believe this also includes the three of you. With us, the virus inspires what I like to think of as strategic violence."

"Management?"

"Take Detective Miller, for example. Angela, you were infected the moment you downloaded my father's book. Yet, you have continued to operate more or less as you normally do. You even continued to function in your role as partner and detective until you realized you could go no further before cutting the cord with the old world. What happened the day you killed your partner?"

Angela heard the door behind her open a split second before she could process the sound for what it was. She watched Abigail's line of sight swoosh left. Riding on instinct, Angela raised her .45 and squeezed off one shot, hit Abigail in the side of the face, sent her cartwheeling to the pavement. To her right, Jim still had his gun trained where seconds ago Abigail had stood.

"Nice shooting, Angie-"

Angela turned and put two in Jim's chest. His body bounced once against the car before coming to rest on the curb, his firearm hanging limply in a puddle of garbage that had collected atop a drainage grating.

Behind her, two twenty-something guys emerged from what might have been an apartment building. She saw the joint look of confusion and terror strike them right before she spent the remainder of her clip on them. All discernible life in the area quieted, Angela exhaled.

Angela sighed, "I'm not talking about that."

"Understandable. Better perhaps to look to Gerald then, what, with his gifts and all."

"How do you know anything about me? About any of us?"

"The dead are here with us, Gerald, just as they are with you. They whisper precious things to those who can hear."

"That doesn't answer my question. Like, not at all."

Murphy smiles, secure in his superior knowledge. It pisses me off, but not half as much as what he says next.

"Think about it! Gerald, ever since you were young, you've been able to see the things that others cannot. So too, with most of us here. Why? Because the dead need a place to go, the same as the living. And they need people to talk to. Live people."

"Why would the dead need people to talk to?"

"Comfort," Murph says, the smile replaced by a matter-of-fact scowl.

"Comfort? Are you telling us you know what happens when we die? Gerald, that book you teased us with earlier, I hope you didn't plagiarize these fine folks."

"Real funny, Angela."

"No, seriously, Murph. What are you talking about?"

"All in good time, Angela. For now, let us retire to the city, proper. Once you're settled, we can sit and take the time to address all your questions and concerns."

Murph turns and the others follow. There's a crunchy, black path of the pulverized glass that leads up off the beach and through the junk jungle. As we filter down into a single-file line on the path's narrow course, I realize there are others keeping pace with us, obscured but visible through the junk. They don't speak or interact in any way. They just keep a perimeter, a buffer around us as we follow Murph and the others to an increasingly uncertain fate.

CHAPTER 46

After a while, the garbage-plants thin. I smell the smoke and can't help but think of William Golding's *Lord of the Flies*. Is someone going to offer us roast pig? I fucking hope so; I'm so hungry I'm practically drooling.

Murph shoots me a smile. I realize I am going to have to be careful what I think around here. A moment later, the lumberjack named Preston at the front of our little parade pushes through a final layer of old, blackened coat hangers, and we emerge into an opening. That's where we see it for the first time.

Paradise.

There is no *Lord of the Flies* here. No firepits, no pigs on spits, no warpaint. This looks like downtown fucking Chicago, the area right by the Riviera theatre, where the 'L' tracks cut across some of the oldest buildings in the city. Only here? The entire thing is made out of garbage.

"Humanity has always built on top of its ruins, always utilized waste in achieving progress. This is because the idea of waste – of discarding - is a product of modern man. A divergent path; a mutation and symptom of the disease we have become."

The path underfoot changes to what looks and feels like asphalt beneath my feet.

"Of course it feels like asphalt, Gerald. It *is* asphalt," Faust says, beaming with pride.

"Everyone here read minds?" I ask. The woman named Mary snickers, but that's my only answer.

The buildings - if that's what they are - tower into the sky. Which, of course, isn't sky at all. We're just so deep underground, we can't see what's above us.

I shudder when it occurs to me that something may have made these caverns. If that's the case, we're talking about an animal that would be bigger than anything we've ever seen on Earth, including the dinosaurs.

I push the thought from my mind by trying to count the number of structures. There are two dozen I can see, all of varying height, half of which look less than functional. A wide walkway snakes between these, invoking images of those aforementioned elevated tracks in Chicago. The windows of the buildings reflect what looks like sunlight but isn't. I can't tell where this light originates.

"Do people live in those?"

"No, Gerald. Those buildings house… other things."

The asphalt forks up ahead of us, running between buildings, creating a cityscape of garbage. It is the definition of organized chaos, and it leaves me feeling a sense of wonder.

"For the last two centuries, civilization has been based on waste. Garbage, the remains of our lives, day by day. Fossil fuels, the remains of animal life from millennia ago. Once, we shared the Earth with those animals and their descendants. We lived as they live: in harmony with the land. When those animals died, we ate them, used their skin for warmth. Likewise, our dead filled the bellies of the wild, whether food for the worms of the Earth or carrion for scavengers. It was, in a word, a perfect cycle. Death and rebirth."

"But that changed," I say, intuiting where he's going. I remember this from a conversation with Roy during my previous visit. The early days of his indoctrination?

"Exactly," Murphy continues, "Once Humanity became infected with the City-State virus, we moved away from the Hunter-Gatherer paradigm. We became greedy, hoarding that previously balanced sustenance. We've turned the gifts of the Earth into imaginary profit. Ones and Zeros: the fuel for our new world. A world where we share *nothing*. A world where we dominate and destroy the very planet that gave us life in the first place. This Death-State, as my father called it, has lasted for nearly two centuries. Two hundred years of draining the planet's lifeblood, along with a total refusal to counteract any of the damage we do to Her on a daily basis. No more. Now, it's Her turn."

"So you're saying this is like that movie by the Shamala-mading-dong guy? It's the Earth making everyone kill each other?"

"Believe it or not, Joseph, this is hardly unprecedented. Nature has always possessed ways of eliminating populations when they become toxic. Look at the dinosaurs, or prehis-toric man, or..."

Murphy hits me square in the eye with a smirk because he can read my mind. He knows that I get it. I've understood all along: this murder virus *is* nature's catastrophe for Humanity. The idea just seemed so... *contrived* up until this point.

"That'a boy, Gerald. There is no doubt you'll make a fine addition to our team."

"What kind of team could you be building if the human race is on the outs?"

"The kind that will see this through. We will pass the

planet back off to Mother Nature, and then... well, that's a surprise."

Murphy is almost comical with his vaudeville gesticulations. He's the kind of guy that speaks to you like he's got the aid of a piano player behind him at all times. Speaking of music, the first strains of a familiar melody hit my ears.

"Is that *Rise* by Doves?"

"I don't know. I'm more of a jam band guy. That's probably Guinevere's music."

Guinevere? For the end of the human race, everyone we encounter seems pretty hard to kill. Might be a good reason to consider joining Team Paradise, after all.

Our current trajectory leads us to one of the tallest buildings. Murph veers around to the rear. As we follow, the light source comes into view: a tower with a massive configuration of lights like you usually see at sports stadiums. The whole thing is fenced off, like a construction site, and a group of people approaches from that direction. They welcome their compatriots and seem excited by our presence. Our escorts flank in from their orbit. Pretty soon, we're in the midst of a large group of people - fifty or sixty at most - who all want to shake hands and introduce themselves to us.

In particular, one catches my eye: an attractive, dark-haired girl, tall with broad shoulders. She's dressed in combat boots and a t-shirt with the word 'SALEM' printed across it as if in blood.

I do not see pants. I try not to stare.

'Rise' plays from a boombox on the ground next to the fence. Just beyond is the entrance to the building the lights are mounted atop. A closer look is out of the question until I can find my way around the fence or acquire a key.

"Well, well. Look what the cat dragged in." Guinevere Speck saunters over to us, steps right up in Angela's face, then surprises everyone by grasping her by the back of the head and swallowing Angela's tongue.

Detective Miller does not resist.

When the two women separate, Angela's forehead and cheeks are flushed red. Her mouth stretches tentatively from ear to ear in what I believe is the first smile I've seen from her.

"What day is it?" I ask, pretending I'm not turned on by what I've just witnessed. No one answers. The idea that we may have been drifting on that black ocean for longer than I'd previously thought crawls in under my logic board and starts to suffocate me. What if we've been gone for weeks? How long does it take for a race of billions to murder themselves?

"Not as long as you think," Preston the Lumberjack says. He gives me a salacious smile and conspiratorial elbow to the ribs, "Pretty cool, eh?" he says, obviously referring to the moment the two women just shared.

"Okay people, why don't we let our new arrivals collect themselves before the party?"

"Party?" Angela, Joseph, and I ask in unison.

"Of course! New arrivals are always welcomed with a celebration. You are, after all, now among the last of our species."

"Murphy, how long have we been down here? It can't be... *over* upstairs, can it?"

"Over? Gerald, there hasn't been a single human being on the surface of the Earth for well over five years now."

CHAPTER 47

"That'll be your place for the time being," Jeffrey points to a shorter structure made from what appears to be hollowed-out dumpsters and trash cans. Some protrude at sharp angles where they've been cut to match the building's overall design.

I absorb all this on autopilot. The idea that we were on that raft for five years, no food or water, without a bathroom break or any sense of linear time, has overtaken me completely. Despite my abilities, I've never been one to look too deeply for the whys and wherefores of life and all its crazy phenomena. Right now though, I'm trying to figure out how five years could pass in what felt like a couple hours at most.

"You'll break your brain if you contemplate it too long. Just accept the facts and move on," Jeffrey says before splitting off, leaving us in the hands of Preston and the girl with no pants, whose name I find out is Blair.

"You guys are gonna love it here. Just wait 'til we get to the orgies."

"Orgies?" I ask, suddenly completely in the moment.

Looking at how the hem of Blair's T-shirt hangs just below the spot where her legs come together, my hunger for food nearly disappears. I've got something else on my mind now.

"Yeah. We're all sterile here, and, you know, without procreation, there's really no expectation of commitment. Why not enjoy life, right?"

"Right as rain, baby," Joseph says, putting his arm around Blair's shoulder.

"Hold on there, buddy," Preston says, moving between them, "You're on a schedule."

"Schedule? There's no fucking schedules in Paradise," Joseph says, puffing up his chest in an attempt to stand up to a man that is, at the very least, twice his size and all muscle from the look of it.

"Back off. I need you to listen to me now, okay? You've been greeted, but you have not been officially sworn in yet. Once that happens, you're one of us, through and through."

"When's that?"

"Tonight, at the party. Until then, head upstairs. There are three rooms for you on the tenth floor. Each of you take one, get cleaned up, and meet me back here when the light begins to dim."

"Let me guess," Angela says, clearly exhausted and cranky, "You dim the lights to create a nighttime effect?"

"You'd be surprised what kind of mental and emotional turmoil you can experience without the deeply programmed cycle of light and dark. We are here in defiance of humanity, not Mother Nature and her paradigms. Now, any questions?"

"No."

∾

O nce we pass through the door, I realize this smaller structure serves as a kind of atrium for the larger one behind it. A wide, open doorway and several flights of stairs greet us as we enter.

"What kind of Paradise doesn't have an elevator?"

My attempt at levity fails to evoke a response.

"This does not look safe," Angela says.

"What about our lives has been safe of late?"

"Good point."

"Touche," Joseph zings, and I have to physically resist the urge to turn around and stick my fist down his snide little throat. The image of tearing his fucking insides out through his esophagus almost overcomes my restraint. I manage to hold on, realizing it's the infection. We're all infected, and the world as I knew it, as all of us knew it, is over. The world that's left? No longer our concern, apparently.

The orgies might help with that, though.

The top of the stairs comes faster than I expect. We split up and take our respective rooms. Inside, there's a bed that looks brand new, if not modern, and a small table with two chairs. The tabletop is vomit-green Formica. The color recalls the decor of the Diamond Access, the memory of which makes me want a drink. Behind the table is a small bathroom. I strip and run the water in the tub, easing myself in once the temperature is a notch above lukewarm.

Calgon, take me the fuck away.

N o sooner do I step from the tub than there's a knock on my door.

"How's your room?" I ask as Angela slips past me and takes a seat at the vomit table.

"They're right, you know."

"Who's right?"

"I've thought the same thing for a long time now. I just never would've done anything about it. Not until I read Harvest's book."

I can tell she needs to talk, but I'm standing here in a towel.

"One sec," I say as I reach for my clothes."

"Don't."

"What?"

Angela stands again and moves swiftly to me. She gets close and slips her hand in through the top of the towel.

"I don't know about you, but I could sure go for a good fucking right about now."

Lucky lucky lucky.

~

I open my eyes in a state of perfect calm. For once in this whole fucked up ordeal, I feel... sated. I don't know if I'll like what's ahead, but now that I've made peace with the situation, it's easier to feel okay with having no choice. I turn over; Angela isn't there.

"I'm here," she says from the doorway to the bathroom. The sex is still dripping from me, clouding my eyes so that I'm seeing her but not really seeing her, thinking only of the way her legs spread out around me.

Angela lights two smokes, passes one to me.

"Thanks," I say, inhaling until my head swims, "I thought you didn't smoke."

"I don't. It's a disgusting habit."

We exist in silence for a few moments. Then, Angela breaks it.

"Jim and I had an affair. It was early in our tenure as partners. I'd just made Detective, and I had a real chip on my shoulder."

"You? I don't believe that for a second."

"Fuck off."

"Sorry."

"I ended up pregnant. Jim self-identified as 'happily married,' to which, of course, I questioned why we ended up in bed together in the first place. He didn't like that so much. Also, he didn't like that his partner was a threat to his marriage. Which I wasn't. I had no interest in a relationship with him, but I guess he got paranoid. That made me paranoid. I thought the other cops were all out to get me. I think a lot of that was in my head, but it didn't seem that way at the time. I remember walking to get something to eat one night, crossing through a small side street. This was as close to an alley as you get in West LA. I heard catcalls close by but couldn't see anyone. I sped up, then a noise from behind made me stop. I looked back, saw a squad car parked at the end of the street. When I turned around, there was one ahead of me, too."

"What'd you do?"

"I sucked in my breath and walked right past them. One of the cops nodded to me, smiled in this way that really fucked with me."

She pauses for a drag.

"After that, I started to really lose it. I took some time off. Drank a lot, I guess, hoping to kill the fucking thing growing inside me. No such luck. Just before the start of the second trimester, I went for an abortion. Afterward, I remember thinking how much it empowered me. I mean, there's too many fucking people anyway, right? This is the exact thing I thought later when I put a bullet in Jim's head. Harvest is right. Humanity is a disease. It's been choking every last resource from this planet for too long. Somebody has to take us out. Why not be a part of that?"

"Yeah. I get it. Still, if what Murph said is true, and we've somehow managed to pass through five years to get to this point, then this really is it. I don't know how that makes me feel. But Angela? Thanks. Whatever happens, this was nice."

"Nice?" The way she repeats my words back to me tells me whatever post-coital peace held Angela in its sway only a moment ago is gone. I look in her eyes, and I see the gallons of blood I did in Murphy's earlier.

Angela stares at me with a look that is both defeated and furious. Her eyes tell me she wants to give up, for this to all be over, but the quaking of her body tells me she's completely aware of the murder gene at work inside her.

"Look," I say, breaking the intensity of the moment by standing and pulling on my pants, "Someone's working the dimmer switch. We should probably get ready to go to this fucking party."

I turn and pull on my shirt, walk to the bathroom, and gargle with some water from the tap.

"I hope their fucking pipes aren't made of garbage, too," I say, returning to the room to find Angela leveling her handgun at me.

"What?" is all I can manage before she pulls the trigger and I die.

CHAPTER 48

PARTY LIKE IT'S THE END OF THE WORLD... BECAUSE IT IS

If climbing the ten flights of stairs to our new lodging felt like an arduous ascent into the unknown, the way back down feels surreal. The colors of the garbage crushed and packed together to form the walls seem brighter beneath the pale-orange recessed lighting. Evocative of candlelight, this new world around me feels labored with hidden meaning, darkness embellished with layers of occult significance.

Something has changed, but I can't quite put my finger on what.

As I emerge from the building, I become especially aware of my feet and the fact that I can't feel the ground beneath them. My head feels too small, like the effects of a particularly nasty hangover, my consciousness squeezed to a tenth of its size. I marvel at these sensations and only return to an awareness of my surroundings when I see the short, round woman named Mary approaching.

"Get any rest?"

"A bit," I say, then watch in surreal horror as Mary's face explodes in a burst of blood, brain, and bone. My adrenaline surges and my vision dissolves into static-ridden nonsense.

When the world flickers back into view, I see it's my hand holding the gun, the barrel still smoking...

Then I realize it's not my hand. The long, slender fingers and chipped, ovular nails tell me something it takes me a minute to process. It's Angela's hand that holds the gun, even though I see it through my eyes.

No, there's the rub. I see the gun through *Angela's* eyes.

My soul screams as I remember her pointing the gun at me, followed by the understanding that I am now inside Angela's body. Does she know I'm here? Does anyone else?

Before I can fully wrap my head around what's happening, we're on the move. I watch, a passenger, as Angela follows the fence until she sees more people.

"Feel better?" a woman I don't recognize asks, and Angela fires at her. The bullet misses, and the next attempted shot reveals the gun is empty.

"What the fuck are you-" the woman screams, but Angela has already closed the distance to her and delivered a hefty blow to her head with the butt of the gun. The woman folds in half like paper. Pinning her to the ground, Angela batters her face into an unrecognizable lump of goo.

In the distance, someone screams. A mob of people rushes toward us.

Preston's the first one to intervene. He snatches the firearm from Angela and punches her square in the face. My consciousness shutters black again, then slowly reknits itself from a series of ghostly impressions.

"This psycho bitch killed Mary and Lenore," Preston tells Jeffrey and a handful of others as they arrive.

There's a tight jolt of pain in my shoulders, and I can tell someone has Angela's arms pinned behind our back.

Those arms are mine now, too.

"Angela, where is Gerald? Is he in on this with you?"

"He's dead," I hear her say. I can feel her lips move when she talks.

"What do you mean, he's dead?"

"I killed him, just like I'm going to kill all of you."

Jeffrey takes a step back and ponders the situation. I focus on his ability to read minds, screaming silently for him to pay attention to me in here. It doesn't seem to be working.

"This isn't good," he finally concludes.

"Oh, give me a fucking break! You've already killed off the entire species; how do another couple dozen deaths sour the deal? It's a little late for the people who engineered the Apocalypse to start acting so fucking precious."

I try to remember my body dying but can't. Maybe that's good. Maybe I'm not dead. For the moment, then, I tell myself I'm merely a passenger here, like when I channel others, except in reverse. This makes me feel better, except for the fact that if they kill Angela, I may die, too.

Jeffrey! It's Gerald! I'm trapped inside Angela! - my mantra, a series of silent screams that go unanswered.

"Let's go," he says gruffly, and whoever has us by the arms twists them back around to our front and applies handcuffs.

"Get moving, bitch."

"Where's the Fed?" someone asks.

"Joseph? He already went on ahead with Blair."

"At least that's on schedule then," Preston says.

I try and ease out of the panic that's eating at my faculties. I have to concentrate. This is a first, being stuck inside someone, so I need to figure out some logistics. I focus and try to make Angela raise her hands. I fail. A moment later, however, there's a tickle in her nose, and I can tell she wants desperately to scratch it. Was that me? Can I influence her *at all*?

We follow the asphalt until a park appears in the distance. Several fires burn at intervals close enough to illuminate what looks like fifty or so people mingling, dancing, and drinking from black, plastic cups. Music plays softly, not Doves, but some noodly, jam band nonsense. Below that, I can just barely make out the hum of industrial machinery.

Murphy emerges from a small, black tent. He frowns when he sees us.

"What the hell happened?"

"Murph, we have a prob-" Jeffrey says.

"Where's Henry?"

"That's what I'm trying to tell you. There's been a bit of an incident-"

"I killed him," Angela says, stepping into Murph's grill. I feel her smile defiantly, "I killed Henry and two of your fucking people."

"Now, why would you do that? Seriously Angela. Not cool."

"Why do you think we came here? You think I want any part of your little murder-happy jack-off party? You're fucking pathetic. "

Understanding dawns on me. Not good: Angela *wants* them to kill her. Is that the point? One last bit of fun for both of us, and then goodbye.

I did you a favor, I hear her say internally.

Suddenly possessed of considerably more grandeur than before, Angela's voice echoes through my thoughts, shorting out what I think of as 'me.' Did she say that out loud?

No, asshole, because unfortunately you don't know when to give up and went and latched onto me. You were a decent lay but in here? Not wanted. Why don't you just fuck off and die already?

I can't believe this. What the hell can I do?

I don't want to be in here with you, you crazy psycho bitch, but if my body's dead, I don't see how I have much of a fucking choice.

Just close your eyes and drift away into your aether, or what-ever you call it. Maybe some other low-rent psychic will channel you, then you can tell all this through them. Wouldn't that be ironic?

"I'm sorry Angela, but there are going to have to be consequences to your actions," I hear Murph say.

"You got a cigarette?"

"We don't allow smoking here."

"Let me get this straight. You're all about facilitating the end of the human race, but you're against killing and smoking? How does that even make sense?"

"Angela, our policies are not open for debate."

"I didn't say they were. No killing? Guilty, and as soon as you let your guard down, I'm going to kill the fucking rest of you!"

"No, Angela. You won't," Murphy says.

CHAPTER 49

D arkness stretches out before me, to all sides, for as far as I can see. It feels like it lasts forever until, eventually, a tiny white dot appears. It grows closer, and after a time, I see it's the raft. Only here and now, it's most definitely alive. I'm looking at it from high above, like a drone shot in a movie. From here, it resembles a dinosaur without flesh, a great, writhing demon whose body is made of bone. Its eyes are giant, flaming marbles, and when it lifts its massive torso from the dark ocean, I can see bright, almost fluorescent organs pulsing inside its ribcage. Desiccated flesh hangs from the bones in tatters.

"Angela," it says, in a deep, drawn-out voice that sounds like a kidnapper's phone call, "You are awake..."

∾

T he darkness drifts from the room like fog across Lake Mendota, where my mother's cousins had a small house we'd spend summers in when I was young. I think of that lake now, of cloudless days with my sister and mother. Laughing, swimming. No ghosts there. One time, though, an old, blind man wandered onto the property, came up and smacked me for no reason. He called me Angela. My mother chased him off, we never saw him again, never learned who he was or where he lived. Also never learned who Angela was.

Until now.

"Mendota…" I say and jump when I hear my voice come out of Angela's mouth. It sounds different; physically, her vocal cords aren't the same as mine, but the defining cadence is there. A tear falls from her left eye as Murphy, Preston, and Guinevere shimmer into focus.

"How…?" is all I can manage.

"Angela's unconscious at the moment. We wanted to talk to *you*, Gerald."

"My body?"

They look to one another, then back to me.

"I'm sorry. There was nothing we could do."

I really didn't think things could get any worse, but there you have it.

"I thought everyone here was psychic? How didn't you see this coming?"

"How didn't you?"

"Touché."

"Now is not the time to mourn the past, Gerald. We have a proposition for you."

"What kind of proposition?"

"Obviously, Angela has to go. Normally, we'd have simply killed her."

"I thought you didn't kill here?"

"Not inside the walls of the city. But we have a special place outside reserved for sacrifices."

"Sacrifices?"

"To the spirit of this place."

"What's outside Paradise?"

"You don't ever want to find out."

There's a gravity to Murph's voice that scares the hell out of me.

"To be clear, we fully understand Angela's motivations for leading you here. She arrived in Paradise intending to kill the people she deems responsible for bringing Harvest's plans to fruition. I thought I could change her mind. I was wrong. If not for the fact that you now occupy a place inside her, there is no question Angela would already be dead. However, we have a particular interest in keeping you alive, Gerald."

"So, you can't kill her?"

"We cannot kill Angela's body. However, there is a way we can help you remain in control of it by... extinguishing her consciousness."

"How?"

"You'll like it," Guinevere Speck says in a sultry hiss. She looks at me like a thirty dollar steak and starts to sweat.

"Sex?"

"Sex Magick."

I get to sit in the driver's seat for full-on sex between two women? How could I possibly say no to this?

"I..."

I'm about to say yes and hit the fast-forward button to bumping fuzzies when suddenly, it feels like my breakfast - if I'd had any - is about to come up. I put my hand over my mouth, but it's too late. Angela's voice explodes from her mouth like vitriolic vomit.

"This is my fucking body!" she screams, momentarily regaining control.

In my head, I imagine Angela standing in the middle of an abandoned street shouting through a megaphone. I run up behind her and swipe the implement from her grip, then smash it into her abdomen. Back in the outside world, our body coughs hard and falls to the floor. Inside, we grapple for control.

You fucking asshole! This is my body! Mine!

I'm the asshole? You're the one who killed me! You did this to yourself! Never fuck with a psychic, bitch!

Rolling around on the ground, grappling with myself, I see the others move tentatively along with us. They try to interject, grabbing for a hold on Angela's shoulders or legs. Anything to help restrain her and turn the tide back in my favor.

Get out of my head! I'll take my chances outside this glorified landfill!

"Gerald, if you can hold her steady for just a second, I can sedate her."

"I'm… trying…"

Angela's thrashing intensifies. I'm trying to hold on, to keep her body still for even just a second, but I can't. I'm saying goodbye, when, without knowing why, an image of her shooting a man snaps hard into focus. I know without being told this is a replay of the moment when she murdered her partner. In the wake of the memory, I feel Angela's determination dissolve like sugar in a flame.

"Now!" I scream, sounding even more like myself. Murphy does not waste the opportunity. A moment later, I hear Angela whisper, "I loved him," an instant before the darkness sweeps back over us, swallowing the world in its wake.

CHAPTER 50

I hear music. The kind of self-indulgent noodling only a hippy could love. Trilling, arpeggiated scales interlaced with lazy banjos and sloppy bongo rhythms; all the bullshit I abhor. I imagine Psalm 69 era-Ministry showing up and setting fire to everything, blasting the place with pummeling industrial rhythms. Then I remember - Ministry are probably all dead.

Shit.

After a while, voices:

"Yes, yes, it is Jeffrey," Guinevere Speck says. Her voice indicates she is not happy.

"Guinevere, your concerns are ill-founded. We've kept tabs on Henry for years. He's easily one of the most powerful psychics we've ever encountered. Surely he's strong enough to push Detective Miller out of her body."

"I don't know. Doesn't help no one can read them since he entered her mind."

"Gwen, we've talked about this. Skepticism is toxic in an ecosystem of this size."

I open my right eye just enough to see what's in front of me without disrupting the illusion I'm still unconscious.

Guinevere stands close to Jeffrey. As the man who, according to Angela, bankrolled the initial distribution of Harvest's book, he is perhaps the person here who is most responsible for *everything*.

"Skepticism? Did I push you when you wouldn't answer my questions? No. I might not have gone 'full hilt' from moment one, but eventually, you guys made me a believer. Now? I would die for this. If you don't believe my commitment after everything I've done, well, you already missed your best chance to get rid of me. This is as much mine as it is yours at this stage, Jeffrey."

"If I wanted to get rid of you, Gwen, I would have killed you myself."

"Bull. You would have had Preston do it."

"You're probably right. That boy does love to kill. Look, we're stressing out about nothing. As for our current predicament," I see Jeff motion toward us, "I think you're idea is the best chance we have."

Gwen smiles ear to ear. She looks at Angela's prone body like a predator stalking its next kill.

"You know what to do, but you have to be careful. If it's Angela in control at the moment of the Little Death, she'll gain the advantage. If that happens, Gerald will be easy for her to push out, psychic abilities or not."

"How do I keep him at the forefront?"

"I seem to remember you're pretty good at keeping a man's attention."

"If this fails and Angela kicks Henry out?"

"Then we tried. Personally - and I haven't discussed this with Murph yet - I'm of the mind we return her to the surface. I can have Parker outfit her with a small video camera and microphone duo. One of those that's so small she wouldn't even know she's wearing it."

"Now who's skeptical?"

"Not skeptical, just... look. Think of it as a second opinion."

"How do you think Murph would react to you wanting a second opinion?"

"He doesn't need to know. I just want to be thorough."

"You have trouble taking things on faith with him because he's Harvest's kid."

"That's not true."

"Sure it is. It's also smart. Does it feel like five years have passed to you?"

Something tickles my nose. I adjust my focus, see a large fly has landed near Angela's left nostril. Disgusted, I involuntarily swat at it.

"You're awake," Guinevere says.

"Yeah."

"Is this Angela I'm talking to, or Gerald?"

"Gerald."

"How do we know for sure?" Guinevere asks Jeffrey.

"Well, I'm not cursing and threatening you, so that should be a pretty good indication."

I sit up and right away, my head feels clearer. I run Angela's hands over her body; it's a creepy sensation, feeling myself as a woman.

"I'm not convinced," Speck says again.

"If you are Gerald Henry," Jeffrey starts, "What is the name of your friend who died sixteen years ago?"

"How the fuck do you know about that?" I ask, finding it difficult to keep my violent urges in check.

"Gerald, Roy told us everything about you. He was very thorough."

So that's how this is gonna be, eh?

"Danny. His name was Danny."

Saying the name, I get a lightheaded sensation, and my

vision swims with memories I've worked a damn long time to repress.

Daniel Ketchkey was a friend. We met when I started working as a Dick, circa 2004. Danny hired me when his sister was framed for killing clients at the Gentlemen's club where she danced. Candy was a sweetheart, but she was self-destructive and had a habit of getting so fucked up she'd blackout and wake up in compromising situations.

But a murderer, she was not.

I got Candy off - turned out one of her co-workers was killing clients and setting her up for the frame. Relieved of the murder wrap, Candy proved very thankful. We became an item, and as I got to know her family, Danny became a friend.

Shortly after all that, I convinced Candy to retire from dancing, and we all let our guard down. I was wet behind the ears then, and I didn't do enough homework on the girl who took the fall. Turned out, her father was a wealthy Senator. He sent some men after Candy and me. I saw it coming, was able to keep us safe. What I didn't see coming was the Senator showing up at their house in our absence and stabbing Danny in the fucking aorta. Devastated, Candy lost her mind. It was about that time, I moved to Los Angeles. On my way out of Chicago, I brought a guest; I dug a hole in the desert and tried to make the world a better place with one less One-Percenter in it.

"Happy?"

"Yes, I've no doubt you're Gerald Henry. Now, let's talk about how you're going to oust Angela from her body, shall we?"

"Sure," I say, but I'm getting that feeling again, like I'm about to lose my imaginary lunch. I try to control it, but before I can do anything, Angela is awake, back in control, and lunging at Guinevere. We clock Speck in the face with a sharp right hook, and she drops like wet denim. Before Jeffrey can process the attack, Angela snares the handgun from his belt and pins him against the wall with it.

"Help him kick me out of my body, huh? Fuck you!"

I watch from the back seat as Angela shoves the gun's barrel into the soft flesh beneath Jeff's chin and pulls the trigger. Having never seen a man's brains explode through the back of his skull before, I can tell you, it's pretty dramatic. Like fireworks, but with flesh and blood instead of sparkly fire. And the smell. Man, oh man.

CHAPTER 51

When I finish puking, I realize Guinevere is crouched in the corner, staring at us in what I can only describe as abject terror. I'd always heard that term in movies and whatnot. Personally, I never actually understood what it meant until now. Jaw crooked, maybe broke, cowering in the shadows, Guinevere Speck defines abject terror for me once and for all. Seeing her this way has transformed her into someone I very much want to have sex with. But that's not me, is it?

"Now, Ms. Speck," Angela says, "We are long overdue for a private interrogation. Wouldn't you agree?"

We lay beside Guinevere, each of us smoking a cigarette. Angela has complete control, and if what I heard Jeffrey say earlier is true, she has the advantage now. Was it worth it for the first-class VR experience I just went through? No. But that doesn't mean it wasn't amazing.

"The others are going to be upset. I was supposed to fuck Gerald, not you."

"Oh well."

"Is he even still inside? Gerald, can you hear me?"

"Honestly, I think he's gone. Probably couldn't hang on."

"Well, consider this your sign off then, because babe, without Henry, Murphy isn't going to have any use for you."

"We'll see."

Angela takes a long drag on her smoke, stares at Guinevere's body.

"My research showed you weren't a smoker."

"Your research?" Angela says, and I can tell she's both freaked out and flattered. I think if things were different, she might have been able to fall in love with Guinevere.

"Oh, we've had eyes on you since you shot your-"

"Don't say it."

There's an awkward silence, then Angela relaxes.

"I hate cigarettes. I mean, like, violently. Cigarettes killed both my parents. But I guess, in some weird way, when all this became horrifying on an existential level, I thought maybe if I could die like they did, maybe we could be, I don't know, reunited or something."

"That's… naive."

This was the exact wrong thing for Guinevere to say. I feel ice move through Angela's veins, and when she begins to speak again, it's with a very business-like regard that I'm pretty sure will prove fatal for Ms. Speck.

"Okay, you know so much about all of us, here's one for you: you know what I don't get? What is it with Gerald and Roy? I mean, why are those two so important? How did they even end up getting involved?"

"Their mothers knew one another, the only two women with Native blood on the Southside of Chicago, probably. Middle class, at best. Roy and Gerald were childhood friends, up through High School. Then, to hear Roy tell it, the day he turned twenty-two, a man knocked on his door, told him that his father had set up a Living Trust, all he had to do was leave his mother, never talk to her again."

"That's fucked."

"It is. Roy did it, though, no problem. He left everything and everyone he knew behind, Gerald included. Moved to Los Angeles and hit it big with a start-up, then sold the company and moved to the Pacific Northwest, set up on campus after meeting Murphy."

"The start-up. Let me guess: Lindsey Corporation."

"Yep. Jeffrey bought it from him. Turned out, their fathers knew one another. Roy stayed on as a consultant. My company spun out of theirs once Jeffrey decided to branch out into media and IPs. They really planned for this, you know. For a lot longer than I've been involved."

"Is that supposed to be my cue to reassure you that you're not as bad as they are? That you simply got in over your head?"

"Not at all. I believe in what we're doing. What we've done."

"Yeah, about that. Murphy told us five years have gone by on the surface. That's not possible. You don't look any older, neither do I."

"Angela, when you made the call to leave me for dead back at the bookstore, Murph sent people for me. Brought me down here. I haven't been back since, so I can't say for sure, but…"

"Yes?"

"There's a contingent of the Executive Team that doesn't exactly trust Murphy."

"Why would he lie?"

"Murphy has one agenda: his father's. You've read Harvest's book; you know how this plays out."

"What is it?"

"The book? Remember I said Roy's part Native American? Algonquin blood. He says his mother told him she met his father while he was on her reservation, researching certain aspects of Native American mythology."

This rouses me from whatever crypt Angela has relegated me to. Mythology was always Roy's obsession when it came to our heritage.

"There are stories from the old world, warnings about what would happen if humanity's greed ever threatened the natural order of things."

"Harvest's book is a recruitment strategy for a bullshit, radicalized murder cult. I see no folklore here."

"You're wrong. Folklore, the old world, it's not about *ideology*. These stories aren't static, finite parables. At least the ones that are based on facts aren't. They change; they grow and evolve right along with us. Lurking just beneath the thin skin we've covered ourselves with in the name of progress."

I remember that, in particular, Roy was fascinated by the mythology of the Wendigo. Then I remember the back of the thing we rode into town on, the deep sounds I interpreted as breathing.

Angela catches this thought. It stirs a minor panic inside her.

"*That* is impossible."

"No, dear. It's not. In the old world, the tribes believed nature had the means to combat humanity's unchecked greed. Back when this country was still mostly plains, its Native inhabitants saw the white man's arrival, felt his ruthless ambition first hand. How he wanted to own everything, profit from things not meant to be bought and sold. In those more intimate settings of campfires and prairies, the Natives told of a great and terrible spirit that kills those who have become merciless in their greed. Now I ask you, when the entire world has become ravaged by that same ruthless greed, how does that spirit fight back?"

"By evolving. By taking a new form. A monster that becomes a virus, infecting everyone and putting us all to work toward the same goal: a clean slate for Mother Earth, free and clear of those who would destroy her. That's why we're down here, why it brought you to us. Our job is to outlast the entire human race, then return to the surface and lower the curtains. Show's over. Next."

"But Gerald?"

"Angela, he can talk to the thing. He already has."

"Well," Angela says, standing us up and walking toward the bathroom. I realize too late Guinevere's gun rests on the crappy steel counter that houses the sink, "it's been fun, Guinevere, but I think it's time I started closing things down now. Show's over. Next."

~

I can hardly believe what I just witnessed Angela do to a woman's body. To flesh that, until several moments ago, was every bit as ripe and alive as her own. Now, the room is painted in blood splatter, shards of bone litter every surface, and her eyes. Her eyes...

I'm staring at Guinevere Speck, but she is utterly unrecognizable.

Still with me, Hank? Hope you liked that. I certainly did. You know, after I killed Jim and those kids in front of the strip mall, everything sped up. The SWAT, my arrest, the weekend in jail. They wanted to try me quickly to make an example, but the virus spiked for the first time, and everyone panicked. The cops, the Feds, Homeland. Everyone. After that, it was only a matter of another couple of days before Joseph and his goons showed up and we were

257

on a plane. But after what I just did to this one, I gotta tell you, Hank. I feel... comfortable for the first time. I think the incubation period may be over. I think whatever the next stage is, it's here.

Angela's bravado is her trying to convince me what a badass she is, but I'm not buying it. Her voice feels incidental at this point; it's the skein that houses her fear, which is abundant. For myself, all I can do is stare at the horror show before me because, for the first time, seeing this has made me understand what things had previously been too seat-of-the-pants for me to accept.

I am dead.

I have no body. Everything I define myself by is gone.

It's interesting how even though we live entirely in our own heads, we harbor a holographic, symbiotic relationship with our actual body. Like we live in it and outside it at the same time. The mirror, other people, expectations, and desires we accrue from encounters with love, hate, joy, prejudice... all of this helps build our concept of what's attractive or fulfilling, creating an *internal* conception of our *external* existence. Stripped of this, with no experience in the world as a frame of reference, the fear starts to set in.

You should be afraid, Henry. Seriously. The worst shit that has ever happened on this planet is about to turn the corner, and neither you nor I are prepared.

What do we do?

What do we do? Why, honey, I thought it would be obvious by this point. We kill everyone in Paradise, and then we kill ourselves.

CHAPTER 52

With no attempt to disguise what she's done to Guinevere, Angela steers us out into the waning artificial night. The first rays of Paradise's sun peek over the tops of the buildings that surround us. The hum from the generator that powers it permeates the entire aural landscape.

We pass buildings, large and small, all made entirely of garbage. I can see driftwood and scrap metal in the DNA of the closest ones. There's a lot. Paradise is bigger than I'd first accounted for.

Back in Chicago, there was a small, fenced-in subdivision down the road from my apartment on the Southwest side. This was after I'd dropped out of college. I rented a place above a liquor store to use as an office while I tried to suss out a career as either A) a psychic, B) a detective, or eventually, C) a psychic detective. This particular subdivision was strictly for the families of officers assigned to a nearby military base. I think I remember someone once telling me the place housed fifty families. This is about the size of Paradise's population, except sans the kids. Of course, the difference is every domicile here is small and practical, only consisting of what the residents have had the ingenuity to construct from garbage. Also, unlike the base housing, there are no children in Paradise.

We make it back to where the party was held the night before. Everything's been cleaned up, no sign of whatever festivities occurred. Joseph must have ended up the default Guest of Honor. It occurs to me that our absence must be generating suspicion.

How long until they find Guinevere? What about Jeffrey?

I find myself wondering if Joseph has already accepted a position inside "Paradise." He'd make a great thug, I guess. Why should his new life be any different than his previous one?

We crest a small rise, and there's the sun, not more than a hundred yards ahead. We walk toward it. Not that I have any say in where we're going; I feel like Angela has me crammed inside a tiny box somewhere deep inside her. I have tunnel vision, and everything has an extra few seconds of reverberation on it by the time it reaches my perception—the proverbial boy in the well.

As we get closer to the light, the hum becomes almost unbearable. From this distance, I can see the ensemble isn't just made up of stadium lighting. There's also a massive grouping of everything from old headlights, flashlights, lamps, and large movie production type lanterns.

The effect is fantastic.

From within probably fifteen yards of the light, the source of the roar is revealed. A massive, gas-powered generator sits fenced off from everything else, barbed concertina wire along the top.

By the time I sense the hand on Angela's shoulder, she is already mid-swing with her right fist. Preston catches the would-be blow effortlessly, squeezing until she shrieks in pain. I convulse along with her as Angela's right hand implodes, drooping uselessly to her side. All five knuckles feel exploded, twisted into a weak, throbbing claw.

"You shouldn't have done that to Gwen. Gwen was one of us."

"Yeah? Guess what? I *liked* it."

Preston's fist slams into Angela's face, and we fall to the ground. I feel my host turn off, like a tv screen dying in a dark room.

"Gerald, you still in there?" Another voice hollers from behind Preston. It's Murphy. I try to move Angela's lips to answer, but I'm still stunned from the blow. I imagine closing my eyes, and in my thoughts, I swim toward the small, illuminated square at the very top of a long shaft of darkness.

"Yes," I say, not loud enough to compete with the racket from the nearby machine. Regaining control, an overload of stimuli almost sends me spiraling back into whatever deep-sea trench I just made my escape from.

"We're going to need you to put a leash on that bitch, Gerald, or you're not going to be any use to us."

"What?" I scream, pain shredding the inside of my thoughts.

Murph repeats himself, shouting this time.

"Easier said than done," I shout back. Screaming back and forth is doing nothing for my concentration.

"Is she still in there with you?"

"I can't tell. I can barely tell you what I'm thinking. That goddamn generator."

Murph stuffs something soft and small into Angela's good hand.

Earplugs.

I put them in, and the sound becomes nearly manageable.

Murphy motions for me to follow as he and Preston

move away from the lights. We walk until we're finally far enough away that shouting becomes unnecessary.

"Things get pretty noisy near the Sun," he says. I follow him toward a small cluster of buildings I hadn't noticed previously, "Parker pilfered crates of these homeopathic earplugs from somewhere on his last mission Topside. They work pretty well."

We walk on. Near the opposite side of the camp where we originally came in, I see what appears to be a medical tent. Behind that, another tent that houses what looks like the kind of bar you'd see on a tropical island, all driftwood benches and tiki torches.

"Bar open?"

"Bar's always open if you're not on the job."

We enter and Preston motions for Murphy and me to sit at a table in the open-air patio's front corner.

"What the hell is a homeopathic earplug?" I ask, taking the tiny buds out and setting them in front of me. Murphy does the same. The light is full-on now. All around us people are beginning a day's work: shifting large cylinders, digging trenches, and laying cable. Preston returns with two black mugs of something from behind the counter, hands one to each of us. I get a POV of Angela's tattered fingernails as I accept the beverage and once again have to call on some inner strength just to keep from screaming.

I have no body.

"Drink it," Murph says, "It might help ease your existential dread."

"That'd be swell," I say with a wink. My attempt at lightening the mood fails. This isn't so much a friendly sit-down as it is a necessary pow-wow.

"Murph," A tall man approaches. He looks concerned.

"How's it coming, Dan?"

"It's looking like a ten-to-one that the transfiguration will work. What's the current timeline?"

Murphy stops and thinks for a moment. His forehead creases with the labor of the decision he is apparently being called on to make.

"Tonight."

"I'll get everything ready."

"Preston, can you check in with Parker, make sure the branches are all on the same page?"

"I didn't think we were far enough along on the upgrade?"

"It doesn't really matter if we move the timeline up."

"Murph, I don't want to sound like I'm questioning you, but -"

"Then don't. Just do as I ask, will you, Preston?"

Preston hesitates, then nods and trudges off toward the sun.

"Tough being the boss, eh?"

"Yeah."

"You guys expanding?"

"Hardly. We've had some technological challenges lately and have been working to bolster the generator to handle a higher output signal from our dialers. Hopefully, thanks in no small part to your friend Joseph, none of that is going matter after tonight."

"Joseph? Really? I wouldn't have pegged him for a techie."

"Oh, he's not. Finish your drink, I'll take you to him."

We drink for a time. The beverage has the heat of coffee but the sting of whiskey. There's something else, too. A hint of... fish?

"So tell me, Murph. How did you get involved in all this end-of-the-world shit?"

"You know who my father was, yes?"

"Yeah, but I mean, did you always know this is where you were headed? Or did something... happen?"

"It's always been inside me, my father's work. He passed it on to all his children."

"How many children did ol' Abe have?"

"He's Roy's father, too. Did you know that? In fact, quite a few people here can trace their origin back to Abramelin Harvest in the sixties and seventies. Peace, Love, and Understanding may have collapsed, but Free Love never loses its appeal."

"The mysterious benefactor that appeared after graduation and coaxed Roy to leave Chicago after graduation?"

"Exactly."

"Well, that certainly explains what a fucking psycho he turned out to be. Roy wasn't like that when I knew him. Nice guy. Sharp dresser, too."

"Let me ask you something, Gerald. Did it ever seem strange to you, the fact that Roy disappeared and you didn't hear from him again until you had a need to disappear, too?"

"I guess. I don't know, isn't that the way the Universe usually works? People come back to you right when you need them the most?"

"It is when everything in your life is monitored, coordinated, and manipulated."

"You have my attention."

"Brass tacks: we need you. I believe Angela realized that, so she killed you. Lucky for both of us, you didn't take death lying down."

"What exactly do you need me for?"

"Finish your drink and let's go see your pal, Joseph. Then I'll explain everything."

CHAPTER 53

We finish our drinks and walk. I have a sense we're not alone, that Murphy has a security detail close by. He's smart; if Angela takes over again, the first thing she's going to do is kill him.

"I'm curious, Murph."

"About what?"

"How did your father end up on this path? I mean, how many other hippies took the 'Love the One You're With' philosophy and ended up with 'End the world' instead?"

"Good question. If you follow the philosophical progression of the sixties, it doesn't take long to see how the "Woodstock" era most people associate with that time actually burnt out fairly quickly. What followed was, in a nutshell, hard drugs and toxic spirituality. My father believed you could measure this by tracking the Love Crowd's dispersal into either New Age Yuppies or narcotics and black magick."

"Satanic Panic. I thought most of that was bullshit, though."

"Most of it was. But an air of malevolence embedded

itself in the cultures of man during that time, and it has only grown."

"Can't argue there."

"From there, the world's simply been one revision after the next of a single creed: Consume. My father and his followers stood in staunch opposition to this."

"Then why Lindsey Corp? Why play that game at all?"

"To eliminate the enemy, sometimes you have to become the enemy. Even as far back as the seventies, anyone with any degree of prescience could see the ultimate outcome of our unchecked Capitalist Aggression would be the destruction of the planet."

"And yet, Harvest and his group were the only ones to do anything about it."

"Distraction. That's how the world continues to devolve. One thing about my father and his protocols: he eschewed completely the lust for distraction. The Omega Council remains rooted in Mindful Occupation of the Moment."

"Sounds New Age."

"It's not. My father and his people became Watchers; Chroniclers of the ramshackle chaos that came to define Western Society. This then, is where the idea of ushering in the Omega Chapter was written; the OC is simply the epilogue. My job is to pen the postscript and turn the lights out when we leave."

I can feel Angela's consciousness coming back online. It's faint, laying low. Listening. I'm tempted to warn Murphy, but I decide not to.

We enter a building that looks like a hospital. I see rooms with unoccupied beds, IVs, sharps containers. None of the stuff is new enough to sparkle; it's all second-hand.

"This a hospice?"

"Sort of. We mainly stock pain killers and birth control,

bandages, and the like. We're not really equipped to deal with anything else."

"It'd be counterproductive if you were, yeah?"

"Does that bother you?"

"No, I'd call you crazy if you were trying to cure cancer or something down here."

"This is a very 'short-term' camp. We're here to oversee and maintain, sort of the janitors of the Apocalypse if you will."

I laugh. I can see how this man persuaded so many people to do so many fucked up things. Charismatic isn't the word.

We pass through another door, this one marked with a large, orange biohazard sign. Ahead of me is a gurney. Joseph is strapped to it, unconscious. Beside him, an array of what I think are bone saws and other gnarly surgical instruments lay aligned on a sterile white sheet.

"What happened to him?"

"Sedated. Joseph is the test subject we've been looking for."

"What's he testing?"

"The Transfiguration."

"Come again?"

"If all goes well, by tomorrow, everyone in the OC will head Topside and assume the Rite of Transfiguration. We will shed our flesh to become something terrible, something that can devour what remains of the human race. From there, the planet will be free of us."

I hadn't expected this. I don't know if I believe Murphy. Hell, I'm not even sure he believes himself.

"That's fucking crazy, man."

"Really? You do realize who it was that brought you to us, right? Whose back you rode in on?"

I knew it!

"I know you heard it speaking, Gerald. I was there. I was

in your head because it's in mine. That's where my power is derived from, and it's been boosting yours since you arrived. It's the only reason you were able to attach your consciousness to Angela's body."

"So you're saying, the Wendigo-"

Before I can finish speaking, the world is sucked away, and I'm thrown back down that well. My perceptions flatten, and I watch through that tiny window as Angela reasserts her control and drives her working fist straight into Murph's Adam's Apple. It takes him as much by surprise as it does me, and he staggers backward several steps. This is Angela's cue; she snags the largest bone saw from the table and leaps at Murphy. There's a sound like torn meat as the instrument's teeth begin to rake across the bridge of his nose. The attack is so preposterous, so ad hoc, Murphy can do nothing but choke on his crushed throat and flail his arms as Angela literally saws through the front of his skull. I can feel both her adrenaline and fatigue as she works the instrument back and forth until a fountain of blood erupts from Murph's face. It coats us, face, neck, and chest, but still she saws.

A few moments later, Murph collapses, and I catch a glimpse of his soft, pink brain matter through the gap Angela has opened in his face. We go down with him, our two bodies next to one another like spent lovers.

What... the absolute fuck?

Was that as good for you as it was for me? I mean, what I wouldn't give for a cigarette right now.

~

I don't know how long we lay there, but at some point, it occurs to me that someone is bound to come in and find us. Where's that security detail?

We need to get up and get the fuck out of here, Angela. We're leaving a body count of VIPs in our wake, and the fine people of Paradise will probably not take too well to our atrocities.

You knew about this Wendigo shit?

What?

This monster shit. You knew about it?

Not exactly.

What the fuck does that mean? Not exactly?

Look, you might recall that I tried to tell you about this while we were floating down the River Styx on the thing's back. I said, 'hey guys, I think this raft might be alive.' Neither of you listened to me.

I'm listening now. What made you think it was alive?

It... talked to me.

It spoke to you?

"I don't know. I heard... something. I felt like it was addressing me, but I don't speak Algonquin, or Wendigo, or whatever, so I couldn't exactly be sure the whole thing wasn't just a hallucination.

Some fucking psychic you turned out to be.

Fuck off.

Inside Angela, we argue. Outside, we walk.

Where are we going?

Angela doesn't answer me. She tosses the bone saw to the ground and heads towards the door.

CHAPTER 54

As we make our way around the camp, what feels like a final, fatal fatigue settles over Angela. It's not her body; it's her mind.

Where are we going?

Look, I hate to tell you this, but I'm done.

What the fuck does that mean?

It means, through this whole nightmare, ever since we left the bookstore, we've done nothing but run from an inevitable fate. It really doesn't matter if Murphy was lying about the amount of time that passed back in the real world. Look how we left it. You really want to go back to that?

What choice do we have?

We end it.

Wait a fucking minute. You killed me, Angela. You took my fucking body from me, and now your body is all I have left.

So?

So I think I should have a say in whether or not you kill yourself.

I'm so intent on arguing my point, I almost miss the fact that ahead of us, a large congregation of people has gathered in the center of the camp. Angela, who is still driving the bus, also almost misses this.

Look out.

We stop sharp and slip behind a group of large steel drums a few feet to our left.

It's Preston, and he's addressing probably half the camp, speaking loudly and with the obvious intent to incite. He does not sound happy.

Methinks they've found our trail of corpses.

I was wrong about you, Hank. You really are a great detective, after all.

"... they are dangerous, but they are also outnumbered," Preston is saying.

"Yeah, but one of them's a psychic, right?" Someone in the crowd asks.

"Your point?"

"My point, Pres, is they killed Murphy. That's... well, I don't know about you, but that doesn't inspire much confidence when I contemplate facing them."

"Jesus Christ. They're outnumbered fifty-to-one."

"Forty-six," someone else corrects.

"It doesn't fucking matter!"

"Look," another person starts in. This time it's Parker, "Before he died, Murphy had us take steps to move the timeline up. The third Outsider is one-hundred percent ready to undergo the Transfiguration."

This causes talk. It doesn't sound like the others realized judgment day was so close.

"I don't know about this," someone says.

"He didn't say anything to me about moving things up," another voice insists.

"I'm not ready," a third person states flatly.

The crowd becomes unruly. I can taste the panic from

here, like pennies or blood on the tongue. Preston rises to the occasion, wrestles back control like a born leader.

"Look! We can talk about timeline later. Right now, I want them caught, and if you're all too afraid to face them, let's be smart. Parker, once the Transfiguration starts, how long does it take to complete?"

"Not sure. That's one of the metrics Murph wanted me to use our lab rat to measure."

"Okay. Everyone needs to go home right now. Bolt yourselves in. That thing gets loose, you do not want to be out in the open. I'll make an announcement once it's safe."

"What are you going to do, Preston?"

"I'm going to turn the Outsider and sic him on his friends."

CHAPTER 55

The crowd disperses quickly. Whatever this Transfiguration is, it scares the hell out of these people.

See? Seems like a great time for getting out to me...

Angela hasn't exactly relinquished control, but she's not actively blocking me, either. The sensation is odd, to say the least. It's like someone is standing next to me. A shadow pantomiming my every movement as I desperately search for something to turn the tide in our favor, or at the very least buy us some time.

There has to be something we can do. What about these barrels? Gotta be gas, right?

My excitement is quelled when I feel the barrel of a gun press against our back.

"What do you think you're doing?"

"Trying to avoid being overrun by that mob of your friends there," I answer Preston.

"Believe me, they're the least of your worries."

"Oh, really?

"I know you were at the hospital. I know you saw Joseph."

"Was your first clue finding your boss's corpse? You're good. I could use an assistant in the PI biz, you know."

Preston whips us across the back of the head with the revolver, sends us to the ground.

"The way some of us see it, you did us a solid, killing Murph."

"Really? The Congregation second-guessing the Priest, eh?"

"Something like that. Let's just say, without Murph, no one here is all that eager to undergo an excruciating process that will rob us of our humanity."

"Sounds like you guys are playing with the big kid toys."

I can't tell if it's Angela or me who's speaking. This worries me more than anything this dickhead says.

"You can ask Joseph when he's tearing you limb from limb."

I hedge our bets and swing at Preston. He steps to one side, easily dodging the blow, then cracks us across the back of the head again. Face in the dirt, we realize in unison that Preston has revealed his hand: he's not going to shoot us. He's too interested in seeing what Joseph is capable of.

"Time to die," he says.

Angela seems to have receded with that last blow. I pick us up, wipe bloody spittle from our lower lip.

"You're a real cunt, you know that?"

This pisses him off. He *wants* to shoot us so badly.

"Don't have it in ya, eh? What a precious bunch of fucking flowers you Paradisers turned out to be."

"Fuck you."

"This reminds me of the time I saw a clip of the singer from my favorite death metal band cry. So fucking embarrassed for you." My voice drips with vitriolic condescension.

That does it. Preston snaps and charges. We're faster; I bring Angela's knee up into his balls and snatch the piece from him, just as it goes off, the bullet missing us by what must be a fraction of an inch. Without a proper center of gravity, Preston slips in some dirt and makes it easy for me to pop him in the nose.

Hard.

Stunned, we drag him into the dark spaces concealed behind the steel drums. I feel separate from Angela for just a moment, almost like I just woke up in an empty room. Kill kill kill repeats somewhere in the sub-basement of this shared mental space, and I'm reminded of Tony Tod's subterranean room. So many metaphors lain side by side with the world I knew, almost like humanity's collective unconscious has slipped its hand over reality. For the first time, I understand how Tod became so dependent on his drugs. The idea of intoxication as a way to escape this ravenous void that beckons ceaselessly.

"You're dead," Preston says on his knees before us.

"You think? Not me. I bet we have everything we need to burn this whole sorry excuse for a subdivision to the ground right here."

"Fuck you," he says again, his tone doughy with the phlegm of a broken nose. There is both realization and acceptance in his voice.

"Be a damn shame if these barrels caught fire. You know, being that your whole Paradise is built entirely of flammable trash."

He stares at us with unrelenting hatred in his eyes.

"See, Pres? No future *here*, either."

"There was never *supposed* to be a future here. We were supposed to martyr ourselves, a final offering to the great and terrible spirit of the plains."

We nod, urging him to continue.

"I'm not even sure how I came to be mixed up in all of this, you know? One minute you stand for something and the next, well, Murphy's father would say ghosts have more than one way of affecting us, the things we do, the way we live our lives."

"You've spent a great deal of time helping Murphy try to finish something his father started. In our book, that's time wasted."

"You're not wrong."

We're about to say something incrementally more judgemental when a sound echoes across the sky. It is, without exaggeration, the most horrifying thing I have ever heard. A cross between the cries of a mangled puppy and flesh caught in heavy machinery. As if on cue, the light from the sun shuts off completely. We are left in total darkness.

"What the fuck was that?"

"*That* was Joseph," he says and laughs. With the broken nose, it sounds like shoes schlepping through wet grass, "Looks like I kept you here just long enough to make sure he has no problem finding you."

This sound, to describe it as a howl falls painfully short of conveying the bitter dimensions of pain and horror contained in its reedy issue. When it recurs, it is considerably closer.

Preston catches us off-guard, snatches the gun. Instead of struggling with him for it, we release it to his grasp and go for his throat. Angela's bum hand might be useless for grip, but with the other around the back of his neck, we lean in with our forearm and squeeze the ball in Preston's throat between the two. He tries to bring the gun up but loses it as the sheer force we apply snatches the oxygen directly from his lungs. He begins to choke, is about to expire when something lands on top of the barrels to our right, reaches down and pulls Preston's head clean off his shoulders. The gun falls to the ground at our feet.

"What the fuck?"

We can see the thing limned by the light from a nearby building. It does not look like Joseph. Doesn't even look human, but whatever this is, it's *enormous*. We're talking at least eight feet tall. We grab Preston's gun and scramble to our feet amid the gut-wrenching sounds of the thing chowing down on his skull. A second later, the rest of his body is hauled up and out of sight.

It occurs to me that if we don't take out this stupid dystopian city, we'll have the Paradisers to deal with as well as the Joseph Monster. Hands shaking with fear, I manage to wrestle several of the overturned barrels into a rudimentary circle. Once there are a good half dozen or so drums, I root around in the dirt until I find a stray piece of metal. Using this, I dig a small moat that connects the overturned barrels to those still standing upright. Using the metal again, I lever off the cap on the drum in the middle, releasing a stream of fresh gasoline. Fumes hit our nostrils, and I shudder. The effect brightens the darkness into a softer, more malleable environment. Nearby, the sounds of the banquet are just getting started.

Hurry...

I ram the metal shard into the bottom of the closest drum still standing. I watch as this second stream of gas joins the first, connecting all the drums.

The eating sounds stop, followed by the sound of the beast running our way, its feet alternately hopping and dragging in the dirt.

We run.

When we get a few dozen yards away, Angela steps in and turns, fires several rounds at the barrels. As the first explodes into flame, silhouetted behind it, I see the outline of something that nature never intended to exist. Or if it did, clearly humanity was the outlier all along.

CHAPTER 56

We run, Joseph's monstrous new form just behind us, driven into a frenzy by the ravenous hunger ignited by Hors d' oeuvres de Preston. Choking back waves of terror, we weave through the dense trash foliage. It is nearly impossible to see the path in the dark. Disaster is only a step away.

A moment later, a gust of foul wind hits me in the face—the creature sails over us, lands directly in our path. Unable to overcome our momentum, we misstep and tumble downhill into a thick tangle of wood splinters, wire, and what feels to the touch like strips of old plastic molding.

Up! Up! Get up!

What did you expect? There's no way out, Gerald. You have to accept that!"

There has to be a way out!

I'm screaming, my voice feels like a mountain inside the space Angela and I have come to share inside her psyche. Not a room, exactly, but a mental projection of one. Parts of it look like my apartment in L.A., parts like my old basement, parts unknown. These, I assume, are hers.

Just hold on! There has to be a way out!

What, like the way we arrived? You really willing to take that ride again, knowing what you do now about what brought us here?

I don't know, okay? I'm operating on pure, vestigial survival instinct here.

Did you see this thing we're running from? They turned Joseph into that, Gerald! It's not human, do you get that? Microscopic organisms that produce human monsters is one thing, but that? That's a whole other matter. How do we run from that? How do we fight it? I'd rather we drown than be eaten alive!

Angela has a point. Still, I'm not giving up.

Let me handle it, then? Okay?

Fuck that.

In the center of our interior room, a door appears. It is shaped like a giant skull.

Outside, I struggle free from the branches, trip, and land face-down on the beach's black glass. I try to catch my breath only to realize that although *my* mind remains acute, Angela's body is wracked by violent, panicked convulsions. She is terrified beyond the ability to control herself, and that terror is robbing me of any and all primary motor function.

The next howl comes from directly behind us.

Look! You want my body? Fine. It's yours.

I feel Angela's presence begin to move toward the door.

What do you mean, it's mine? Angela?

Just remember, you have to rub the little bump if you want to get anything out of it.

Her voice fades to an ethereal whisper as Angela passes through the skull's maw.

Hey, wait a minute, where the hell are you going?

It's too late. She's gone.

My head swims with the after-effects of her departure. I measure my breathing and feel my heart begin to slow. Control returns, albeit too slowly to make a difference in what is about to happen.

Behind me, another explosion lights the sky. It's so loud my hearing fades to a static-tinted whine. I fight to steal a glance over my shoulder only to see flames have lit the sky beyond the beach like a forest fire at midnight. Illuminated by the Halloween glow, I get my first good look at Abramelin Harvest's monster.

It's tall, probably not the eight feet I estimated before, but close. Despite this, there's no doubt this was once the man I knew as Joseph. The eyes harbor the same, duty-bound dogmatism that carried him through a night most could not survive. I know it well. It's the same obstinate nature that has sustained me since I put three holes in a wealthy Senator's chest and dropped his corpse in the desert. Inertia that begins as hardship but eventually becomes unrelenting compulsion, the fundamental tool I used to rebuild my life after watching my friend lowered into a hole destroyed it.

What little of Joseph's flesh remains doesn't look so much like skin but a loose-fitting garment. Its face is nearly all skull, and its jaw lacks a mandible. Because of this, I can see directly into its throat. Something slithers out, a grossly elongated organ that looks and behaves more like the tail of a rat than a tongue. It lashes at the small bits of burning rubble that fall from the sky around us.

"Can we talk about this, Joseph?" I say but can't commit to the levity. My eyes stare into the fleshless abdominal cavity that looks like an enormous bear trap. Fluorescent green organs pulse within, just like in my dream.

The monster stares into my soul and I feel like my insides die. This time when it howls, I answer it back with equal gusto.

"I'd *much rather drown than be eaten alive,*" Angela's words come back to me as I turn and run toward the incoming tide. The creature follows, but just when I think I'm done for, something miraculous happens. I turn in time to see a chunk of burning metal arc out of the jungle and across the sky. It collides with the monster.

"Well, I'll be a -"

The creature bursts into flames. It's so close, I can feel the heat licking at my face. I watch in an odd mixture of relief and horror as Harvest's abomination flails uselessly, its body dissipating in thick billows of black smoke. It burns for several minutes, then collapses and dissolves into dust.

Horrified but thankful, I drop too, content to watch as, on all sides around me but one, Paradise burns.

As I lay, I feel the tide of sludge finally reach me, its cold, torpid touch prompting me to wonder for the first time, what force inspires its cycle? The sky overhead is empty of constellations, not a firmament at all, but a hollow void that conceals this beach from the underside of the world above.

My answer reveals itself by emerging from beneath the sea. Preceded by the sound of a gargantuan wave, I turn and watch the ultimate horror rise from the murky depths of the tainted black ocean.

Finally then, this is enough to convince me to accept that my survival ends here. Despite everything I've experienced during the past twenty-four hours, I now know *this* is the true face of the world in which we live. I'd had it wrong all along. We all did. Monsters are real; the fiction is the world I *thought* I knew. School, family, career: these are the folklore, stories made up and enacted to distract humanity from living with the knowledge that nature is far more hostile than they would ever feel safe knowing.

I scream. I can't help it. My mouth opens, and it's like my voice just explodes from it. The sound sustains for a little under a minute, but by the time the thing takes its first great step onto land, the only sound left to me is a thin and scratchy cackle. If the monster is offended by my rage, it makes no sign. There is a moment when we stare at one another, and I can see it contemplating extinguishing my life. Angela's knees, now my knees, are sunk in the wet, black sand of glass, a worshipper before my new god. Before I can fully comprehend what I'm looking at, I hear its voice again, like I did on the raft. This time, though, I understand it. The Wendigo tells me to rise.

Just like the song: rise.

I stand and look my death in the eyes. It holds my gaze, and then - and I can't be sure of this - I think it smiles at me. After that, it moves on.

The beast's first step up off the beach knocks me over with its sheer seismic force. I watch as it stalks off toward the flames. I realize now there is a chorus of wordless screams issuing from the burning city. Perhaps their savior will begin its culling with their surviving numbers. Or maybe the beast is every bit as lazy as those it's meant to destroy, opting for the quick snack instead of the long walk to dinner.

Either way, I'm not waiting around to find out.

~

E verything is green.

"Well, yeah, it should be that way, don't you think?"

"What?"

I raise my head and see the sun for the first time in what feels like a long time? Five years? I'm still not buying that, but some time has passed, for sure.

Around me, amazingly, the trash jungle is gone, replaced instead by soft soil and real, living plant life. I'm sprawled out next to a small copse of trees, and I'm in *my* body. Not Angela's. Also, inexplicably, I'm naked.

"What did you expect? You didn't come into the world with any clothes; why would you leave with any?"

I immediately recognize the voice, even though I haven't heard it in a long time. I scan from side to side but don't spot him until I look up. Sitting on a low-hanging branch of a gnarled old Oak, Danny Ketchkey smiles at me.

"Danny?"

"One and the same, boy. How's it hanging?"

Danny's kicking his feet back and forth in front of him like a kid on a lazy summer day. I'm so elated, I forget my nakedness, stand and approach.

"How are you here? Is this like Roy?"

"Nope."

"Then, what?"

"Two guesses, dude."

"I'm dead?"

"Congrats on the obvious. You must be one helluva private dick, eh?"

His chiding is good-natured, welcome even. I used to love when we'd bust each other's balls. I laugh with him.

"What is this supposed to be, Heaven? Why do you get pants, and I don't?"

Danny laughs. He looks good.

"C'mon Hank, I know you don't believe in Heaven."

"You got me. Then where are we? You've been dead for some time, man. This doesn't look like the other place."

"The amazing thing is that even guys like us, who know all that religious shit doesn't exist, we end up defaulting to those stupid myths once we get here. Naw man, there is no Heaven or Hell, there's just a return to that which all things are from, dig?"

"Did I hit my head or something? Really…"

Danny hops off the branch and lands upright before me. He smiles. I have no context for what is happening right now.

"C'mon man, give me a hug. Shit, it's been too long."

Left to my own devices, I'm not sure if I'd hug him, but he moves in and grabs me in a big, bear-hug kind of way.

"Okay, so what the fuck is going on, exactly?"

"You're dead. You can put it off for as long as you want, but there's not much you can do to hang on to your humanity without a body. Specifically, those marvelous attributes of the human mind that prevent us from interfacing with anything outside our own selfishly small understanding of the cosmos. Floodgates are open, bro. You're standing in a dark room holding a torch. No hiding."

"So you're, what, delivering a message on behalf of … the cosmos?"

"Something like that. See, the Universe really bumps and grinds on the subatomic level. Normally, for a living brain to come into contact with someone like me - a personification of what I'll just call The Cosmic Soup - is almost unheard of."

"The Cosmic Soup?"

"I think you used to call it the aether."

"I like that better."

"Poh-tay-toe, poh-ta-toe. Point is, after everything that's happened, all the shit you've witnessed, you're a special case, Hank. You're kinda halfway between both planes of existence, and that makes for some interesting shit comin' your way."

"Why is the subatomic interested in talking to me now?"

"It's not. *You're* talking to it. Also, in case you haven't guessed, I'm not really Danny Ketchkey."

"A personification?"

"Yeah."

"Why…"

Before I can figure how to properly phrase my question, a scream in the distance silences us. Danny smiles, makes a conciliatory gesture, and then vanishes. As with everyone else in my life, it dawns on me that I've missed the opportunity to tell him I love him.

I open my eyes and find that I am lying on my back, surrounded by trees. The screaming continues, but it's far enough away that I don't feel threatened. Besides, I'm not the one who reneged on a deal long ago signed in blood.

How long were you out?

At first, I mistake the question as having come from Angela. But no, everything that's left in her body is all me, Gerald Henry, psychic detective. No one else is here with me. I look around, inside and out.

I am alone.

CHAPTER 57

I walk, and as I do, my mind wanders. I think about Danny and his sister, Candy. I didn't love Candy, but there was a time, nothing more than a brief instant when I thought she could make me happy. You know, buy a house, have a kid. Uncle Danny comes over on the weekend for barbecues and beers. Then Danny was murdered, and I couldn't face Candy, knowing his death ultimately led back to her. So much has happened in the years since then, much more than the number of days would seem to allow if you added them up and plotted their course.

So I walk, slowly adjusting to my new body.

I follow the Black Ocean for as long as I can. The creature hasn't returned to finish me off, but at one point, just before I find the passage back Topside, I see it. From a distance, the giant, misshapen skull looks like something out of a big-budget sci-fi flick, moving above the tops of the few remaining refuse trees. That's actually how I find the passage - I watch concealed in the distance as it leads a troop of several dozen similar, smaller creatures through the mouth of a cave. Looks like some of Murphy's people got their

Transfiguration, after all. What will the murder-happy denizens of the surface world think when they see a parade of monsters emerging from subterranean depths to finish off their ravaged world? Will they even notice or care? Or, was Murphy right? Is the world finally empty of humanity?

I walk. Time passes. When my surroundings change, I find I can't remember the journey. It's difficult to remember what happened after following the creatures into the cave. I remember moving carefully along a narrow, ramshackle path, out of the light of the fires and into the darkness of more foraged detritus – stockpiled corridors built with endless equipment, supplies, rations, and of course, bones. But that's it. Everything stops after that. The exact last thing I remember is carefully placing my left foot in front of my right. Then?

Nothing.

Well, not nothing. I can remember part of my dream (it didn't feel like a dream), Danny telling me how special I was. That I was neither living nor dead. What else did he say? A warning?

I'm startled out of my thoughts by a nearby sound. I turn and see that I am on the top of a hill, surrounded by trees. Off in the distance are high rises. I'm above ground, in the 'real' world. Still Seattle, I assume, although I don't recognize this part of town. An almost paralyzing feeling rips through my muscles and finds my spine as I scan for murderheads. There is no sign of anyone, hostile or friendly.

I hear the sound again.

I spin around this way and that, looking for a weapon of some sort, hoping to find something - anything - I might use to stave off the hordes when they arrive.

There is nothing.

The sound recurs, and I realize what it is. The creatures are nearby. Fear settles in, but I force myself to ignore it. I turn, and behind me, I see something low to the ground moving within the trees. I step forward to get a better view. It's a cat, a small tabby, brown and black. It looks at me from within the cover of many leaves, and in its eyes, I see the same fear I know it sees in mine.

AFTERWORD

I wrote the first version of this novel back in 2007/2008. I was working retail at a Borders Book Store. The company had gone from being a haven of intelligent interactions with like-minded people to barbaric moronity from both the daily customers and the Corporate overseers who eventually drove the company into the ground. Needless to say, the first version of this book had a lot more "Charters" in it, and a lot more violence within those walls. Writing was my therapy.

2007/8:

    Doves - Lost Souls
    Brand New - God and the Devil are Raging Inside Me
    Twilight Singers - Powder Burns
    Afghan Whigs - 1965
    Underworld 1992-2002

I restarted the process of editing/modernizing the story on March 14th 2020. The first wave of COVID-19 madness had descended with the Stay-at-home order lurking nearby, toilet paper and essential supplies being hoarded, and a palpable sense of uncertainty the likes of which, I had not experienced as an adult. Humanity, it seemed, deserved everything that was happening. I woke early on a day off to go to a nearby grocery store. Human Impact's eponymous debut had just dropped the day before, but I was getting my first listen while shuffling through the isles, grasping at scraps of supplies. To say it was the perfect soundtrack to the experience would be a gross understatement. It dawned on me, while waiting to check out, that I would be wasting the experience if I did not pull my weird little novel about a Murder Virus Pandemic and retool it. I wanted to hone what was there, because I very much liked it, but I also wanted to synchronize it with the thoughts, experiences, and emotions many of us were feeling while staring at a most uncertain future.

2020:

    Human Impact - Eponymous

    White Lung - Paradise

    Code Orange - Underneath

    Blut Aus Nord - Memoria Vetusta III: Saturian Poetry

    The Atlas Moth - Coma Noir

    Burzum - Filosofem

    Blut Aus Nord - Memoria Vitusta II: Dialogue with the Stars

    Underworld 1992-2012

If this was a movie, it would have Beach House's *Elegy to the Void* playing over the ending credits. Thanks again for that, Chazberg!

NOTES

CHAPTER 2

1. I Shakespeare, W. (1609). Sonnet 130